THE SEER OF KINTAIL

I put my hands to my face and waited for him
to seize me and run shrieking to the sea, for
I had spoken to him and the enchantment was
on me. I waited on a breath, but he moved away
from me. Through a chink in my fingers I saw
him sitting on the sand, his head sunk in his
hands. I would have risen then and run with
the wind at the back of me, but I could not
move. My limbs had stiffened. I would stay
there till the tide rose. I would die unshriven
with the marsh creatures in my body.

Elizabeth Sutherland

THE SEER OF KINTAIL

ARROW BOOKS

Arrow Books Ltd
3 Fitzroy Square, London W1

An imprint of the Hutchinson Publishing Group

London Melbourne Sydney Auckland
Wellington Johannesburg and agencies
throughout the world

First published by Constable & Co Ltd 1974
Arrow edition 1976
© Elizabeth Sutherland 1974

Made and printed in Great Britain
by The Anchor Press Ltd
Tiptree, Essex

ISBN 0 09 912000 3

To Hugh C. Rae in gratitude

FOREWORD

There is no documentary proof that Coinneach Odhar (dun-coloured Kenneth) also known as Kenneth Mackenzie, the Brahan Seer, ever existed in the seventeenth century, and yet to the Highlander of Ross-shire he is as real and romantic as Bonnie Prince Charlie.

Throughout the Highlands and Western Isles of Scotland his fulfilled predictions are remembered with awe and his unfulfilled prophecies awaited with apprehension.

Probably the earliest written reference to him may be read in the *Bannatyne History of the Macleods* (1832) at Dunvegan which represents him as being a Lewisman from Ness.

Hugh Miller, the Cromarty stonemason, writer and geologist, writes in *Scenes and Legends of the North of Scotland* (1874) that he was a field labourer near Brahan Castle when he first began his career as a seer.

The most detailed account of Coinneach Odhar may be read in Alexander Mackenzie's *The Prophecies of the Brahan Seer* (1899) which is a collection of oral tradition and folklore concerning his life, prophecies and death.

Briefly, according to Alexander Mackenzie, Coinneach Odhar was a member of the Mackenzie clan born in Baile na Cille in Lewis some time in the first half of the seventeenth century. He received his gift of prophecy when he was a child in the form of a charm or divining stone. He travelled east and was prophesying at Brahan Castle during the time of the third Earl of Seaforth after the Restoration. He offended the Countess Isabella who had him arrested for witchcraft and burned at Chanonry Point (Fortrose) between 1665 and 1675 AD. Just before he was burned he uttered the famous prediction

7

foretelling the end of the House of Seaforth which was to come true many years later in uncanny detail.

The most mysterious fact about this shadowy prophet is that there is no reference to him whatsoever in contemporary writings. The seventeenth century was a well-documented period in Scottish history but there is no proof anywhere that he existed.

Alexander Brodie of Brodie and his son James, who kept detailed journals from 1652 to 1685 and who knew and disliked the Seaforths, do not mention him; nor does the Reverend James Fraser, Minister of Kirkhill, and author of the *Wardlaw Manuscript*, which traces the history of the Frasers from 916 to 1674. James Fraser also knew the contemporary personalities and wrote of them in an intimate, almost gossipy way, but nowhere does he mention Coinneach Odhar or his trial and death, although he showed great interest in other witchcraft trials of the day.

Thus there is no written evidence that Coinneach Odhar was a Mackenzie, that he was born in Lewis or died a criminal's death at Fortrose. Nor is there mention of him in the ecclesiastical archives of the day.

There was a 'Kennoch Owir' (possibly an English-speaking clerk's rendering of Coinneach Odhar) who was ordered to be arrested for witchcraft in 1577 and 1578 for being a 'principal enchanter' connected with the Munro Witchcraft trials. Had he been caught and brought to trial, he would no doubt have been burned at Chanonry, the seat of the diocese of Ross, but as the cathedral archives for this period are missing there is no record that he was even arrested, nor was it ever said that he was a seer.

It does not seem likely that the Kennoch Owir mentioned in the old commission could be the same prophet as the Coinneach Odhar who lived at Brahan during the Countess Isabella's lifetime. The title of Earl and Countess of Seaforth did not exist until 1623 when Colin Mackenzie of Kintail was made first Earl of Seaforth.

Who then was the Brahan Seer? In a land that abounded

in seers, augurs and believers in the Second Sight, could his perhaps be—like Isaiah—a collective name for a number of lesser seers? Was he the 'principal enchanter' and black witch who was perhaps burned at Chanonry a century before, or was he, as Alexander Mackenzie believed, a strange being, strangely gifted, whose life and death were to affect not only the Seaforth family but nearly every other branch of the Mackenzie clan?

There is no doubt what Lieutenant-General Lord Francis Humberston Mackenzie, Baron Seaforth of Kintail, ex-British Governor of Barbados, believed as he watched that awesome prophecy come true down to the last detail one hundred and fifty years after it had been uttered. Nor is there much doubt in the minds of most Ross-shire Gaels as the commemorative stone recently erected on Chanonry Point indicates.

AUTHOR'S NOTE

I would like to pay tribute to the memory of Alexander Mackenzie, FSA(Scot), author of *The Prophecies of the Brahan Seer*, published by Eneas Mackay, Stirling, 1899, and reissued by the Sutherland Press, Golspie, in 1970. Without his book, mine would never have been written.

The outcome of Coinneach Odhar's prophecies described in the text of my book may be found in the Appendix on page 217.

Part One
THE ISLANDS

Chapter 1

LEWIS

Jonet

I needed a son. God knows since the death of the Old Eagle, my father, I needed the hands and the strength of a son. Aye, God knew well enough, for it was He, according to the Preacher, who had given the Sallow One to me.

'The gift of a son, a child of God,' said the Preacher, with piety wetting his eyes. 'You will both come to the burn for baptism, daughter.'

But how could I take the bairn down to the burn with the rest of the crofters and they knowing who had fathered him? I stood at the door of the Black House with the child in my arms and watched them pass. Thirty-one of them there were, for the Preacher had said that everyone under the age of forty was to go down to the burn to repent and be born again. They all went, even the Dancing Hag who had seen more than seventy summers and could not recall her baptism but wanted to make sure of a shieling in heaven. They passed my door but not one of them looked at me or the Sallow One in my arms. Not one of them, not even Callum the Crab, who had the biggest boat in the village, stopped to say, 'Will you not come with us, Jonet?'

As for the Preacher, he never noticed that the dark woman with the bastard bairn was not at the service. They say he baptized a thousand souls in the Lewes on that journey, so how would he remember one who was not there?

When it was all over and the women snug in their cottages and in the belief that they were saved, I went down to the burn to look for the Preacher. The soft wet turf by the bank of the pool was muddy and trodden and the machair above flattened and bruised. Flies whined over the peat-dark pool and a fish jumped twice. I set the child down on the grass, propped between three stones. His head lolled, too heavy for his puny body, for he was scarcely a month old. I climbed down the bank to the pool and, kneeling, put my face so close to the water that I felt its cold caress. What need had I of the Preacher? The power lay in the water itself, not in the words or the hands of a man. I plunged deeper and, gasping, lifted my head quickly. Water ran up my sleeves and down my bodice, finding the channel between my breasts, and my hair hung in wet strands down my back.

The child whimpered and I turned. Whether it was a trick of the setting sun, or the water that stood like tears in my own eyes, but it seemed to me that he was on fire. The shawl had slipped from his head and the soft black down on him shone red as with flame. I was afraid, as afraid as I had been when the Fat Midwife cut him from my belly and held him up for me to see. A peat had settled in the fire, setting loose a shower of sparks, and a leaping tongue of flame had lit up the bairn so that he seemed to have come to me from the very pit of hell. I had screamed and turned away, hiding my head in the straw, aware of nameless horror which stunted the impulse to love.

'You have a fine son,' the Fat Midwife had said disapprovingly. 'Put him to your breast.'

I looked at the bairn fearfully and saw that he was yellow all over, the colour of bog-myrtle when it has been boiled to dye the wool. I had no milk for him. Would you believe that? The Fat Midwife had never in all her years of experience come across a mother with no milk. She tried to suckle him along with her own bairn, but he could not keep the milk down. In the end it was the thin milk from the lame cow that kept him alive those first few weeks, though it also kept him small, shrivelled and yellow.

I struggled up the bank and seized the bairn, but the image was still with me. The flaming sun turned the dripping water on my fingers to liquid fire. I could feel the heat of it, searing, scalding my flesh, and I was filled with the same nameless dread that had frightened me at his birth. Water was stronger than fire. Water alone could save him now. I plunged the child deep into the pool, so deep that his head was bruised by the stones at the bottom. It seemed to me that the water fizzed and sizzled as if I held a glowing peat in my hands.

At the same time my shoulders were seized by strong hands and I was flung aside so roughly that my cheek struck a sharp stone. Staunching the blood with a corner of my shawl, I saw the Preacher crouching over the sodden body of the babe. He pressed his feeble little frame roughly and breathed his own strong breath into the gaping mouth. The small yellow face crumpled and vomit seeped between his lips. Presently he began to whimper. The Preacher reached for my shawl and wrapped the bairn in it. I felt nothing, nothing, I tell you. It was then that I knew that not only was there no sustenance for him in my body but also there was no love for him in my heart.

'Is there murder in your soul, daughter?' the Preacher asked me sternly. He had powerful eyes that would not be lied to.

'I came for baptism,' I whispered.

'Why did you not come with the others?'

Held by his eyes, the words came out before I could stop them.

'The child belongs to Shoni.'

The Preacher was angry then. 'Woman, what kind of a mother are you to speak thus of one of God's children? What harm has this innocent done to you that you should seek such a revenge?'

Beyond him I could see the crofters creeping close, drawn by the loudness of his voice and the anger in his words. Bairny Reid, Callum the Crab, the Widow Macdonald, Ian the Cormorant and Mairie, the Dancing Hag, all were there waiting and watching. The Preacher raised his voice, aware of them, though it was to me that he spoke.

'This is indeed an evil generation where superstition and idolatry have supplanted the worship of God. I tell you,

17

woman, the pit of hell is gaping wide at your feet; see that you do not stumble into it. It is well known to me that this place is the abode of the Evil One. Drive him out, daughter, drive him from your hearth and from your heart. As for you,' he cried, turning to the group of watchers on the bank, 'you are no better than she. I have heard of your idolatrous ways. Be sure the Lord will find you out. Remember the children of Baal.'

And so he continued for an hour or more while the bairn whimpered in my arms and the crofters looked meekly at the Preacher but saw only me. Their minds were busy counting back the months to the Feast of Shoni, nine months from the day my babe was born. I saw their closed hostile faces and I knew that the hate they had for me because of my father had been supplanted by guilt for what they had made me do. I knew too that guilt breeds a greater hatred than suffering.

I stared back at them, no longer ashamed, no longer desiring to be one of them. So be it, I thought. They had made me what I was. They were responsible for what I had almost done. As for the Preacher, he ranted on till the darkness came, then he left, whipping the reeds with his staff as he crossed the Long Bog. The crofters went home in close whispering groups. As I followed alone, it came to me that the child was still un-baptized. He became known as Kenneth because my father had been of the Clan Kenneth, but to me he had no name. He was always the Son of Shoni, the Sallow One.

I had never known happiness in the Lewes. My father, the Old Eagle, had been kinsman to Red Colin of Kintail, who had brought peace of sorts to the island and had been made Earl of Seaforth for his trouble. My father it was who had seen to the building of the round tower at the head of Loch Seaforth and had been given the tack of Baile na Cille for his pains. In those days my father had been a man of strength, well able to control the Macleods and the Macdonalds whom the Red Earl had dispossessed. His thirst for the blood of the Macdonalds earned him his byname, for when he came upon a party of them roasting oxen stolen from his own herd he attacked them so mercilessly that it was said that all the eagles in the Long Island were glutted with the blood.

He was not forgiven either by the crofters or, it seemed, by God, for his wife, a Munro of rank, and his sons were drowned on the waters of Kintail. There were times when I wondered about the man my father had been, for I was a child of his dotage born of a serving wench who had died in giving birth to me. The Old Eagle called me his curse, for he had wanted a son to inherit the tack. If I had been a son it is doubtful that the tack would have come to me anyway, for my father fell out with the Earl of Seaforth and when he died, senile and impoverished, the tack was given to a Macaulay. I was left to fend as best I could in a small croft let to me by the new tacksman, surrounded by the old enemies of my clan.

Aulay Macaulay sent word to the Earl, who, after all was my kinsman, suggesting that a place might be found for me among the women at Brahan, but I never heard tell of a reply. The Earl had troubles of his own by all accounts and I held him no grudge for not adding me to the list.

But all this is past history and I only mention it to show how I came to be living alone in a hostile village with no man to protect me and no woman to call friend. In that first year after the Old Eagle had gone I learned to live with loneliness. Perhaps that was why I went wild on the night of Samhuin.

In the Lewes there are two livings to be made, one from the sea and the other from the land. There are plenty of fish in the sea but they are hard to take, just as there is a living in the land, though I sometimes think it is harder to find. The Feast of Beltane is held in a blaze of light and laughter when blessing is sought for the land. The Feast of Samhuin is different, dark and secretive in honour of the God Shoni in whose gift lies the seaware which in some strange way is able to make the land fruitful.

There was a stillness about the Black Houses on that particular October day. The women were busy preparing the feast of salted fish, oatmeal and cream, and the children, busy with their fancy clothes, were plastering their faces with soot and threading necklaces of scarlet berries round their necks. After the family feasted the children and the old folk went to their beds. When all was still the rest of the people came out of their houses in twos and threes furtively, not eyeing their neighbours or calling out in greeting. Dark fleeting shadows sped past my door and I watched them as I had watched from childhood, half-afraid, and wholly curious as they hurried towards the ruined kirk on the hill.

No one asked me to go, but I needed no invitation. I was no longer a child. The Old Eagle had been dead for a year, a skeleton at the hearth long before he was laid in his grave. Had he been alive I would not have left the cottage, for he was a religious man in his way and would take no part in the dark rites of Samhuin. Now that he was dead there was no reason to keep me at the hearth against my will.

I waited until all the crofters had passed my door, then, taking my shawl, I crept after them. I was trembling with excitement and fear, for this was Shoni's night, Shoni, the God of the sea who could also feed the land.

The door of the old kirk was closed against me. I pushed it cautiously, hoping to creep in unseen, but it was as if they had been waiting for me. The crumbling old building was ablaze with lights, for each man and woman there had brought a cruisie lamp and the flames danced and flickered in the windy vault. The crofters had their backs to the altar stone. They were facing me as I entered and a sigh came from them that was half satisfaction, half anticipation.

Then Callum pushed through the crowd and pointed at me. 'It will be Jonet,' he said loudly.

There was a murmur of agreement from the men and the women nodded their heads. I felt a tremor pass through me, but I was not afraid. The speculating eyes of the men filled me with excitement. As I stood there before them it seemed to me that this was the first time they had ever looked at me in the whole of my life. It was the first time anyone had looked at me properly and it was an intoxicating feeling. For a moment I belonged to them and I felt dim stirrings of affection for them. I wanted to please them.

Then the women came forward, shrouding me with their skirts. The Fat Midwife unpinned my shawl and loosened the ties of my bodice so that presently I stood before them naked. Then the Dancing Hag pushed forwards and with mumblings and shakings placed a white shift over my shoulders and a necklet of shells over my head. When they stepped back, Callum came forward, holding out a drinking horn.

'Drink, Jonet,' he said, his eyes devouring mine.

The first mouthful made me splutter, for I had expected ale or the crude whisky my father used to drink, but this was special; this was the water of life thrice distilled and it slid down into my belly like liquid fire. Callum watched me till every drop was gone and then Donald Squint-Eye came forward, his left eye staring sideways, but his good eye as hot as Callum's. He filled my cup to brimming.

'Drink,' he told me, and the others picked up their horns and did the same. Laughing a little, I drained every drop. Others were quick to come forward and make me sup from their own cups. I did my best to please them and then, when my head was spinning, Callum opened the kirk door.

Only the men came with me. Although a breeze had begun to blow softly off the sea, I did not notice the cold. The water of life was flowing so thickly in my veins that I did not feel the grass under my feet or the shingle, nor yet the sand. The men did not speak nor did they touch me, but I felt their breathing all around me and once when I stumbled a hand reached out to hold me steady. It was as if I were being carried along on the strength of their movement, half-flying, half-running on winged unfeeling feet. We did not stop until the wet fringe of a wave lapped over my ankles. Then Callum spoke to me, his voice distinct over the murmur of sea and wind. He gave me a horn brimming with the water of life.

'Take it to Shoni,' he said, pointing across the water.

I looked at the black moving expanse of the bay.

'Take it to him,' he urged, and I nodded wisely, aware of the importance of my task.

The men stood in a line between me and the shore. I could not see their faces, for though there were stars pricking the dark skin of night, there was no moon. The shape of them was as solid as a stone dyke. Nodding again, I took the horn carefully in both hands and at the same time a wave leapt up my thigh.

'We will be waiting for you,' Callum said, and as I turned towards the sea, I heard him cry, 'Shoni, we give you this sacrifice hoping that you will be so kind as to send up plenty of seaware in the coming year.

Holding the horn high, I stumbled forward. The sea was not as rough as the moaning wind implied, or else I was too drunk to be aware of it. It seemed to me that the waves were long and lazy and friendly towards me. A strange joy was in me and the water of life that I had taken so freely kept the cold from freezing my limbs.

You will perhaps think it strange that I was not afraid, but I had known this bay all my life. I could walk for a quarter of a mile through the water and had done so often, and still be within my depth; I was not at all afraid. Besides, the men were there waiting for me and so I moved on through the clinging water, murmuring Shoni's name and trying in vain to stop the water of life sloshing away before Shoni came to take it.

Soon the men were snatched away by the darkness and the water circled my waist and sent fingers to touch my breasts. 'Shoni!' I cried, and he came, a darker shape on the dark water. I lifted the horn and poured out the drop that remained.

'Shoni, take this sacrifice,' I said, at least that was what I meant to say. The words came out differently because my teeth were chattering and my tongue was numbed.

He spoke to me then in his own language, for I understood not one word of what he was saying, and I felt him take hold of me. Looking back on it now, I realize that he must have had a boat, but at the time it seemed to me that I was lying in

22

a great rocking shell, wrapped in something soft and smelling strongly of fish. Shoni spoke to me again and I could hear the question in his voice, but I could make no sense of what he said. The words were incomprehensible, but his movements were kind and there was concern in his tone. He rubbed my feet between his hands, but the coldness would not let me go. My body shook and there was a dizziness in my head, so that I truly believed that I was at the bottom of the sea and drowning. And then Shoni moved on top of me and I felt a wonderful creeping warmth. The terrible shivering eased into a different trembling, and comfort flowed into every part of my body. I worshipped my sea-god then for the bliss he could bring to me and when eventually his movements grew rougher and his body strange and hard, I welcomed it although there was pain at the end. I remember thinking that if this were dying I would wish to die many times. And then I knew nothing more until I awoke. It was morning and a grey sky drizzled over me where I lay in a deep drift of heather about a mile south of the village. I was not cold. I was wrapped in a blanket of sealskins. That was how I knew I had been with Shoni in the night. No Lewis man would dare to kill a seal.

The crofters were still sleeping when I returned and no one saw me creep into the cottage clad only in a bloodstained shift and a blanket of sealskins. No one spoke to me of the event; if any were surprised to see me, none showed it. Later I remembered tales of unaccountable drownings which made me realize that I had been fortunate. Shoni had been in a benevolent mood. Far from taking my life he had given me a son.

That was the last Shoni sacrifice to take place in Baile na Cille. By next Samhuin the Preacher had put the fear of God into the hearts of his flock and although there still remained other ways of appeasing the sea-god, he was never again offered such a sacrifice.

It was many years afterwards when I was visiting the market at Stornoway to sell my plaiding to the merchants there, that I happened to go down to the harbour. I passed a group of foreign fisherman who were talking among themselves and I thought I recognized my Shoni's language, but I could not be sure. It was all so long ago and I had not been in my right mind at the time. I put such suspicions right out of my head. If Shoni wished to speak with a Dutch tongue, that was his affair. He was the only man to play God to me.

No man ever asked to marry me. At the time I believed it was because of my father. As I grew older I thought it must be because of what I had become, or what the crofters had made of me, but now I am convinced it was because of my son. Even as a child he was different, with black rages and strange moods that would gather in him like a winter storm.

Life was not easy for a woman alone in Baile na Cille. I was more fortunate than some, for I was young and strong and I had a son. The widow Macdonald found it harder than I did and there were some who lived entirely on sowans and charity. I had a handful of sturdy sheep and five cows and never once lost a beast to the Morrisons when the season of 'lifting' came round.

' 'Tis easily seen that Shoni looks after his own,' the crofters would grumble with a sly look at me when a toll had been taken of the missing beasts.

During the summer months we lived almost entirely off those few beasts, the Sallow One and I. There was milk, butter and cheese in plenty and in winter the warmth of their quiet bodies gave out a heat in the Black House that was like a second fire.

Strange, but I remember the ways of those five beasts better than many of the folk who lived in the village. Not so strange, perhaps, when I recall that they shared roof and diet with us during the long winter months which was little enough, Shoni knows. I remember the day when the Sallow One and I had to drag the beasts to pasture, so weak were they from the long slow hunger of the dark months.

Besides the beasts that shared the common grazings both on the machair and at the summer shielings up on the moors, we had a good infield which grew a fine crop of bere and oats with a strip for willow to make the creels, but harvest can

24

come late to the Lewes and many a dish of nettle-tops and wild mustard have I set before the Sallow One when the meal kist was empty.

We had a lazy bed too, but the ground was poor and never improved, however much seaware and cow-dung we laid there. As for the hay crop, it was always thin, full of rushes and marsh weeds.

There was little time for leisure on the croft. Until the Sallow One grew up I had to do my own ploughing, weeding and reaping. There was also the threshing and grinding, as well as the baking of the meal. There was the thatching, the spinning, the weaving and the dyeing and, most important of all, the winning of the peats. I was fortunate there, for Callum always cut my peats after the birth of the Sallow One. Perhaps it was his way of making up to me for what had happened on the night of Samhuin. Certainly I was grateful for his help.

Although we worked hard, we found time to play too. There was not a man or a woman who did not sing, and the old white-headed story-teller could take us into a world of wonder and magic, while the piper's music could make even the Little Folk come down from the moors to dance.

I waited impatiently for the Sallow One to grow strong enough to take his share of the work on the croft, but when the time came all he wanted was to go fishing with the men. He was a true son of Shoni, never away from the wide white sands and the restless water. The only work he enjoyed was collecting the seaware and spreading it on the upper shore to dry. Here he could watch the boats come and go without interruption.

There were three boats in Baile na Cille at that time, each carrying a crew of four men and a boy or two. Dangerous craft they were, to my way of thinking, with woollen sails and ropes of twisted heather roots. The men who sailed them were strong and fearless, pecking for fish like sea-chickens in a gale. It was every boy's ambition to go to sea and mine was no exception. I was not the mother to try and stop him. A few extra fish to salt down against the winter would be a welcome addition to the cooking pot.

25

When I heard that Ian the Cormorant was willing to take a boy on his boat I put on my best shawl and, wrapping a fine cheese in dock leaves for Mairie, told the Sallow One to wash his face and come with me.

It was a fine June evening with primroses scenting the banks of the burn and a cuckoo calling from a thorn bush. The sound pleased me, for it is well known to be a bird of good omen. The cuckoo is a fairy creature and the thorn a fairy tree. There is an old tale told of a man who was once so foolish as to kill a cuckoo while it was singing in a thorn bush. The Little People turned him and all his clan into seals. I began to tell my son the story.

'Only when the moon is full can they cast off their sealskins and become human again,' I told him. 'No one in the whole of the Long Island would be so foolish as to kill a cuckoo, or a seal either,' I added.

The boy was silent, as was his custom when I told him of the old beliefs.

'Are you not interested, my son?' I asked sharply.

'Why should I be interested?' he replied.

'There is generally wisdom in the old tales for those with a mind to understand.'

'I was wondering why you sleep on a sealskin blanket,' he said.

It was like him to catch me out.

'Because it is warm,' I replied tartly.

'Well,' he said, 'there is wisdom in that, just as there is wisdom in saying, "Do not kill a cuckoo because the noise he makes is pleasing." There is no wisdom in saying, "Do not kill a cuckoo because if you do, you will be turned into a seal." '

'How is it that you know so much better than your mother?' I asked, hearing the sharpness in my voice. What he said was sensible enough, but the way he said it angered me.

He was silent, but I could not blame him for that. My question was not worth the answering.

'Ian will never take you on his boat if you talk lightly about killing seals,' I added. 'He has more respect for the old ways.'

26

'The Cormorant will not take me into his boat whatever,' he said, playing with the white pebble he kept in a pouch about his neck.

'What nonsense is this?' I cried.

'Hector of Uig will go on the boat.' He laughed suddenly but without much joy. 'He will be very sick.'

'Enough of this foolishness,' I said, vexed, for he had the habit of making such uncalled-for remarks, but I was uneasy.

Ian was whittling away at a creepie stool at the door of his cottage, while Mairie, immaculate as always in a snowy curtch tied neatly under her chin, worked deftly with distaff and spindle. Mairie's weaving was famous as far as Stornoway and I knew what I was talking about being no novice at the work.

We talked of this and that and the calm evening while the Sallow One played quietly with his pebble. There was no hurrying this matter, though Ian knew well enough why we had come. I gave Mairie the cheese and we talked of its making. Although I could not call Mairie a friend, there was a bond between us born out of a respect for work well done. Mairie's cheeses were second only to my own. As was fitting, it was Ian who opened the subject.

'The boy will be a help to you, Jonet. He is growing fast.'

'He is beginning to take a man's place in the croft,' I said carefully. The Sallow One was sitting very still and stiff and the stone was clenched in his fist. I wished he would put it away. He looked as daft as Bairny Reid.

'Mm hm,' said the Cormorant, turning the stool and examining it carefully. 'What do you make of this, boy?' he asked, holding it out to the Sallow One.

The boy glanced up but did not seem to see the stool.

'Take a good look at it now,' Ian urged, and it was all I could do to stop myself shaking my son, for he showed no interest.

Ian placed the stool on the ground where it shifted unevenly on its three legs.

'What would you do with it, Kenneth?' he asked.

It was such a simple test and Ian was only waiting for the

boy to point out that the ground was uneven, that he had better test it inside where it was destined to be. Instead he said, 'There is a whale stranded at the mouth of Finn's Cave.'

The Cormorant looked at him as if he were foolish. Even Mairie paused in her work to look sideways at him. What a time, I thought, to indulge in one of his dreams. I was used to his strange utterances and had learned to ignore them. To argue or question him would often bring on one of his black moods, but Ian was not to know this.

'What is that you are saying, boy?'

'There is a whale stranded at the mouth of Finn's Cave with meat on him sufficient to feed the whole of the Lewes.'

Ian laughed, but the sound was false.

'I'm thinking this boy of yours has a sense of humour, Jonet.'

The Sallow One looked up at him. His eyes were very dark and there was that blind look in them that I had come to dread.

'There is a whale at the mouth of the cave. It will escape when the tide turns.'

Ian frowned. He picked up the stool and began to whittle at the legs.

'Will you be letting it escape?' the Sallow One asked anxiously, coming close to us.

'So you would be skipper before you have caught your first fish?' Ian said quietly.

The Sallow One turned to me. 'Tell him, Mother.'

That was the day I learned never again to make light of my son, but the words were out before I could stop them.

'It's only his fun, Ian. Pay no heed.'

The Sallow One turned on me then and the black rage boiled up out of him.

'Fool of a woman!' he cried. 'You know that the whale is there. May the nine rays of the sun blister your tongue for the stupidness in you!'

I wanted to cry out, 'He does not mean it. He cannot help himself. The mood is like a sickness,' but I was too late. Ian's fingers lashed across his cheek like five leather thongs.

28

'Never speak to your mother like that!' he cried.

The boy fell back with water starting in his eyes. He must have bitten his tongue, for his spittle was red with blood.

'You have just lost yourself a good whale,' he said, and turned away.

The worst of it was that Callum reported sighting a whale blowing in the neighbourhood of Finn's Cave. There could have been some truth in what the Sallow One had said. Lately I had come to realize that many of his queer sayings had truth in them. Ian might have found a lie easier to forgive. As it was he took Hector to his boat and that in spite of Mairie's pleading. Mairie had her own reasons for not wanting to cross me at that time, but I was not an unreasonable woman. Ian's decision was natural. The Sallow One had only himself to blame.

I believed at the time that this was the first occasion that the crofters learned of the Sallow One's strangeness, but I was wrong. They had known of it as long as I had myself.

'What else would you be expecting from a son of Shoni?' the men would mutter.

'As to that, he is also Jonet's son,' the women would add darkly, and they would all murmur in agreement.

The strangeness in the Sallow One first came to him at the Beltane Feast when he was in his fifth year. It was as good a Beltane as I can remember that year, for the weather was warm and windless and the crofters in the mood to celebrate. For days the bairns had been busy collecting fuel for the great bonfire on the Round Mound and there was ale and whisky in plenty.

It had always been the custom for the Dancing Hag to place a sprig of rowan at the door of every byre in the village before the cattle were released from winter bondage and taken to the further grazings and higher still to the shielings on the moors for summer pasturage. The old woman was no longer able to walk so far and Callum had asked me if I would perform the task for the crofters. More and more of late I had been asked to take on the Dancing Hag's rituals and I was glad enough to do them. If I could not be liked in the village, I could at least be respected.

One of the most important rites was the making of the nead fire to stop cattle sickness when the beasts first cropped the sweet new grass of summer. I had been practising the ritual for days and found it no easy matter to make fire from the friction of dry wood. It would be for me to light the Beltane Bonfire with every man, woman and child watching me.

Once the baking of the Beltane Bannocks was done and they had been spread thick with custard, the hearth fires were doused, cleaned out and set with fresh peats to be kindled by fire from the Beltane Bonfire. When I had finished planting the rowan sprigs, the Sallow One and I looked to our own poor beasts and a fine time we had of it trying to keep them off the infields as we drove them with birch twigs up towards the Round Mound. There they mingled with the other beasts and I saw the Sallow One laughing with the rest of the bairns as the Widow Macdonald pulled away at the tether of her beast that could not be much younger than herself. I particularly noticed the Sallow One's laugh, for it was a rare event. He was like me in that, for though I see much to make me smile inwardly, I seldom have cause to laugh aloud.

At dusk the time came to light the great fire. As the sparks fell on the heather I had carefully soaked in fish oil, the new fire sprang into flame and the whole hillside came alive in the light. Then it was the turn of the men and boys to drive the cattle three times widdershins round the crackling furnace, and how the women laughed at the unhandiness of their menfolk with the beasts. In all the confusion I was glad to see how gently the Sallow One tended our lame cow. Some of the lads were close to drawing blood in their efforts to spur the poor creatures to wilder antics.

When the ceremonies were over and the cattle allowed to graze at their leisure under the care of Bairny Reid, the feast began. When the serious eating was over, the young girls brought out their own crossed bannocks and, with much shrieking and excited laughter, rolled them down the hillside.

If her bannock arrived intact that girl would be married within the year. The lads teased them raucously and pretended to stop the flying cakes and crush them underfoot. Even the younger bairns rolled their own bannocks, choosing steeper slopes and vying with each other for distance. It vexed me a little that the Sallow One did not join with them. He was sitting alone in the light of the great fire and nibbling evenly round a custard bannock, absorbed in some dream of his own, but I felt for his aloneness and related it to my own.

As the night wore on, the singing and the drinking grew wilder. The fire was built up with peats which would be used later to kindle every hearth before dawn. I could have had any man I wanted that night, for it was considered good luck to sleep with the Beltane Woman, and it had been many years since the Beltane Woman was young enough to be desired. Callum sought me out where I sat apart and in the shadows with the Sallow One drowsing at my side. He handed me a cup of whisky, not the sweet fire with which he had filled me at Samhuin, but a hot drink none the less. I took it from him and he sat down at my side. When I had drunk a little he took my hand and carried it to his groin. His breath was heavy with the drink.

'I'm hard for you, Jonet,' he said, squeezing my hand against him.

I let my hand stay on him for a moment but felt no answering heat in myself. To tell the truth, Shoni had spoiled me for other men. My dreams were all of him as I lay under my seal-skins at night, a poor substitute, no doubt, but better than the Crab.

'Do not spill your seed in me,' I told him, and took away my hand.

The Sallow One awoke and whimpered. I turned to make him more comfortable and when I looked back, Callum had gone. I drank the rest of the whisky and felt strangely unhappy.

The old story-teller had begun a rambling tale about mermaids, water horses and rope spun from the gold hair of a Northland princess. The older folk listened or dozed while the

31

younger couples made beds for themselves in the heather. It was considered the best night in the year for making bairns.

I was not tired, though it had been as long a day as I could remember, but I had a wish to be by myself for a while. Leaving the Sallow One curled up in his plaid, I wandered down from the Round Mound. Two of the younger men who had not yet paired off followed me. I knew well enough what they were after and told them they were wasting their time. I was more interested in the whereabouts of my own five beasts. Tomorrow the younger folk would be taking half the herd up to the high summer shielings and I wanted to make sure that my beasts were left behind. I had served my time in the shielings and when he was old enough the Sallow One would take his turn, but that would not be for a year or so yet.

The cattle had found their way to the old burial ground where the grass was sweetest and greenest. I found my own five beasts easily enough, for they were all together as close as if they had still been in the byre, and chewing as if another winter depended on it. When I had tethered them to a head-stone, I saw Bairny Reid. He was propped up against a stone cross, crooning to himself in the moonlight.

'Are you not weary, Bairny?' I asked him.

'I'm hungry,' he said, eyeing my bundle.

'I just thought that might be the way of it,' I said and gave him a bannock, all that remained of my Beltane Feast.

He snatched it and ate it, totally absorbed in the act of eating.

'Away you go now and listen to the old father's tales. I'll mind the beasts.'

He shambled off happily. Bairny was one of God's children and though he had lived for the best part of fifty years, he had never grown up in the head. The crofters cared for him and in return he did what he was told to do, such as watching the beasts when the others were feasting.

I sat down in Bairny's place, thinking that this was something we had in common. We were the only two souls in the village not afraid to spend a night with the dead. It occurred to me that this was another reason why folk shunned me. I had no proper respect for ghosts and water bulls and the Little People. Shoni had cured me of that.

I must have fallen asleep, though I had not intended to do so, for it was my responsibility to see that the beasts kept away from the infields. Certainly I had a strange dream. A woman came to me where I sat wrapped in my plaid. She was tall, with long yellow hair woven into thick plaits that fell as far as her thighs—put into my head no doubt by the old man's tale of hair rope—and she was dressed in white with a jewel round her neck that glowed like the moon.

'Let me in!' she cried, twisting her pale smooth fingers. I particularly noticed her hands, for they were so different from my own that were as rough and calloused as my feet.

'For the love of Shoni, let me in,' she pleaded. 'It is nearly dawn.'

I knew then, the way it is in dreams when explanations are not needed, that this was a woman of rank. She was also dead and I was barring the way to her grave.

'What will you give me if I let you in?' I said without shifting. She reached up to her neck and took off the shining jewel.

'It is for Shoni's son,' she said, and I felt the coldness of her hand on mine as I awoke.

It was dawn and great dark clouds were massing to the west. The Sallow One was tugging at my hand.

'The great fire is nearly out,' he said accusingly. 'Did you make the new fire in the house?'

I had forgotten to kindle my own cold hearth from the Beltane Fire, but I could not see that it mattered.

'The Beltane Woman can make her own new fire,' I told him.

He seemed satisfied. I stood up stiffly, for the old grave had not been a comfortable bed. As I moved, something fell from my clothing. The Sallow One stooped to pick it up.

'What is it?' I asked, drawing my plaid close.

He opened his hand. A stone lay there, smooth, white, the shape of an elfin moon.

'Where did it come from?' he asked me.

I shook my head. It would take time to work out an answer that would satisfy myself, let alone my son. He was a man before I told him.

He held it up, caressing it, loving it, and it did not strike me as strange that he should want it. It was a beautiful thing.

'Let me look at it,' I asked.

'It's mine,' he said, holding it possessively. Later he asked me to make a pouch for it out of cow hide which he kept on a thong round his neck.

It was after that when I first noticed his wild predictions, and though I could not see the sense of it, I had the feeling that the stone was somehow involved.

As for the woman in my dream, I asked the story-teller if there were any tales about the old burial ground. He told me that the Northland warriors were buried there. A ship carrying a fine princess to her betrothed was wrecked close by. 'She was so fair,' the old man said, 'that it was said Shoni himself took her for wife.'

Perhaps this pretty moon-smooth pebble was Shoni's gift to his son. On the other hand, Bairny Reid collected stones. Every so often the Fat Midwife who gave him shelter had to throw away great heaps of them which he kept hidden under the dry heather of his bed.

'Bonny stones they are, some of them,' she would say, 'but if I kept them all there would be enough to build a dyke to Stornoway.'

Education was not for the likes of crofting families. In truth it was feared by many and for good reason. An educated man was often a discontented man who had no wish to return to the crofting life, and crofters needed their bairns as they needed the sun and the rain.

I am not certain why I wanted it for the Sallow One. It came to me gradually that if he had an education, the black rages and wild predictions might not trouble him so. An education might teach him not only an understanding of the English language but also an understanding of himself. I believed that the rages came from some tangled web of confusion in his own mind. It was possible that education might help to unravel that web. Education, however, cost more than half a dozen hens, a length or two of cloth and the few cheeses that were left over when the tacksman had taken his rent. I did not have that sort of wealth.

When the Dancing Hag died, the opportunity came. For years I had undertaken more and more of the village rites, performing them at least as well as she did. Two days after her burial I had my first private consultation. The Widow Macdonald, leaning heavily on her stick, paused outside my croft when I was spinning wool, a task I particularly disliked and was glad enough to set aside. Wondering what she wanted from me, for I seldom had visitors, I offered the old soul a bowl of broth which she refused with an impatient gesture.

'How then can I help you, Mistress?'

'That remains to be seen,' she said tartly. 'It is my shoulder.' Her face twisted with pain as she tried to show me the place. 'She-who-was-lain-in-the-grave gave me a soothing physic.'

I did not know what sort of physic the Dancing Hag would prescribe for such an ailment. I was ignorant of such matters except for the simple measures that all the world must know, such as goat's milk for the consumption and a singed butter cloth for a burn. I suspected that the Dancing Hag was not much better informed than myself and that if she had survived on her wits as a wise woman, then I could do no worse.

I took the Widow into my home and asked to see the painful place. With my help she removed her curtch and several layers of clothing. She turned her bent old grey back towards me and a strange feeling gushed into my heart at the sight of those pitiful shoulders. So strong was the feeling that my eyes ached with tears and my hands, full of a gentle strength, moved of their own accord over the afflicted spot.

'Ach,' said the old woman, 'that feels so good.'

Her shoulders seemed to straighten under the power of my hands and presently she closed her eyes and seemed to fall asleep. After a while my hands grew tired. I helped her to dress and fasten her shawl.

'You have healing in your hands, Jonet,' she said, and there was a new humbleness in her.

I remembered times when I had quietened a sick beast or soothed the Sallow One to sleep when he had a fever, and I rejoiced. The old woman reached into the pocket of her skirt and brought out two small brown eggs carefully wrapped in plaited reeds which she laid on my table. I would not have insulted her by refusing them.

Those two eggs were the start of the long slow climb to the Sallow One's education. My patients were not rich but I had plenty of them, for the Widow Macdonald was not one to hold her tongue. But I quickly realized that healing hands were not enough. I had much to learn about the use of herbs and charms. Still more important, I had to learn to read the minds of my patients. There were some who preferred their physic to be bitter and unpleasant before they would trust in its effectiveness. Others needed no physic at all but preferred to sleep with a charm under the heather in their beds. To begin with, my physic was mainly whisky flavoured with herbs, but as I grew more interested in curing my neighbours, I learned which plants were effective, and grew a plot of them in a corner of the infield.

I had other clients too who were not sick in the accepted sense. These would come—some from distant parts—for love-charms, protective coloured threads, incantations and advice. Then there were others again who would come for darker purposes in the belief that I had the knowledge of hurting. Here there was real wealth to be made, but it was dangerous. One careless deed and I would be denounced as a witch. A wise woman, yes; a healing woman, yes; I was finding much satisfaction and sufficient material reward in that profession, but witchcraft was something else.

When I had enough put by to pay for an education for the Sallow One, he was ten years old. He was still a dun-coloured bairn, small for his years but neatly made with brooding black

36

eyes and black unruly hair. There was always a frown between his eyes which troubled me. No other bairn that I knew had this look of drawn anxiety. It was to be hoped that education would smooth away the trouble, whatever it might be.

Looking at the boy on the eve of our journey to Stornoway, I realized that I was putting much store on education, too much perhaps. If I had stopped to think more deeply I would have realized that I was deluding myself. Education might indeed cure some of the problems, but it would no doubt bring others and these I could not anticipate.

You will be asking me what the child thought of this business of his education and I am ashamed to tell you that I never knew. I did not ask him or consult him in the matter. I assumed he wanted it for himself and I hoped that he would not spoil the opportunity by behaving as he had done with the Cormorant.

It was a fine April morning when we set out for the town. The Sallow One had his first pair of shoes for the occasion but he would not wear them until we stood on the doorstep of the Maister's house, and then he grumbled at the weight and discomfort of them. I had no pity for him, for I had worn my shoes for most of the fifteen miles across the moors and my feet were hot and blistered. I was not so particular on the way home.

A servant lass opened the door of the fine stone house and took us into the room that was used for teaching. It pleased me that she knew who I was and when I told her there was good fortune as well as beauty in her brown eyes, she turned as pink as clover. The Sallow One had retreated into one of his dark moods but at least he waited until she had left the room before saying:

'She will have two bairns, the one deaf and dumb and the other simple. Is that what you call lucky?'

'Wheesht, my son,' I said hastily, 'and put away your stone. The Maister will think you simple if he catches you playing with it.'

I was relieved when he slipped it into his pocket, but I believe he was as nervous as I was when the Maister came in.

To tell the truth, I did not take to him. He had the appearance of a gentleman, which indeed he was, for it was said he was kinsman to the Macrae. I could not help wondering why he was content to concern himself with the education of humbler folk, but the ways of gentlemen are as difficult to understand as the language they speak. His clothes were elegant, his body long and thin and, to my mind, useless, but it was his eyes that I mistrusted, old yellowish devouring eyes that did not quite fit their sockets.

'So,' he said, his eyes swivelling from me to the boy, 'we are to make a scholar of you, Kenneth.'

His Gaelic was so bad that I doubted his ability to make a scholar of anyone.

'Our first task will be to teach you the English,' he said haltingly, and then he started to speak in his own tongue so that the Sallow One and I could only stare at him without understanding, and yet not entirely without understanding, for the tone of his voice and the soft easy rush of his words made me uneasy.

'Do you have other pupils, Maister?' I asked when the opportunity came.

'They come and they go, Mistress,' he replied with his wavering eyes still on the boy.

'What are your terms?'

They were lower than I had expected, which, strangely enough, did not please me at all.

'Will that cover the cost of a good education?' I asked doubtfully.

'It will cover the cost of his board. A good education is beyond price.'

He raised his hand and when the lace cuff fell back from his wrist I noticed a strange thing. The nails on his fingers were smoothly cut, rounded and clean, but his thumbnail was long and sharply pointed and rimmed with rusty dirt. Though it in no way resembled an eagle's claw, yet that was what came to my mind when I saw it. Seeing the direction of my eye he lowered his hand and turned to the boy.

'I will have no Gaelic spoken here, boy, remember that or it will be the worse for you.'

Although he spoke lightly enough and there was even a smile on his lips, yet I was increasingly uneasy. I looked at the Sallow One, determined that the decision must be his. If he showed the least disinclination to stay I would be glad to take him home.

'I will stay until the harvest,' he said.

'In English, boy, say it in English,' the Maister said quickly and though I could not fault him, yet the uneasiness remained.

Afterwards it struck me as strange that the child who could predict the wildest of fortunes for the unlikeliest folk was as blind as the rest of us when it came to his own future.

Three weeks later he came home, scaring the wits out of me as he fumbled his way into the croft some time before dawn.

'Who is it?' I whispered, raising myself in the bed and staring into the smoky gloom beyond the smoulder of the fire.

'Me,' he said in a soft uncertain voice that was so unlike himself that I was afraid.

'What are you doing here at this time of night?' I asked, my voice surly with anxiety as I rose and wrapped a shawl about my shift.

He did not reply but drew the stool close to the fire and held out his hands to the heat. I blew life into the smoored peats and a flame shot up lighting his face and reminding me uneasily of that moment by the pool when I had seen him framed in fire. I shifted the porridge pot closer to the heat and stirred the mixture that was thickening nicely for the morning.

'You will be hungry I suppose?'

He shook his head. The small hunched loneliness of him hurt me so that I ached to put my arms round him. I had missed him more than I had thought possible and I was glad to see him now, but I could not tell him so. There had never been a show of love between us.

'Well?' I demanded more harshly than I intended. 'I am waiting for an explanation.'

'I was not wanting to miss the Beltane Feast,' he said, not looking me in the eye.

I was angry then. 'What is this nonsense? I send you to the town to be educated when Shoni himself knows how much you are needed here. I have given you the chance to enter another world and you are fool enough to turn your back on it. Why?'

I cupped his chin in my hand and forced him to look up at me. His face was sallower than ever, as if he had not looked at the sun lately. His cheeks were streaked with the smudges of tears. Worse; there were rusty traces of blood on his neck and about his ears. I looked more closely. The fragile skin behind his right ear was scarred and suppurating. The lobe of his left ear was almost severed. With horror, I remembered the Maister's sharpened nail.

'Shoni!' I exclaimed, gripping his shoulders. 'What has he done to you, my son?'

He winced and whimpered at my touch. With mounting dread I removed his plaid. His shirt was stuck to his back with dried blood. I had to cut it free and soak away the parts that seemed to have become part of his flesh.

'Why? Why?' I cried when I saw his back criss-crossed with open lashes, but all he would say was, 'He took my stone.'

There was no sense in questioning him further, for he was all but dead from pain and weariness. I went to my own bed and took the sealskin blanket still warm from my body and wrapped him in it. After a while he slept, but I sat on watching and wondering until the cock reminded me that day had begun.

It was my plan to confront the Maister that day, but the Sallow One stayed so close to the hearth that I was reluctant to leave him even for the sake of reciting the curses I had been practising under my breath for the past hour. It seemed to me that he was still afraid. Whatever had happened to hurt the child could only be resolved by time, so I set him small indoor tasks that kept his hands and mind occupied but not overtaxed. Nor did I question him. I could not trust myself to think, let alone speak calmly of the affair.

40

That evening while we sat at our meal there was a clap at the door. To my surprise it was Catriona, the Maister's servant, who stood there, her weary face drawn with anxiety. At the sight of her the Sallow One rose.

'So you found your way home—thank God for that!' she cried. 'I thought—' but she did not say what she had thought. Instead she added, 'I brought your clothing.'

She laid a small bundle on the table. He looked at it eagerly, and then tore it open. He picked up his shirt and shoes and shook them carefully, but the slate and primer he left lying.

'Is this what you are after?' Catriona said, opening her hand to reveal the leather pouch that contained his stone.

When he had taken it from her he did a strange thing. He took the girl's hand and carried it to his cheek. It was a gesture of love and gratitude such as I had not thought him capable of making. Then he ran to the door and went out into the soft pink dusk. I let him go without fear. I could see he was himself again.

I set Catriona down close to the fire and began to prepare a meal for her. There was much she could tell me.

'Why does Kenny set so much store by that stone?' she asked, loosening her shawl and holding her hands to the warmth.

I shook my head. It was a question I had often asked myself. If the crofters knew how it had come into his possession, they would have had no doubts. The stone was from Shoni and Shoni's gift to his son was the Second Sight. To me it was not so simple. Perhaps the stone had indeed come from Shoni, but it seemed to me that the strangeness in my son was no gift but a curse bestowed by the other God in punishment for my misdeeds.

As I listened to Catriona speaking I realized that my uneasiness in the Maister's presence had not been misplaced. Seemingly he was a terrible man for punishment. A single word in the Gaelic produced from him a sharp nip behind the ear from that sharpened thumbnail. And there were other equally unpleasant punishments. He kept a grinning skull on his table

41

to hang around the neck of any boy who gave a wrong answer. Fingers were caned for untidy writing, and the whip used for insolence.

When the Sallow One joined the school, the Maister had but two pupils. The rest had run away or been taken home by compassionate parents. The two who remained were the motherless sons of a sea-captain who had nowhere else to send them. A week after the Sallow One's arrival, the elder boy had run away to sea, leaving his younger brother and the Sallow One alone with the Maister.

'I did my best for the two poor bairns,' said Catriona with tears rolling over her cheeks, 'but it was not enough. That poor little motherless creature! He was so afraid of the Maister that he lost the use of his tongue. The more frightened he was, the stupider he became, and stupidity always provoked the Maister to violence.'

Catriona had not been allowed to interrupt the Maister when he was teaching but on that last morning she could not in the name of pity ignore the cries of the sea-captain's younger son. She had run into the class-room just in time to see the Maister, his eyes glittering, standing with whip in hand over the insensible body of the boy.

As she ran forward to tend to the child, she looked across at the Sallow One. He was standing with his back to the small window. Although she could not see the expression on his face, for it was a dark morning, she could see that he was trembling. At first she thought he was transfixed with terror, but when he spoke his voice was strange and strong. She could not remember the exact words he said, for she had been too occupied with the other bairn, but she thought it was something to do with a hillside, a tree and a great crowd of angry strangers. The Maister strode over to him, seized the pouch containing the stone and was about to shake the life out of him when she had cried, 'Is one dead bairn not enough for you?'

He stopped. 'Is the child dead?' he asked with a fearful expression.

'If he is not, it will be a miracle,' she told him.

He left the room then in a great hurry and seemingly he took the first boat out of the harbour.

'I had to leave Kenny then,' Catriona said. 'I had to get help to the other child, for he was still insensible. Kenny was in a bad way too, huddled in a corner of the room, his hands at his throat and his eyes strange and unseeing. Perhaps I should not have left him, but what was I to do? When I came back, he had gone.'

She was silent for a while, remembering the horror.

'Do you know what was the most terrible thing about the Maister?' she continued presently, in a low voice, not looking me in the eye. 'He enjoyed hurting those bairns. Until that day I thought he was doing it for the sake of education, but I was wrong. He was using those boys the way a man will use a woman, to give himself pleasure.' She paused. 'I often wondered why he did not ask to come to my bed, for I was the only woman in the house and he had never taken a wife.'

'What of the other bairn?' I asked, sick to the stomach.

'He will live. His body will heal in time, but only God can cure the hurt to his soul.'

I asked her then where she had found the stone. She flushed as red as a poppy. 'You will be thinking me a terrible creature when I tell you,' she whispered. 'The Maister owed me money. He left in such a hurry that the clothes he had been wearing were lying all over the floor of his room. I looked in the pockets of his coat. That was how I found the stone.'

'It is well that you did,' I told her.

We talked for another hour and again later when the Sallow One was sleeping peacefully in his bed, but the question in my own mind was still unanswered as we lay down to sleep together. Was the power of seeing such strange sights in the Sallow One or was it in the stone?

Three years later Shoni's son was to get his education even if I were to lose my soul for it.

I have told you how the tack that had belonged to my father was given to Aulay Macaulay. Some said it was an unlucky

43

tack, for my father had been left with an only daughter and now it seemed that Aulay was to be the same. His wife was a woman of an age with myself but as unlucky in childbearing as I had been in husbands. It was Aulay himself who told her to speak to me for news of Morag—like most village gossip—had reached the laird's ears.

I had been lucky with Morag. She had come to me after a year of childless marriage for a charm to help her conceive. Poor little Morag and her clumsy witless man! They would have been the laughing stock of the whole of the Long Island if I had repeated what Morag had told me. But their secret was safe with me. I kept my place as wise woman not only because of my skills but also because I knew how to hold my tongue.

You would not think it possible for a man to be so ignorant or a woman so innocent. They had seen the beasts coupling often enough, and he had approached her in the same fashion. Her marriage had been a year of agony and she was still a virgin. Weeks after her visit to me she had conceived and the good news must have reached Aulay's ears.

'Speak to the woman in Baile na Cille,' he told his wife. 'If anyone can help you, it will be herself.'

So Mistress Macaulay sent for me to come to the big stone house by the sea. It was a great inconvenience to me to walk the two miles along the shore at that time, for the Lame One was about to calf and as she had not given birth for three years now, I was anxious to be present at the event. However, I did not want to offend Macaulay, for he had been good to me when my father died, so I set off leaving instructions with the Sallow One to come after me himself if the birth-pangs began.

It was a grey-and-silver afternoon, with the sea like wet sealskin and a silence that turned every bird's cry into an intrusion. My thick skirts were too hot on such a day, so I bunched them high to let the air get at my limbs. All the while I wondered what I could do for a woman of breeding. I had never spoken to such a one in all my life, though I had seen her often enough, for she bought plaiding from Mairie and

44

fish from Ian, and very particular she was about them both, I had heard.

The house was scarcely a dozen years old, for Aulay had not thought the old place where my father had lived fitting for his family. It was a grand house indeed, three storeys high, with a round tower and a turret. The servant took me up a winding stair and into another world where my feet were welcomed by soft skins and carpeting. There were pictures and hangings on the walls and I would have liked time to look at them properly, but the servant was in a hurry.

I was shown into a room that was altogether the most beautiful place I have ever seen. Mistress Macaulay was sitting on a high-backed carved chair, her feet in satin shoes crossed daintily on a footstool. A fire burned in the chimney place, but what took my eye first was the bed, so big was it, with four posts and rich heavy hangings. The room was full of fine things, but the prettiest of all was the girl that sat on a stool at her mother's side. Like her mother, she was sewing with coloured threads, but her work held no interest for her. There was a restlessness in her blue eyes and in the backward sweep of her thick gold hair. She must have been near to fifteen at the time, for although she was small, she was a perfect woman. It gave me pleasure to look at her.

'Leave us, Grania,' the mother said without paying heed to me.

The girl rose gracefully. As she passed me at the door she gave me a wide knowing stare from her bluebell eyes as if we shared some secret. When she had closed the door, Mistress Macaulay looked at me with distaste. Then she said something in English which I did not understand.

'Tch,' she said impatiently, 'so you have no English.'

Her Gaelic was strange and hard to follow until I remembered that she was a Caithness woman and spoke a different form of the language.

'You must realize that this was not my idea,' she continued in the same aggrieved tone. 'However, since you are here, you had better be seated.'

She waved towards a chair some distance from the fire which I ignored. I felt foolish enough on my feet; seated, I would have been vanquished. She was beautiful in a dark bitter fashion with passionate eyes and a sulky twist to her mouth. It came to me that she was a woman who blossomed in the presence of men. With her own sex she was as dry and prickly as winter whin.

'You may as well know from the start that there is nothing, absolutely nothing, you can do for me. You are only here because Macaluay desired it and what Macaulay desires, Macaulay gets—most of the time,' she added, and her mouth twisted momentarily.

'What is it that Macaulay wants?' I asked.

'A son and heir, but I fear he must be disappointed.'

'How is it that you are so certain?' I asked, for I had learned that nothing is sure where conception is concerned.

'Macaulay's seed is damaged. Oh, he has plenty of it and he plants it often enough, but it will never bear fruit. That is all you need to know.'

She reached out her hand to pull the bell-rope that hung on the wall by her chair.

'You have one child—a perfect child—' I began, but she interrupted me impatiently.

'A girl,' she said harshly, 'conceived before Macaulay caught the pox when soldiering on the Mainland, so do not tell me to tie a red ribbon on the bed-post or offer a fresh cheese to the fairies. There is nothing they—or you—can do.' She leaned back in her chair and added with a sigh, 'Unless, of course, you have the right words to convince Macaulay that it is his fault that I am barren. He blames me.'

I moved towards the window. The girl Grania was standing on the shore, a golden creature in a grey world. Below and beyond a figure was running along the sand that might be the Sallow One in search of me.

'He blames me,' she continued. 'Because he has plenty of seed he thinks the fault is mine. He does not realize that my desire for a son is at least as great as his own. He will die

46

sooner than me, for he is ten years my senior and diseased. If I have no son to protect me and to inherit the tack, what is to become of me?'

'Then give him one,' I said softly. I could see that the running figure was the Sallow One and my mind was already fixed anxiously on my poor cow. I could not afford to lose her.

Mistress Macaulay turned in her chair, her eyes blazing in her pale face. She stared at me, demanding my full attention.

'What are you saying?'

I did not reply. There was no need. She had interpreted my advice so quickly that I knew the thought had been planted already in some dark corner of her mind.

'How could I arrange such a thing?' she murmured.

Still I did not reply.

'It is impossible,' she said, flushing, for she knew she had betrayed herself to me. 'You are wicked to suggest such a thing. Macaulay would have you evicted for less.'

I smiled. Let her protest a little. I was not afraid of eviction. I was afraid only for my beast. I went to the door.

'Where are you going?' she demanded. 'I did not say you could leave.'

'I have a cow about to calve. I must go to her.'

She came over to me quickly and put her hand on my sleeve.

'Would you do it? Would you take such a risk?' she asked, but there was such an excitement in her that I knew she had made up her mind. I had only told her what she had wanted to hear.

'You forget, Mistress,' I said with a faint smile, 'I already have a son.'

She let me go then.

'There was a boy here,' said the servant when I entered the kitchen. 'They are wanting you at home.'

Although I was in such a hurry I had time to look down to the beach. The girl, Grania, and the Sallow One stood there side by side on the long white sands close to the edge of the water. Suddenly she danced backwards, laughing and shaking her restless hair. It was not a loud laugh, but soft and delightful, and it disturbed me. She was too pretty, too clever and altogether too much of a woman for the Sallow One. 'Go home,' I urged him inwardly. 'You are playing with fire.' Fire, always fire I thought, trying to drive away the old images that would keep returning to my mind. I opened my mouth to call to him as he trailed along the shore after that sunlit girl, but I said nothing. There were some forces too strong even for Shoni himself. What if he did fall in love with the girl? Nothing could come of it. Such a girl could draw the great Fionn's love himself. She would never so much as notice my son. So I thought no more about it at that time and for the rest of the day my mind was fully occupied with the Lame One's calf which was born with some difficulty later that night.

Mistress Macaulay conceived in due course and I was to hear the news from Aulay himself. He rode up to the croft one day with a great clatter of hooves and swung heavily off his horse. A woman was with me at the time. When she saw who had come, she bobbed to him and called out a blessing, but I stood where I was and waited for him to come to me.

'Well, Mistress Jonet,' he said in his rough, bluff way. 'I don't know what you did, but whatever it was, it worked.'

Looking at him, I could see where Grania got the colour of her eyes and the springing life in her hair. There was no mistaking her fatherhood. I wondered who in the Lewes the new infant would resemble.

The Sallow One came round the corner of the Black House. He had been creeling peats and he was black with the work. Macaulay eyed him with interest.

'I would like to do something for this boy of yours, Jonet. I could find him a place at the Big House perhaps. What do you say?'

I looked at my son. His eyes were black and intent and there was a stillness about him that told me he wanted to go to the Big House, but not as a servant; indeed no! His grandfather was a man of standing born out of a proud race as good as any Macaulay.

'There is plenty of work for him here,' I said stiffly.

'Aye, granted, but would you not have him better himself?'

'I am wanting him to have an education.'

He threw back his big fair head and laughed loudly, slapping his thigh with his whip.

'Still piping that tune, eh, Jonet?'

I flushed. It had taken months to live down the disaster of the Sallow One's first attempt at education. I had not realized that I had been a joke at the laird's table too.

I glanced back at my son. He was watching the tacksman with the look I had come to dread. Before he had time to make one of his outrageous remarks, I said slyly, 'It will be a pity if the child in your wife's belly turns out to be another girl.'

He took my meaning instantly and the bluff good-natured heartiness dropped from him like a cloak.

'Your son shall have an education, woman,' he said abruptly. 'My daughter has a governess who is not over-occupied.' He turned to the boy and said, 'Be at the Big House on Monday three hours after dawn.'

He looked at us both coldly and mounted his horse.

As I watched him go there was both shame in me for what I had said and also triumph. Why should not the grandson of a tacksman share an education with the daughter of another? My son was as good as his daughter. The Sallow One was standing beside me.

'Make the most of the next few months, my son,' I said soberly. 'This education may be as short-lived as the last.'

'He will have his son, my mother,' he said, and there was such certainty in his voice that I believed him. Over the years I had come to believe that there was truth in most of his predictions though the knowledge did little to comfort me or, I suspect, himself. That frown which I had first noticed on his yellow infant face was still notched between his brows.

On the Monday as I watched him set out for the Big House dressed in shoes and his good plaid, I did not doubt that he wanted an education but I also knew that he wanted Grania more.

I stood watching until he was out of sight. For the rest of the morning as I worked at my tasks my heart was unusually heavy. I felt that where my son and I were concerned we had reached a toll-gate in our lives. His childhood was at an end. My part in his life was almost over. What had I accomplished? What did I know of him? Had I done enough for him? Had I prepared him properly for the life that was to be his to spend as he chose? The answer was no, nothing and no again.

Who was he, this creature that I had given to the world? He carried the proud blood of the Kintails in his veins. They had given him his looks, his moods and his pride, but who had given him his strange gift of foreknowledge? Was it a trick played on him by nature? Was he in truth the son of the sea-god or was it a madness caused by damage to his head that terrible moment I had held him in the baptismal pool?

The Preacher had once told us the story of the Mother of the Christ, how she had known of His strangeness before His birth. Was it not the same with me? Was my son half-god, or was he, perhaps, half-devil? The Preacher called Shoni the 'One from the Abyss'. To worship him is to worship Satan himself. They had crucified the Christ who had been part-God; what would they do to my son who was part-devil?

The more I thought, the more I was afraid.

All that day while the Sallow One was at the Big House, I was afraid, so afraid indeed that I could no longer work. The Sallow One found me late in the evening with no meal prepared, cowering over the dying hearth. He stood at the door of the Black House looking in at me. Seeing him there, black in the darkening light, I could well believe that he had come from the Abyss. I stared and then turned away, hiding my face in my shawl.

'Mother?' he called uncertainly. 'Are you unwell?'

I rose stiffly and reached for the bellows, but there was no spark left in the hearth, another omen of ill fortune. I wanted to cry out to him, 'Who are you? What are you? What will become of you?' But the words stuck in my throat. I knew then that I did not really want to know the answers to the questions that had been tormenting me all day. Ignorance is easier on the mind.

'I am well enough,' I told him. 'See you to the beasts. Your food will be ready in an hour.'

Grania

Jonet did not look like a witch, at least not the sort of witch that Sheena described with crooked back and hairy chin. She was far too beautiful with those dark blue eyes that saw into the very soul of me. I believe she is the only truly beautiful woman I have ever seen. Not everyone at home thought her beautiful. My mother said she was like all crofting women, old and haggard before her time, but I did not notice the lines and shadows in that strong wise face and nor, I am sure, did my father who treated her with more respect than he showed to most women. I was also a little afraid of her, which made me act foolishly the first time I saw her. I always do stupid things when I am nervous, but I don't believe she minded. I wanted her to think well of me.

It was the same with her son. He was beautiful too, but in a different way. There was a peacefulness in the mother's presence, a quietness, as if she had come through suffering to accept her way of life. The son was unpredictable and disturbing.

I had never had much to do with boys of my own age. I had cousins whom I saw rarely, odious creatures, rough and boastful and never content unless they were slaughtering the deer or shooting at the birds. When they were tired of outdoor sports they turned on me, pulling the ribbon in my hair and behaving in a truly abominable fashion. I hated them, but the witch's son was different. It was wonderful for me to have someone to talk to; someone who would listen to my fancies without laughing at me. Mistress Grant, my aged governess, used to say that

51

I twittered as foolishly and ceaselessly as a blackbird. With the witch's son I used to have the sort of conversation that included silence.

He knew much more than you would expect of a crofter's son, not book-learning; he was never much better than I was when it came to reading and writing and his English had a stilted lilt to it that sometimes made me smile. But he knew about the tides and the seasons. He knew when a storm was coming and how to catch a trout in his bare hands. Most of all he knew about people.

My governess, Mistress Arabella Grant, a distant kins-woman of my mother, did not know what to make of him at all. She was deeply insulted by my father's request that he should be included in the daily lessons. She did not like boys and she did not understand them, so she said. The truth was that she was afraid of them and avoided contact with them as if they had been wild dogs. When she realized that the witch's son was quieter and better-mannered than I was, she gradually began to take notice of him, but she was never at ease in his presence.

Once after she had kept me at my studies an extra hour I said to him, 'I hate Mistress Grant. She is old and ugly and she stinks.'

He looked at me strangely. 'I see her sick and weeping and alone,' he said sadly.

What could I answer to that? He often made strange remarks, sometimes during our lessons which angered Mistress Grant who believed that he was trying to divert my attention from the complexities of English grammar. If that had been his aim, he succeeded, for I would fall into fits of helpless laughter, but soon I was to learn that his intention was not necessarily to interrupt. He could not help himself.

If my mother had known that he waited for me every afternoon behind the Red Crag, she would have been astonished and angry, but she never found out. When I had done an hour at my needlework and another hour at the clarsach, I was free until the evening meal. Those were the happiest hours I spent with the witch's son. Sometimes we would walk along the shore as sedately as a couple going to the kirk, or we would sit and talk together as seriously as old wives at a funeral. Other times we would play as wildly as bairns. He had taken me bird-nesting and I had clambered after him in search of gulls' eggs. He had taken me fishing and lent me his own long wand. With his help I had caught a trout which we cooked over a fire of dry seaweed.

He had taken me to the loch where the water-bull lurked and to the little round dwelling on the hillock where the Fairy Folk lived, but he had not yet taken me to Black Ian's Cave which I had a mind to visit.

'Why are you wanting to go to such a place?' he asked.

'You know why.'

'I know you are always wanting to go to places which make you afraid.'

'There is no fear in me,' I protested, but he was right. I would not have dared to go near any of those places on my own. Sheena had filled my head full of tales of enchantment and mystery and I was curious to see these places in the hopes that I might catch a glimpse of some of the strange creatures she had told me about.

Part of me knew that her tales were foolish fancy, but part of me was not sure. In my mind's eye I could see a water-bull or a sea-fairy; above all, I wanted to see them with my natural eye, but not alone. The witch's son would protect me from being whisked into the water-bull's whirlpool or snatched into a fairy mound.

'It will not be easy to get to Black Ian's Cave,' he said doubtfully, eyeing my long gown and stuff slippers.

'You said that when we went after the cliff nests,' I complained, 'and I managed as well as you.' He eyed me questioningly. 'Well,' I compromised, 'almost as well as you.'

His anxious face was transformed suddenly by that rare beautiful smile of his.

'I have never met a woman like you for exaggeration,' he said, and I was pleased that he called me a woman.

'Well, then, when are we to go?'

'The tide will be low this afternoon. I'll take you there then, but mind, there is to be no screaming or the ghost of Black Ian's mother will be haunting you for a whole week.'

'But what if the old woman is still there? What if it is lies that Black Ian took her home to be buried?'

'Certainly she will still be there,' he teased me. 'She will be guarded by a monster with two heads, a goat's beard and a horse's tail.'

My tasks seemed endless that day, and when I thought I was finished, my mother sent me to the dairy for a cheese. She had a passion for cheese and as her time was near I would not have dared to disobey her, though privately I would not have been surprised if the baby turned out to be made of crowdie.

The witch's son was waiting for me in the usual place and we set off to walk the four miles along the shore to the cave. I quickly shed my shoes, bundled my dress high, the better to keep up with his long easy strides. As I hurried along beside him I began to think about the strange story of the cave.

Black Ian was fishing near by when a great storm arose, forcing him to seek shelter in the cave. He had his old mother with him, for she had been recently widowed and was in no fit state to be left alone in the croft. During the gale the old woman suddenly died. Black Ian attempted to leave the cave to take the corpse back to the village for burial, but the storm was too strong for him. As the days passed, the body began to stink, so Ian, knowing that it was unthinkable for her not to be buried with her husband and family, disembowelled the corpse and hung it up in the smoky cave along with the fish to dry. When the gale had blown itself out, he took his mother's remains back to be buried as was fitting.

It was a sad little tale and one that had haunted me from the time Sheena had first told it to me in my bed one night of wind.

The tide was out and the sea lazy over the wet white sand. There was rain in the air and no sign of the sun. Gradually the sand changed to shingle and the shingle to rocks and boulders that were harder to cross. I had never been this far before and I felt a shiver of excitement as the shore rose up into high craggy cliffs. The darkening sea and the sky lowered at each other. Sharp-beaked terns, disturbed on their ground, dived at us and black shags shook their long necks in unfriendly greeting. Soon the rocks gave way to sheer cliff and there was scarcely room to scramble between the deep green water on the one hand and the soaring rocks on the other.

Several times the witch's son suggested that we go back, but a stubbornness was in me and I refused to be turned from my intention. I had often been told that I was as thrawn as a wild pony. My mother constantly complained of it when her own wishes were thwarted, but that afternoon I was aware of it in myself. Nothing short of a broken limb would have stopped me going into that cave.

Soon the witch's son was having to help me in the worst places. When we reached a gulf where the sea came right into the side of the cliff in some gurgling underwater cavern, it was his hand and the strength of my own purpose that carried me across. I could never have jumped over on my own. My feet were torn by the little white sharp-spined barnacles that covered the rocks that were usually submerged, and the great green slimy patches of sea grass were as treacherous as ice.

We came upon the cave suddenly. It was set a little above the high-tide level and quite dry. The mouth was sandy, but further back the floor was carpeted in bats' droppings. I soon found what looked like the remains of a long dead fire. Turning excitedly to the witch's son, I saw that a change had come over him.

'Let us be going,' he said abruptly.

'But we've only just come,' I protested. 'Besides, I'm tired.'

He was seated hunched with his knees to his chin, one arm tight round his legs, the other hand clutching the small white stone he used to play with when he thought no one was looking. He was staring at me in a strange way as if he were not really seeing me at all.

'Whatever is wrong?' I cried, but he did not seem to hear me. 'Are you sick?'

I was beginning to feel frightened and fleeting memories of Sheena's tales of possession and madness raced through my head. I reached out timidly to touch his hand. He was stiff and there was a cold clamminess on his skin that made me wonder for one terrible moment if he were dead.

'Wake up,' I urged, shaking his shoulder, 'don't leave me here in this terrible place.'

In a little while the stiffness left him. He dropped his head on his knees and the stone fell from his hand. I picked it up. It was wet as if it had been lying in the sea.

When he looked up the horrid vacant stare had left his eyes.

'Grania?' he whispered, almost as if he did not recognize me. 'Oh, Grania,' he added on a sigh.

'What happened?' I asked, but at that moment he saw the stone in my hand and held out his own.

'Give it to me.'

I don't know what made me act so foolishly. I have since learned that there are times to tease a man and times to be quiet. On this occasion I was unwise. My only excuse was that I was still frightened and upset.

'Not until you tell me what happened.'

He was mad at me. He threw himself against me and grabbed my wrist, twisting it cruelly behind my back and prising open my fingers until he had the stone safe in his own possession.

'Never do that again,' he said coldly.

I began to cry.

Perhaps he had never seen a girl cry before or perhaps he was aware that he had been the cause of my terror. Whatever the reason, he was suddenly on his knees before me.

'Don't cry, my little one, my brown swan, my star.'

He reached out to brush the tears from my cheek that fell the faster for his tender words.

'I cannot help what happened. It is the way I am.'

'I don't understand,' I sobbed.

56

'It is not easily explained.'

'If you don't tell me I will say that you are mad and I will tell my father and he will stop you coming to the Big House.'

I had stopped acting as a woman and had become a child again, but as the words poured out of me, I knew that I did not mean them. Quickly, before he had time to turn away from me, I moved closer to him and said, 'Forgive me. I should not have spoken like that. It's just that you frightened me so.'

He sighed and said, 'How can I explain something to you that I cannot explain to myself.'

'You could try.'

He pulled his plaid over his shoulders as if he were cold.

'There is another place,' he said slowly, seeking for the right words. 'I go there sometimes.'

'What do you mean, another place? There is only here and now in this cave.'

He shook his head. 'You are wrong. There is the past. You yourself are always hoping for a glimpse of it. Why else did you come here today? And,' he added softly, 'there is also the future.'

'You mean you can tell the future,' I cried excitedly, 'like the old wives at a ceilidh?'

'No,' he said, shaking his head. 'With me it is different. I go there—and sometimes—' he hesitated, the frown on his brow deepening, 'sometimes, it is hard to get back.'

He looked at the stone and began to roll it gently round and round in his palm.

'How can that be?' I asked. 'How can you go anywhere and your body remain behind?'

'Sometimes,' he continued, as if I had not spoken, 'I only go there for a moment in time. I see senseless things, people that mean nothing to me, places I cannot recognize. At other times—' He paused, his eyes darkening at some memory.

'Go on,' I urged.

'At other times I see terrible things.'

'Tell me.'

He no longer seemed to be aware of my presence. It was as

57

if he had gone back into that terrible place and was witnessing some dreadful sight.

'There was a hillside and a tree with a rope hanging from it. There were crowds of strange people all shouting and cursing. There was a man on a horse and the rope was placed round his neck. The horse bolted and the man was left there dangling. I knew that man. I felt that rope as if it had been round my own neck and the stone was not there to bring me back.'

'Now I understand!' I cried excitedly. 'You have the Two Sights.'

Sheena had told me that there was talk of it in the village, but she believed he put it all on for show and that the Wise Woman, his mother, encouraged him.

'The Two Sights are a great gift from God given only to those who are wise and worthy. How would a young lad like that come by such a gift?' she had said, but she was wrong. I had never met any one who had the real Second Sight before, though plenty claimed to have it, and I was excited.

'What was it you saw just now when I took your stone?' I asked.

He did not want to tell me.

'You saw me!' I cried eagerly. 'What was I doing? Was I a grown woman? Was I wed?'

He stood up and looked out of the cave. 'The tide has turned,' he said. 'We must go or it will soon be too late.'

'You have not answered me yet,' I said, catching hold of his plaid.

He turned to look at me then, and I knew that if I pushed him too far I would destroy our friendship. Yet I could not let go altogether.

'Tell me one thing. Was I beautiful?'

We stood very close, so close that I seemed to drown in the depths of his eye.

'You will always be beautiful,' he said and I had to be content.

A fine rain had started to fall which made the rocks

treacherous and soaked us to the skin. The sea was lashing the cliff now and I was frightened as I had never been frightened before. This was no game to be played with fear, a delicious tingle of the flesh and creeping of the skin, but a fight for survival as the sea leapt up at us with green greedy fingers. But I was afraid of more than the sea. Suddenly there seemed so much in the world to fear. There was the future itself, that is if I were to have a future and not drown here and now; and there was the witch's son with his uncanny knowledge. Now it seemed to me that Sheena's tales of ghosts and fairies and the world they inhabited were nothing more than the dreams of childhood. I had had a glimpse into another world, another reality that was beyond my understanding.

When at last we reached the safety of the shore beyond the cliffs, the witch's son turned to me.

'I will be going back to the croft now.'

'Yes,' I said quietly.

I watched him until he was out of sight. His loneliness cried out to me so that my own fears were submerged in a nameless dread for him.

That was the moment I fell in love with him.

My mother had a son, Aulay Beag, and my father gave a great feast to celebrate the birth of an heir. Tacksmen and lairds from all over the island came to pay their respects to the red-haired, red-skinned infant, and the crofters were invited to eat their fill of mutton and bannocks washed down with ale and whisky in honour of the babe.

There was not room in the Big House for such an assembly, so it was decided to hold the feast in the barn immediately following the sacrament of baptism. It made me smile to watch old Sheena's face smooth with relief when the holy words were spoken. She had worn herself thin with worry over the un-baptized bairn. First she hid a smoothing iron under his cradle, then she knocked nails into the back of my mother's great bed to protect the child from the fairies who were ever on the watch to substitute a changeling of their own and bear away the human babe. In my new-found wisdom, I smiled at Sheena's efforts. Not so long ago I too would have listened by the cradle for the sound of fairy pipes.

I did not see the witch's son again until the night of the feast. When I had reached home after visiting the cave, I found my mother in labour and Mistress Grant far too occupied to consider continuing my education. Now that my father had a son, he was no longer interested in seeing that I was taught to read and write. Besides, summer had come and book-learning was a winter occupation.

I had given much thought to that 'other place' and had told Sheena of the strange experience in the cave. When she had done scolding me for the foolishness of the escapade, she questioned me curiously about the witch's son.

'He's a queer one right enough,' she muttered, 'but it is not to be wondered at considering—'

'Considering what?' I asked.

'Considering who he is,' she muttered evasively.

I supposed not. Not everyone in the Lewes could claim a wise woman as mother.

On the night of the feast the lairds and their families dined with us in the Big House. I was impatient to go over to the barn to see if the witch's son had come with the other crofters, but my mother needed me at her side to entertain the guests and there was much to see to. My rough cousins were almost civilized and for the first time I found myself enjoying their companionship, but always at the back of my mind there was this excitement at the thought of seeing the witch's son again.

At last the time came to go over to the barn. The ceremony of the christening was beautiful, the bairn being too sleepy to cry. There was a bard from Stornoway who had composed a Rune of Creation, and the story-teller from Baile na Cille gave an invocation that brought tears to my eyes.

'May the grace of courage and fortune, of goodness and wisdom, of whole-souled charity and winning speech be thine,' he cried in his trembling old voice.

A woman sang the Lullaby of the Birds:

The nest of the curlew
Is in the bubbling peat-moss,
My little one will sleep and he shall have the bird.

The nest of the wild duck
Is in the bank of the little loch,
My little one will sleep and he shall have the bird.

A seer foretold a life of prosperity and good health. All the time my eyes were darting this way and that in the crowded barn for a glimpse of the witch's son.

It was not until the music started and the dancing began that I saw the witch herself. She was wearing a red gown with a blue and white plaid fastened by a silver brooch and she was sitting apart in the shadows. She had an air of prosperity about her that was new since the last time I had seen her.

'Are you well, Mistress?' I said, but my mind was not on my words and my eyes kept searching for her son.

She turned her head slowly and following the line of her gaze, I saw him standing in the doorway, his dark face shadowed. I was about to go over to him when she caught my wrist and I was compelled to look back into those blue soul-seeing eyes.

'Be very sure that you know what you are doing, child,' she said quietly.

'How so, Mistress?' I replied, trying to put surprise into my voice, but she knew that I had understood her.

'He is not for you.'

'Are you threatening me?' I asked indignantly. 'Will you call down a curse on me if I disregard your witch's warning, or are you afraid I might break his heart?'

I had never spoken so freely before and I was amazed at my own daring, but there was something about this woman that called for truth.

'It is too late for that,' she said on a sigh.

I left her then, threading my way through the crowd that danced or sprawled on the straw, eating and drinking and jesting among themselves. I went straight up to him.

'Dance the reel with me?' I said, holding out both hands and teasing him with my eyes.

He looked at me with a strange expression, turned and went outside. Across the barn I caught his mother's eye and, in defiance, I ran out after him. He was sitting on a stone dyke playing with his stone.

'Why would you not dance with me?' I asked him.

'I am not fond of the reel,' he replied.

'But I am.'

'Then find a partner suited to your tastes.'

He slid off the wall and began to walk away into the moon-lit darkness.

'Where are you going?' I asked, tripping over my white dress as I tried to keep up with him.

'For a walk.'

'Let me come with you.'

He did not reply but he did not try to stop me.

For a while we walked in silence over the close-cropped turf towards the moor at the back of the Big House. When we reached the heather, we turned at the same time to look back at the sea beyond the blaze of light from the barn.

'Have you been to the "other place" lately?' I asked him, desperately trying to establish some sort of contact between us.

He turned on me and I was afraid of him again as I had been afraid of him once before. This time his eyes sparked with anger.

'Never speak to me of that place—never again, do you hear me? Never ask what I see or seek to know what I know. Swear it in the name of Shoni.'

'I swear it,' I said, not understanding the cause of his anger, but he was already gone, running down the hill leaving me alone in the dark.

Later that night I was to find out that Sheena had repeated everything I had told her about the witch's son. Baile na Cille was still laughing.

His hurt at my hands twisted in me like colic. As soon as I was free, I rode into the village to ask his forgiveness. I found the witch alone spinning at the door of her dark hovel.

'Will he forgive me, do you think?' I asked her.

She looked at me with that strong blue gaze. 'How much do you care?'

'Enough.'

'Your beauty drew the secret from him. It may—in time— make him forget the betrayal.'

'Will you give me a charm?' I asked on impulse.

She smiled at me fleetingly.

'I will do no such thing.'

Three years were to pass before I knew that he had forgiven me. I saw him from time to time on the shore gathering sea-ware with the other men or cutting the corn at harvest time. His mother had given him a boat so that he went fishing as Black Ian had done and was sometimes away for weeks at a time. Although, in all that time, I never saw him alone I heard news of him often enough for his strange predictions set him apart from the other crofters and turned him into an object of derision or sometimes an object of fear. Even though I had plenty of interests and pastimes of my own, every time I heard his name spoken, my heart beat a little faster.

My cousins had grown into fine men and one wanted to marry me. I had other suitors too and now that I was past eighteen my father was anxious to see me settled. His choice for me was Rorie Maclennan whose land marched with my father's tack and who was a suitable match from every point of view. I liked him well enough, for he was easy to look at with a fine head of brown hair and gentle blue eyes. I liked my cousins too and the other men who came riding over to pay their respects to my mother with their eyes on me. I was not, however, in love with any of them. There is a flaw in my nature as a woman. I like a man well enough until he shows a weakness, and that first weakness is usually an over-anxiety to please me. It seemed to me then that I was faced with a loveless marriage, for I was unable to love a man weak enough to show his feelings for me. I tried to explain some of this to the witch, for I still saw her occasionally in the village or visiting at the Big House, but she only smiled and told me that I had not yet met the right man.

I could not, however, wait for such a chancy happening and I had all but made up my mind to marry Rorie when I met the witch's son again.

I had gone for a ride along the wide sands towards the village. It was a mild afternoon, the sea like cream under a milky sky, when I came upon him digging for bait, his boat pulled up on to the wet sand below. He looked up at me and I caught my breath as I saw the soft black fall of his hair, the dark shadow of beard under his sallow skin and those strange deep eyes. He had not grown tall, only an inch or two above my own height and there was a slenderness in his wrists and neck that betrayed a lack of physical strength, but to me at that moment he was extraordinarily beautiful.

I dismounted, leaving the pony to wander home at will.

'Blessings on you, witch's son,' I said softly.

He moved his head in a greeting, but his eyes did not move from mine and I knew that the magic that was beginning to soften my limbs had reached him too.

'Have you nothing to say to me?' I asked half-teasing. 'Surely you have forgiven me by this time.'

'You have changed,' he said presently.

'And so have you,' I told him. 'I see you have got your boat. Is the fishing good?'

'Fair,' he said. I was suddenly impatient of the shyness that stood like a wall between us.

'Take me to the Grey Island,' I said on impulse.

'The island?'

'Do you not remember? I always wanted to go to the island to see the seals, but there was no boat.'

64

He smiled that same transforming radiant smile that flooded my heart with warmth.

'The enchanted clansmen, is it?'

'You have not forgotten!' I laughed with pleasure. 'Let's go there now.'

It was madness, but then I would soon be wedded and bedded and bound for ever and there would be no more opportunities. I thought he was going to refuse and I knew with a thrill of pleasure that my pleadings would make no difference to his final decision. He would go because he wanted to go.

The island was barely a mile from the shore, a hillock of heather and cliff with a stretch of sandy bay. A ruined bothy stood near the beach which some say gave shelter to a holy man; but now the only inhabitants were the sea-birds that plastered the cliffs with lime, and, of course, the seals. There are many tales told in the Lewes about the seals. Sheena believed that they were sons of the Clan MacCodrum enchanted by the Little People for some violation of nature. They regained human form on the night of the full moon in order to come ashore and find a mate. Fortunately for the local girls they were easily recognizable by the brown colour of their hair and the way it grew like fur down the back of the neck.

The seals crowded round the little boat as we approached the shore and it was not hard to believe that they were once human. There were dozens of them, fearless and curious as children. I reached out to touch them in delight.

'Take care!' I cried as the witch's son dipped the oars into the heaving water. 'It is not lucky to hurt a seal,' but my warning was unnecessary. I knew that he would not willingly hurt one of these creatures any more than he would hurt me.

When he had beached the boat, the seals lost interest in us and we were left alone on the white sand under that bright white sky. Normally I would have wanted to explore every rock and stone of that beautiful island, but on this occasion my limbs felt strangely languid, and, instead, I lay down on the sand cushioning my head on my linked hands.

'How has it been with you these past years?' I asked him presently.

On the journey across the bay we had hardly spoken, but now the awkwardness had gone. He sat down on the sand beside me.

'As always,' he said. 'Winter follows summer.'

'And then it is spring,' I said softly. 'We are in the spring of our lives.'

'It is the shortest season of them all.'

'Just at this moment I feel it could last for ever,' I said on a breath.

He turned round and leaning on one elbow looked down at me so that my soul seemed to melt. 'You are so beautiful,' he said.

'And you,' I whispered, reaching up to touch his face.

He caught my hand and his fingers intertwined with mine.

'Oh, Grania, I have had this dream in me for too long,' he said, drowning me in his black eyes.

'Tell me.'

'I dream that you and I are the only people in the whole wide world.'

'Go on,' I whispered, already wrapped close in a web of enchantment.

'We are alone on an island such as this. I am fishing and you are working the croft. We are tranquil, carefree like children, and yet not like children.'

'More,' I urged as our fingers tightened.

'I would keep you safe, Grania. I would protect you, my heart's pleasure, until the end of our time.'

'It is a beautiful dream,' I said, though if I had not been under the spell of his closeness I would not have thought so, for I am one who likes company and soft living.

He let go my hand and touched my face.

'My treasure, my soul's delight, my love is to you, Grania, my sun.'

'And mine to thee,' I whispered.

His lips touched mine.

'Hold me, hold me close, witch's son!' I cried, putting my arms round him.

We lay together mouth to mouth, breast to breast. Ah, that first wonder of love, the tenderness, the sweet joy, the gentle delight. The minutes turned into hours and the sky became grey above us.

Then he said, 'Will you wed with me, my white swan?'

I suppose I should have felt some sort of shock at the proposal. My father would have laid him on the floor for daring to think it. It was not just that he was the bastard son of a bastard daughter of a Mackenzie. He had no property except for a small boat. He had nothing to offer except a black house and a bleak future and, of course, himself.

I never for one moment contemplated marriage with him. The pity was that I did not tell him so in words that he could understand. Instead I said, 'I will love you, witch's son, until the end of the world.'

We kissed again, but this time there was a strength and a hotness in our embrace. He moved from me quickly and, standing, held out his hand to me.

'Come, I will take you home. It will soon be dark.'

It was I who broke the spell. 'Wait!' I cried. 'Remember that day in the cave when you saw me in the "other place"? What was I doing? It can do no harm to tell me now.'

He did not answer me, and I saw that the frown that had so nearly been wiped away by my kisses furrowed the space between his brow.

'Come,' he repeated, 'they will be out looking for you.'

'Why will you not tell me?' I pleaded, but he was already dragging the boat down to the water. I knew then that I had met a man who had no weaknesses where I was concerned. I could never turn him or change him. Oh why did I not follow my heart and marry him?

When I returned home that evening Rorie was with my father. They had been discussing a marriage settlement. He pressed me for an answer and, still hot from the kisses of the witch's

67

son, I accepted his hand. Why? you will ask. Perhaps you will understand better when I tell you that only crofting folk married for love.

To my father I was a valued property. The time had come for him to invest in me. In exchange for a marriage portion, his grandsons would become Maclennan lairds. Besides, I was fond of Rorie. He was a fine man and would make me a good husband. So I did not throw a tantrum or break my heart. I accepted him gratefully and went on dreaming about the one I loved.

What I did not know was that the witch's son also believed that I had accepted his offer. A few days later he was at the door of the Big House in his best bonnet and plaid, his hair smooth and his chin clean-shaven. He asked the servant for my father, but as he and I were out riding together he spoke with my mother instead.

I do not know what possessed him to do such a thing. He must have known the sort of reception he would be given. My mother was too astonished at the time to do more than hear him out, but she was in a fine state of anger when we returned.

'Have you ever heard such impudence? He is altogether above himself, encouraged by that mother of his, I've no doubt. I never in all my life heard of such a thing. He should be thrashed, and you, Aulay Macaulay, are the man to do it.'

When she had calmed down sufficiently to explain that the witch's son had asked for my hand in marriage, my father had roared with laughter.

'The lad has taste and courage,' he said, wiping the tears of enjoyment from his eyes. 'He shall not be punished for that. Meanwhile the betrothal to Rorie must be made public. That will put the nonsense out of his head.'

My father decided to give a feast in my honour.

'But not for the crofters, I beg you,' said my mother. 'I could not bear to have to speak to that creature or his upstart of a mother.'

'As you wish,' he agreed reluctantly. He loved to be free with his hospitality.

My heart was torn in pieces, for I did not want the witch's son to be hurt. I had to explain to him before word of my betrothal reached him by other means. I wanted to make him understand that although I was to wed Rory, my heart would still be his, so at the first opportunity I rode over to Baile na Cille.

The witch was making butter and crooning to herself while she worked the plunger up and down in the wooden churn. She did not give me her attention until the butter had come and she had laid it in a shallow dish of water.

'Will you tell him how it is?' I begged her when I had explained everything. 'I have no wish to hurt him.'

'You can tell him yourself,' she said dryly. 'He is in the room sleeping. He has been at the fishing for the past two nights trying to make his fortune—and yours, I believe.'

I hate the Black Houses with the stink of dung from the byre mingling with the smell of food. I hate the peat reek that stings the eyes and the throat and the dark inner room with the boxed-in beds of scratchy heather. I could never have lived in such a place. I hated even to go inside. The witch watched me with unsmiling eyes. She had always known that I would be no good for her son.

He was sleeping in the inner room. In the dim smoke-crossed light he looked young and unprotected, but as soon as he opened his eyes he became a man and ageless.

'Grania, my sun,' he whispered, and reached up to draw me down to the sleepy warmth of his body.

I was prepared to give myself to him then, but he would not take me. We lay together for a long time kissing and caressing, but it was always he who controlled the passion in us both. It was then that I knew how much he loved me.

'I went to see your father,' he said as we lay entwined on the sealskin blanket.

I tried to tell him then, but I could not break the spell of our love. I could not bear to see him turn his back to me. I tried again when the mother's movements near by told me it was time to go, but every time I tried, he silenced me with kisses.

'I'll come again,' he said confidently. 'Be calm, my heart; your breast is trembling like a bird.'

As I left I looked at the witch with beseeching eyes. There was nothing but scorn in hers.

He came as he promised, on the night of my betrothal feast. God and St Michael, but it still gives me pain to remember.

I had presumed that his mother had told him of my second betrayal, for I did not see him again, though I looked hard enough in the village and on the shore. I still dreamed of him, of his body and our lying together, but I had made up my mind to Rorie and although his strong hairy limbs did not excite me, they did not revolt me either, and it did not occur to me to break my troth.

My cousins and most of the young men of the island, some with brides already, came to my feast. It was a fine gathering, the Flowers of Lewes, as the Bard said, had gathered in my honour. I wore white with a circlet of gold in my hair, a gift from Rorie's mother. We dined on the best the island had to offer; venison, salmon, wild duck and roast mutton with claret and whisky. The Bard composed a verse in my honour and there was piping, fiddling and dancing with a great deal of laughter and not a little drunkenness before the night was done.

And then suddenly the witch's son was among us. Small and slight he might be, but that night he seemed like a giant in the crowded room. When he spoke the whole company fell silent.

'Macaulay,' he cried, and I knew by his eyes that he was far away in that other place.

My father looked up, his jaw loose with surprise.

'Macaulay, this marriage will not take place.'

There was a buzz of angry comment in the hall.

'Get rid of him,' my mother urged, while Rorie was on his feet, his hand to his knife.

It would have been natural for the witch's son to speak in anger, and if it had been so, no doubt he would have been thrown from the room, but it was the appalling air of tragedy about him that silenced the room.

'Men of Lewis,' he cried. 'The Great Stag is bellowing for

your blood. Even now a messenger is riding across the heather
on a horse that is flecked with spittle to call upon the sons of
Lewis to take up arms. Shun the rock jetty of Uig, my proud
Islanders, for, I tell you, three hundred men will perish in
Auldearn and only three will return.'

There was a silence in the hall that was broken only by the
sob of a woman. The witch's son moved forward until he stood
in front of my father.

'You, Aulay Macaulay!' he cried, pointing at him with a
long finger. 'You will be the first to fall, and you—' he turned
to my cousins, '—the four fair sons of Donald will drown in
your own blood. As for you, Norman of the Ness, the raven
will drink his three fills from your heart, and you, Red Angus,
you will be buried without your sword arm.'

One by one he pointed to all the men in the hall until at last
he came to my betrothed.

'As for you, Rorie Maclennan, it would be better for you
if you never left the Lewes, for you will be dead with a sword
in your heart long before you reach the field of slaughter.'

There was a terrible sadness that shook his voice when at
last he turned to me.

'Weep, Grania, weep until your eyes are blind, for you will
never again know happiness until you lie shrouded and still the
way I saw you long ago in Black Ian's Cave.'

He paused then and I saw by the movement of his fingers
on the stone as he turned and left the hall that he had come
back from the other place. Nobody moved and then it seemed
that the whole hall surged after him.

'He shall die for this!' Rorie cried, as he leapt forward, but
I caught his sleeve.

'No!' I cried, weeping. 'Let him be.'

'Grania is right,' said my father. 'The words of a madman
and a jealous madman at that cannot harm us.'

Raising his voice, he managed to pacify the company, assur-
ing them that justice would be done, but the heart had gone
out of the feast and the guests either got drunk or rode home.

Next day the Earl of Seaforth's messenger arrived. Within

a week my father, cousins and my betrothed, together with three hundred Lewismen, embarked at the Uig jetty to raise the standard at Auldearn. It all happened as the witch's son had seen it. My poor Rorie was murdered for his gold by a band of cut-throats in the mountains. Only three, the three men who had not embarked from Uig, returned.

As for me, I know it is only a matter of time.

Chapter 2

BENBECULA

Marsali

Ach, there is always wind in this place. Wind is the man of the house chilling my feet under the bed-mat, ill-tempered at the hearth, and wind is the sickly bairn, restless by day, moaning at night. But now when I hear the wind I remember only the Stranger from the Sea. It was the wind that brought him to the island, and it was I who found him.

In the remembering time by the winter hearth, I still see clearly the slow sunlit seasons of my youth, but I find it hard to remember a single hour in the dreary passage of recent years. The day I found the Stranger is as clear to me as my wedding day.

The sea was green and violet under a tossing sky. There was a single swan in the bay, a blessing on the restless water. It was her presence that drew me down to the wide white sands. While she was there it was safe to glean the high-tide line. The wind caught me as I stepped down to the shore. There was a time when I could stand up to the wind's harsh embrace; when I would hold out curled fingers to feel the velvet presence against the cushion of my hand and slowly close my fist on nothing. When I was young I would be shaking off my shawl to welcome those tugging fingers in the tangle of my hair, but those days are long since past. Now I cringe before the enemy. I draw the outer skirt up over my head and creep close to the sand while the wind draws tears from my eyes and dashes them away before they have time to fall on my cheeks.

That day the sea was not in a generous mood, or so it seemed, for there were only a few white sticks to gather for kindling and a dead gull no more than a cage of feather and bone. A finger of sun pointed at the wet sand close to the water's edge and turned it gold. A great wonder came into my head. It was here in this place that the Black Women of God had found the Melodious Lady Lord and her Princeling Son in the time before the time that was. The Lady wore the blue of the summer sky with stars in her hair and her Bairn was brighter than the sun. What a blessing to come to the Black Women of God! I prayed that I might so be blessed. Aye, but blessings pass as surely as girlhood and womanhood must pass. The Black Women had long since been numbered with the dust and their House was a heap of ruins. It was said in the island that Clanranald's lady was thinking of taking the stones to build herself a fine new house. Black Donald attend her for such a deed! The Augur would have to speak to the laird when he returned from the wars. Ach, but it is always the same with the young folk. They have no respect for the old ways. Yet why should I curse the young folk? How often I have wished to sail to the Island of Youth and drink its enchanted water; to feel myself rise straight and slim from the painful prison of old flesh.

The wish was hard on me when I looked down and saw the Stranger at my feet. At first I thought it was my youth that lay there, still and cold, my dark hair that lifted in the wind, my face closed and pale. My heart and my hand rose to my mouth in terror of the enchantment until the wind tore at his tattered shirt and I saw that he was a drowned man.

Alas, alas, my love, thou that art lying dead at my feet;
How still thou art, my pride, my joy, my beloved.

The words of the lament crowded into my mind as I looked down on him. Tears misted my eyes and brought the cough to my throat shaking my body so that I sank weakly to my knees.

How I would raise thee, my star, my strong lover,
Had I been there.

74

I put out my hand to touch his black hair. It was salt-thick to the touch. How many men had I thus caressed. He was all of them.

> Oh my dead lover, my son, my brother, my kinsman,
>   the beloved;
> Come back to me from the green burial place under
>   the waves.

I took his head to my lap. My tears fell on his face, my breath touched his mouth. I cradled him in my arms.

Then it was that the change came. I still do not know if it was my breath that gave him life or some dark miracle performed behind God's back. All I know is that he stirred and opened his eyes. Such blackness, such power! Holy St Tarran and the three brothers hold me now. I was drowning in their depth. The feeble strength of me drained away into those eyes, for surely they were not mortal. A thousand fears possessed me. I remembered the gainisgeag who haunted the peat hags waiting only to find escape in the body of a drowned man. Death to me if he were one of them. Or maybe I was holding a water kelpie in my arms who would lure me to the sea to feast with his brothers on my flesh.

He spoke then. 'Is this hell,' he said, 'for surely it cannot be heaven.'

'Michael the Brave give me courage now!'

I clamped my mouth shut so that I should not be drawn into conversation with the monster, but my lips trembled. There was an incantation that would protect me from this sea changeling if I could but remember the words. Ach, you must be knowing it as well as myself.

'Crab and lobster, cowrie, limpet; mussel, whelk and seashore flea. Spin urchin, starfish . . .' My head was spinning with the words, but my mouth shook so that the sounds would not come.

'What is this place?' he asked, and there was a power in his question that I dared not ignore.

'The Place of the Fords,' I told him. 'Benbecula.'

I put my hands to my face and waited for him to seize me and run shrieking to the sea, for I had spoken to him and the enchantment was on me. I waited on a breath, but he moved away from me. Through a chink in my fingers I saw him sitting on the sand, his head sunk in his hands. I would have risen then and run with the wind at the back of me, but I could not move. My limbs had stiffened. I would stay there till the tide rose. I would die unshriven with the marsh creatures in my body. For me there would be no resurrection, no paradise, no blessing from the Holy Family, no welcome from the Great Father.

The man moaned and spewed on the sand. Ah God, he was a man after all, a man in pain. It is strange how a man's weakness will put strength into a woman. I took the shawl from my own shoulders and covered his shivering nakedness. Strength flowed into my limbs and I was able to stand. I put out my hand to him. He was my son, the one in need of succour, the stranger at the hearth. I took him to my home.

I called it home, for so it was to me, and had been since the day of my curtching. To the islanders it was called the Accursed Place and not without reason. Long before the time that is, it was a place living and full of laughter until a terrible storm rose suddenly and took most of the men while they were at the fishing. Then had come the Great Sickness when we lost most of our bairns and many of their mothers. Those who had not died had long since left the place and built new homes where the machair is singing with sweet grasses and pink clover. But some of us stayed in the old place. Why should we leave our homes where we raised and shrouded our children? We who had watched night after night with death were not afraid of the black water from the Long Bog which seeped through the floor and moulded the dung. The rain which dripped through the thin thatch no longer troubled us. True, winter brought aches and agues and the terrible spitting cough, but so it did to those who lived on the machair. The peat reek reddened our eyes and scratched at our throats only a little more than it did to the other islanders. No one who came new

76

to Benbecula would choose to live in the Accursed Place, but we seven old women who called it home would not live else-where.

Mad Mag, shaking and mumbling, was at her door when we passed, the Sea Stranger and myself. I knew the others would be watching from the dark midden of their homes. A visitor to the Accursed Place was no common event.

I took him to my hearth and blew the sullen peats to flame. I drew the pot to the heat and he ate a little thin porridge. Soon he curled himself close to the warmth and fell asleep. I covered him with my own bed-mat. Mad Mag was the first to come in but the others were not slow to follow. One by one they stared down at the sleeping stranger, poking and pushing like ravens at a corpse, and all the while the wind rustled in the thatch like an uninvited guest matching its mood to the whispering women who coughed and sniffed and spat into the hissing hearth.

They were still there when the stranger awoke. As he stirred and lifted his eyes, the fear that had come to me so strongly on the shore trod into every heart. He seemed to look deep into the very soul of each one of us though his eyes never moved.

'I took my boat to the place where the sea rises to the wind,' he said softly. 'I rode between the black rocks under the white foam. The boat splintered beneath me. I had hoped to die.'

The death wish lay on him like a shroud.

'There was no place for me in my mother's land. There was no room for me in the sea. Why could I not die?'

'Only the innocent die young,' I told him, for I knew there was some curse on the man's soul that could not be laid aside for the wishing.

'Do not put your trust in death,' said Baraball. 'Death takes only those whom death desires.'

'Death does not come for the wishing,' said another.

'Nor life either,' said Mad Mag, and began to sing in a high reedy keen.

My love lies fathoms deep bound in the clammy weed.
How cruel are the wild waves that have taken my beloved.

One by one we took up the lament and a strange noise we made of it.

> Alas for the days that are gone,
> Alas for my love that is drowned,
> Alas for my sorrow and me,
> For my love that lies dead in the sea.

When the singing was done, the man stared at us, his eyes black and mad, his fingers fumbling at the leather pouch he wore round his neck.

'It is the way he looked when I found him,' I told them.

'He has the Eye,' said Baraball fearfully. 'See how he watches us.'

'Surely he has the Eye. He will be a curse to us all.'

We cowered back shrinking into our shawls. Baraball who had had some experience in this matter took charge. Standing up, she pointed to the stranger and said in a voice that trembled:

'May the Eye be on thee thyself, sender of evil, and on all thou lovest best.'

Well said, Baraball, bravely spoken. The Incantation of the Reversed Eye is a powerful protection, but still the Stranger stared, his eyes seeming to grow larger, blank like pools in the Long Bog.

'Holy St Tarran, protect us all! Black Donald is in him.'

Someone else said, 'The Little Island.'

Afterwards I could not remember who had first said it, for it seemed that the idea entered our minds all at once. Baraball told him to wrap the blanket round his shoulder. Then she bade him follow and he rose like a sleep-walker. We lifted our skirts over our heads and went out into the twilight.

It was raining, fine driving rain that wet our faces and soaked through our clothes. Our feet slapped and squelched as we trod between the water-holes. Mad Mag leaned on a piece of driftwood. My bones ached with weariness, for I had already walked too far that day, and the cough racked me cruelly. The man came with us as docile as a motherless lamb as if he knew what we intended and welcomed it.

I am telling you this in case you should wonder at the strangeness of our ways; we felt no guilt. Had he belaboured our bowed backs with sticks we would not have resisted; had he robbed our kists and stolen our poor few beasts, we would have stood aside, but we had to protect our souls.

The loch was not large but there were two islands, mounds of rock and heather, the nearer smaller than the other. A boat bobbed on the edge of the water, for the loch brought a living in fish to him who dwelled on its shore. The Boatman was short, with bowed legs and powerful shoulders. He was afraid of no man, but he feared us. There were few folk in Benbecula who did not fear us and the knowledge that was in us, and we accepted their fear. It was our only protection against the ill-wishing of others.

Without question, the Boatman rowed the man across to the smaller of the two islands and did there as he had been bidden. We watched and waited until he returned alone. Then we went slowly and singly back to the Accursed Place, our minds at peace.

The Augur

I was sure that the Stranger had been in trouble as soon as I saw him, but it is not my custom to pry. Besides he was in no fit state to give an answer to the questions that crowded my mind. Therefore it was in silence that I carried him back to the croft that evening. As for the Bowlegged One, poor fellow, he was anxious to have nothing more to do with the affair.

He had waited until the Women of the Accursed Place were out of sight and then he had hurried off across the bog and the machair until he had come to my house.

'They have done it again,' he said shamefacedly.

'Man, can you not stand up to them,' I said, reaching for the deerskin cloak that my friths had won for me once on the Mainland. 'What are you afraid of?'

'You ask me that when you are the only man on the whole island who is not afraid of the power of the old hags?'

'What can seven old women do to a man with shoulders like yours?' I told him, closing the door of my house behind us.

'I have been cursed once too often,' said he, glancing down at his misshapen legs. 'My mother offended just such an old woman as one of those in the Accursed Place when I was still in the womb.'

'Well, well, but that is all water under the bridge. Who is it this time?'

The Bowlegged One, half-running at my side, explained.

'A Lewisman by his tongue. They found him on the shore.'

'A Lewisman allowed himself to be treated so?'

'A mad Lewisman or else they have put a spell on him. He spoke wildly of the sea and death and he had the eyes of Black Donald on him.'

It had stopped raining when we reached the loch. A shaft of moonlight slanted across the water. Although the Bowlegged One took the oars, he did not get out of the boat. His courage took him thus far.

I went to the centre of the island. There was a rock there with a deep round hole in the middle of it. The Lewisman stood in it knee-deep in water, shackled by a rope made of heather roots to an iron stake. He did not seem surprised to see me.

'This must seem a strange welcoming,' I told him as I cut the rope. 'Benbecula is not usually so unfriendly.'

He did not reply. Indeed he would have fallen if I had not caught him and carried him across my shoulder to the waiting boat.

Anna found him some clothing and set before him a meal of hot broth. The children, round-eyed, watched him eat and

80

even the infant was quiet in her mother's arms as he told us something of his story. Seemingly he had been fishing Harris waters. Three days of wind had blown his boat off-course so that he missed the Toe Head and was driven on south until his boat struck rocks. He had known nothing more until he had regained his senses in old Marsali's lap.

'The Holy Angels must have held you in their arms,' said Anna gently. 'Most men are dead before they reach these shores.'

The man looked at her strangely. 'The Holy Angels are not the only guardians of the waters,' he said with a bitter edge to his voice. He turned away and covered his eyes with his hands in a gesture of weariness and despair.

Anna and I looked at each other.

'It is not to be wondered at,' she said with the compassion in her voice that I loved, but I had the feeling that there was much more he could have told us if he wished.

Anna gathered the little ones and shooed them into the inner room. Then she turned to the Stranger. 'You will be tired. There is plenty of clean straw in the barn. We are honoured to share our home with you.'

He rose then and, thanking us both, accepted our hospitality. I lighted him to the barn. When I held out my hand to bid him good night, I noticed that he held a small white stone. Right from that moment I perceived that the stone played a great part in the Stranger's life. When he held it clenched in his fist all was not well with him.

As I lay with Anna in the dry warmth of our bed, I listened to the contented noises of the night: the breathing of my gentle woman, the movement of the cows in the byre, the stirring of the hens in the thatch and the settling of the smoored peats. I could not get the Women of the Accursed Place out of my head.

In the old days, before the time of law, the hole on the Little Island had been a place of rough justice. Cattle thieves and murderers had been put there to die in the teeth of the wind. It was a place haunted with tales of horror and cruelty, but it

81

had not been used in the name of justice for at least a hundred years. Recently, however, the old women had taken to using it for their own mad purposes. They had tied there one of their own number with a shaking disease, for they had been afraid of the evil spirit within her. Mercifully, the Bowlegged One had told me in time to save her life, if not her mind, as he had done this night. There was no doubt that the old women were becoming a threat to the island. I would have to speak to Clanranald about them as soon as he returned from the wars. If he did not return, then I would have to speak to his lady. I would have done so sooner if I had believed good would have come out of it. She was so taken up with building a new home at the House of the Black Women that she had no time for the affairs of her lord's people.

I sighed and turned over, sleep as far from me as when I had first lain down to rest. My mind returned to the Stranger in the barn. There was something about him that disturbed me, though I could not rightly say what it was. It was moments like this when I was filled with a premonition of uneasiness that gave me my right to be an augur. Pitifully few these moments were, but I treasured them when they came to me. The more I thought about the Stranger, the more certain I felt that changes lay ahead, not only for my own family but for Benbecula. I made up my mind to cast an augury on the first Monday of the next month for the future of the Lewisman among us, and so, murmuring a prayer to the Holy Father, I fell asleep at last.

The Mondays came and went but the frith remained unread. The Lewisman, as he came to be called, soon made a place for himself, both in my croft and among the islanders. His usefulness to the community lay in the fact that he could read and write the English. Certainly it is true that there were not too many demands on his knowledge, but on the few occasions when it was needed it was easier to consult with him than to seek out one of Lady Clanranald's household.

He was gentle with the little bairns, friendly with the older ones and particularly courteous to my Anna, who took him into her warm heart as she took all lonely souls. He was a great hand at the fishing and would never come back empty-handed from a day at the lochs. He was not a talkative man, either in the croft or in company, but he could sing a few tunes and taught us some new verses in the ceilidh-house. There were times when I would try to question him about his past, but he was not inclined to tell me anything, so I did not press him. A man's past is as much his own affair as his future.

There were times too when he did strange things that perplexed me. For instance, there was the occasion when we were crossing the flat land at Bailevanach on a day that was all summer blue. Suddenly he stopped and turned his head upwards to look at the sky with an expression that was both frightened and incredulous.

'What do you see, man?' I asked him, shading my eyes as I peered up into the cloudless blue.

He did not reply. Instead he clapped his hands to his ears as if he could hear some terrible noise and he flung himself flat on the ground as if he were afraid of being struck.

Something of his wonder and terror communicated itself to me.

'What is it? What do you see?' I cried, but all I could see was a curlew crying a moan as it flapped across the great flat moor.

I do not think he heard me. When he rose I could see that his eyes were strange, like a man in a dream. He began to run, but whether he was running from me or the vision I had no means of knowing. When I reached the croft he was there before me, seated at the hearth, with the younger bairns crawling all over him while Anna chatted to him across the steaming pot. By the way he avoided my eye, I knew he did not want to speak of what had happened and I did not press him. I respect a man's right to hold his tongue.

Those queer turns did not occur often, but I suspected they happened more frequently than I knew and that he had grown skilled in concealing them. I wondered from time to time if he suffered from some sickness of the mind, but in view of his general behaviour, I came to the conclusion that this was unlikely. It did occur to me, however, that he might be interested in my work with the auguries, so I asked him to accompany me to the home of a family on the other side of the island who had lost a dun cow.

We walked in silence over the flat land, a hardship for me, for I am a sociable sort of man, but necessary on this occasion for the casting of a good frith. It was my habit as an augur to prepare myself with prayer and this I found easiest to do under the canopy of heaven.

For the casting of a good frith it is of the greatest importance to obey all the rules. My father, who was an augur before me, often said that the prayer, the fasting and the meditation were more important than the signs themselves, so as I walked I repeated the Frith of Mary.

God before me, God behind me, God over me, God below me.
I am Thy path, O God; Thou, O God, in my steps.

It was near darkness when we arrived and the man of the house met me in silence and took me to a prepared bed where I lay fasting till sunrise.

I came out of the barn as the sun's first rays slanted across the sea and tinged the moors with gold. The man of the house blindfolded me and took me to the door of the house. I placed a hand on either post and called upon God to guide me.

'I am going without from the doorstep of this house in the Holy Name of God.'

The man and the woman, their bairns and neighbours led me to the place where the cow was last seen. The sun was lifting itself clear of the horizon when I made a horn with my hands and blew through it three times before crying on St Bride to open my eyes. Then I took off the blindfold.

I looked first to the west. The Lewisman was standing there, facing towards me, his eyes blank and wide. This was a good sign, for he was a dark stranger to these folk.

I looked to the east and behold there were three sheep grazing with their heads turned towards me, another good omen.

I looked north and saw the head of a duck bobbing on a small loch which pleased me well. The duck is a blessed bird, for it covered our Lord with straw when His enemies were after Him.

Then I looked south and saw the group of anxious folk. One of them stood a little apart from the rest. A hen pecked in the ground at his feet. This was a very ill sign, for it was the hen who exposed our Lord to His enemies by eating the corn that covered Him. As I looked into that man's face, his eyes shifted uneasily and I had my answer.

'The cow is well!' I cried with confidence. 'You will find her at the mouth of the Cave of Rueval at sunset. Be sure you do not go to the cave before the hour of sunset. The Little People will not be spied upon.'

Before I was taken into the croft to be served with the best there was to offer, I had time to look meaningfully at the thief. He knew that I had let him off lightly and that if the occasion arose again, I would not be so lenient.

I have often been criticized for my softness with wrong-doers, but I am a man of peace by nature, preferring to make a friend rather than an enemy. I knew that the man who had taken the cow was not necessarily wicked. More than likely he had a hungry wife and bairns to feed. A couple of days of milk-ing, with butter and cheese, would not be missed by the owner of the cow who had been prosperous enough to employ an augur.

On the way home I tried to find out what the Lewisman's reactions were to what he had witnessed. To my joy, he showed a deep interest.

'How could you be so sure that the cow would be returned if you did not "see" it at the cave?'

'Seeing with the eye is one thing,' I said. 'Seeing with the mind is another.'

'Do you never make mistakes?'

'Of course, but it is also possible to misinterpret the evidence of the eyes.'

'Do you say so?' he said and sighed.

'My son,' I said, stopping and turning to look him in the eye. The time had come to speak what had been in my mind for many months now. 'My son, I believe that you have the Sight. Is it not so? You "see" more clearly than I do, but we are cast in the same mould, you and I.'

He shook his head. 'You "see" because you want to "see". I "see" because I cannot help it.'

'It is a great gift that you have, my friend. Do not run from it.'

His eyes burned darkly.

'What do you know of it? You with your prayers and in-cantations, your signs and your interpretations! I am cursed with an evil that taints every part of my life.'

I reached out both hands to him in friendship.

'That is because you have not yet learned how to use it. The Second Sight is a gift from God.'

'Or the devil,' he said, twisting away from me. 'That cow you saw in the care of the Little People, I saw it too. One of those men there in the crowd had it hidden in his own byre. His woman was milking it as you were blowing your horn.'

So I had been right. There was a strangeness in this man that set him apart. There was no connexion between his 'see-ing' and my guessing.

'I know that, my son,' I told him gently. 'But I would ask you to think of the consequences to that poor woman if the truth were known.'

It was his turn to be silent. I saw understanding flit across his sallow face.

'Would you like to learn from me the secrets of a good frith?' I asked him. 'You are the one to take my place when the time comes.'

He shook his head. 'No, indeed. The things that I see can only bring disharmony and hate. Your insight brings peace.'

'If you were to change your mind—' I began.

'I will not change my mind,' he said firmly.

In spite of his quiet ways, or perhaps because of them, he was a great success with the womenfolk. My Anna soon loved

86

him as if he had been one of her own and he repaid her by taking his full share of the work of the croft. He also helped the young folk herd the cattle in the long summer evenings and the young girls would argue with each other as to who would go with him. I knew that my little Elizabeth was interested when she started coming out to the fields with bannocks instead of sending her younger sister.

'My mother sent me with some oatcake,' she would say, her pink cheeks aflame and her shy eyes downcast.

'That was kind of her,' I would reply, longing to wink at the Lewisman but afraid my daughter would see.

I would have liked it fine if the Lewisman had responded to Elizabeth's shy advances, but he was not interested in her, nor in any other of the maidens who flounced their skirts at him in the reel or sang their sweetest songs to him at the eilidh.

'Give him time,' Anna would say to me hopefully, for she was as anxious as me to keep him in the family. We needed young men on Benbecula. Too many had gone to the wars or been lost at sea.

But if he were not attracted to the young girls of the island, he began to show an uncanny interest in the old women of the Accursed Place, an interest which I never fully understood or approved. It was this interest that was to be the cause of a rift between us. Perhaps if he had told me about it at the beginning I would have acted differently, but by the time it came to my ears it was too late. Strange, you will be thinking, how there could be secrets on an island such as ours. Now I look back with shame at the way we treated the wretched old creatures. The truth was that we were afraid to meddle with them, for they were not above casting an eye or uttering a curse for no good reason but that it suited them. Even so, it took a man from Lewis to show us up to ourselves.

It was the Bowlegged One who first told me what was going on.

We were all at the gathering of the peats that summer day. Not together, mind. We were careful to choose different banks, for although we knew well enough what the others were doing, it was shameful to be seen at such a task.

It was still more shameful to have no man to win the peats and though we knew that none of the islanders begrudged us a creel or two from their banks, it was an ignominious thing to have to steal. I was at the Augur's bank. Beautiful peat it was, three weeks cut and dry enough to creel homewards, dry enough almost to burn. I filled the rush basket to overflowing, set it against a steep slope the more easily to lift it to my back. My limbs ached and my head was spinning with the effort, and the cough was so hard on me that I thought I would drop my burden.

On the way home I saw Mad Mag. Her creel was scarcely half filled and she was standing with her head tilted for listening. I would have passed her without a greeting, for I had no breath for talk, but she called out to me.

'Are you hearing them, Marsali?' she asked with wonder in her voice.

'Who is it that I should be hearing?' I answered her with impatience in my voice, for my back was paining me sorely.

'It is the Little People of Sorrow. Ach, how they weep. Surely you must be hearing them.'

I listened then, for none can afford to ignore the Little People of Sorrow when they cry a lament. I heard a curlew call and the trickle of water in the burn. I heard the sweep of wind in the machair below and faintly, a watery whine that might have been the breath in my chest or the midges in the warm air; or something else that I could not name.

'And are you seeing them, Marsali?'

'Where?' I whispered, looking fearfully about me.

'Everywhere,' she told me.

I stared at a patch of moving reeds, but my sight was poor

I could not make out if the rushes bent under the weight of the Little People of Sorrow or whether they bowed to the wind.

'Who are they crying for, Marsali? Whom do they mourn?'

You will be thinking that with all the knowledge of my years I would know the answer to her question, but I knew as little as she. All the way back to the Accursed Place I seemed to see those tiny green creatures swaying with sorrow, moaning their lament on every blade of grass, and I trembled.

When I reached my home I shut the door and built a strong fire round the small red heart under the peats. As long as there was fire in the hearth there was life in the home. I was not afraid of death. Death could not be harder than life in the Accursed Place. Indeed I had great hopes that it might be better. I was afraid only of dying. Sometimes when I have been torn apart with the cough, and unable to draw breath, I have believed myself to be dying. How long will the struggle for breath last before I am free of my flesh? How will I know that I am dead? Will the Great Father be looking my way when the time comes or will I go spinning down into the Abyss while His back is turned. If the laird's mother were to die at the same moment surely it would not be my soul He would be seeking. I seemed to hear the keening all round me. In my mind's eye those small sad faces pressed down against the thatch, pressed up on the latch. My heart was quivering like an old hen before a storm.

Presently I opened the old black kist and took out my treasures one by one. The spoons the father had fashioned for the bairns with fish heads for handles: a charm against death in childbirth and several thread charms to protect the beasts; a drinking cup that the old laird's father had given to my father in gratitude for some long forgotten service; a sword my man had taken from a dead seafaring man; my wedding dress, a gift from my lover that I had worn the once, and, under all, the winding-sheet I had made as a bride. It was damp and greying. I aired it at the fire and put it at the top of the kist so that it should be easily found. It was a task I had been meaning to do for many months. I was ready for death.

A great peace was in me as I lay down to sleep that night and murmured the evening prayer in the words I had known since childhood.

> With God will I lie down this night,
> And God will be lying with me;
> With Christ will I lie down this night,
> And Christ will be lying with me;
> With the Spirit will I lie down this night,
> The Spirit will lie down with me:
> God and Christ and the Spirit, Three,
> Be they all down-lying with me.

But it was not for me that the Little People of Sorrow were grieving that night.

It was the Lewisman who found Mad Mag's creel on the peat bank. It was the Lewisman who packed it full of the best turf and lifted it to his own back and it was the Lewisman who walked as bold as a bull-calf into the Accursed Place the following morning.

'I am looking for the owner of this creel.'

None of us stirred. Like me, perhaps, they were remembering the last time the Lewisman had visited the Accursed Place and they were afraid. In the end curiosity drove us out. Mad Mag's door was the only one to remain shut. He stopped in front of it and called out. In the silence that answered him, we all saw there was no smoke curling through the thatch. He knocked again more loudly on the warped door. We followed him into the house and when our eyes became used to the gloom, we saw that she was dead.

Death smooths away the ravages of time for death is ageless.

> Weep for the companion at the hearth;
> Weep for the maiden who has shared my joy;
> Weep for the woman who has known my sorrow;
> Weep for the one who cannot be replaced.

We did what was necessary, each of us wondering who would be the next to be taken, each praying not to be the last, for who would then do what was needful? Who would be left to mourn and to keep watch in the dark hours of the night?

From that day the Lewisman belonged to us. After the burial, he went up to a part of the moor that was used by no one and spent his spare hours cutting peats for us. Before the summer was out, each of us had a small peat stack at the end of the Black House to call our own. Every roof had been strengthened with new heather and every barn contained a sufficiency of hay for the few poor beasts we still possessed.

And there were other changes too. Those of us who had been soured by hunger and hardship seemed to grow sweeter. We would smile and cry a morning greeting to each other and meet at the hearth to remember the past and ponder on the present. For those short summer weeks the Accursed Place was blessed with more than warm wind and sunshine.

A mother may have many sons to provide for her old age. We had only the one to share between us, but none of us would have exchanged him for a blood kinsman. Sometimes I would watch the slim dark strength of him at his work and wonder why he drove himself so hard for the sake of six old women. True, I had given him his life, but had I not also tried to take it away from him? Once I tried to question him on the matter.

'My destiny was never in your keeping, old Mother, but yours may well be in mine,' he said quietly, and with that I had to be content.

But most of our woman's talk was on how best to bless our benefactor.

'I will be gathering the root of St Tarran's flower to make a charm to put on his byre to protect his milking cows,' said one, nodding her satisfaction with the plan.

'Ach,' said Baraball, the woman of the house, 'he has no cows of his own and surely you would not be wanting to waste our charms on the Augur's beasts.'

'I was thinking to gather Mothan to fashion into a ring to protect his woman in childbirth,' said another, who in the summer of her life had been aid-wife to the island.

'He has no woman and a good thing too,' said Baraball sharply. 'There is none fit for the likes of him in Benbecula.'

'He could always be wearing it himself,' said the other. 'They say it is a powerful protection should he fall out with the sheriff.'

'Ach,' said the woman of the house scornfully. 'I am not one for the Mothan. I prepared it myself once and gave it to a cousin of my cousin who was accused of burning the laird's long barn in Barra. He was hanged.'

'It is a great protection against the Evil Eye,' said another, and we all fell silent remembering how we had once treated the Lewisman.

'We owe him much,' I said at last.

'It is so,' the others agreed, nodding at each other.

'If we could but look into his future and see what life holds in store for him, we would be the better able to help him,' said Baraball.

'That is for the Augur to do.'

'The Augur!' Baraball spat contemptuously at the fire. 'He can see no further than his own long nose.'

The others cackled and dug each other in the ribs and slapped at their knees.

'It is not an easy matter to see into the future of a man,' said I when the laughter had ended.

'The One whom I will not mention knows,' said the woman of the house, 'if we had a mind to ask.'

The words dropped sharply into my mind like diving gulls, and we all fell silent, for Baraball had not spoken lightly. There was little enough we could do for the Stranger. We had no gold, no cattle worthy of the name, no treasure. The gift of foreknowledge was a worthwhile offering, costing to the giver and valuable to the receiver. There was a great excitement in my head as I put my head forward and joined in the whispers which mingled with the peat reek and caught up in the black thatch. Such a divination had not been done for many seasons.

'It is decided then?' asked the woman of the house at last.

'It is decided,' we told her.

She rose then and fetched some straw, cutting five stalks of equal lengths and one that was but half the size of the rest; then she bunched them in her fist and told each of us to draw in turn. Fearfully my twisted fingers fumbled over my choice, for I knew that if I were the elected one I would not be able to endure the ordeal. The woman who drew the short straw gave a small cry. Then she shawled her shoulders and left the house. The rest of us remained to question and instruct each other until all was plain. Then we returned to our own hovels to doze away what remained of that restless night.

The moon was rising the following evening as we straggled down to the shore, each bent double under the burden of what was necessary for the night's work. She who had been chosen followed more slowly, dragging a fine young bullock, the best available, by its tether. When we reached the place chosen by Baraball for its seclusion and closeness to the sea we built a great fire. Then Baraball slit the bullock's throat.

Blood brings strength to feeble frames and we needed all the strength we could find for the task of skinning the beast, so we drank our fill. Although this was a task usually left to the menfolk, we were as quick and skilled as our years allowed. Within an hour or so the work was done. Then she who had been chosen took off her outer garments and lay down in the still warm skin. We bound her up in it with thongs of hide and rolled her over the sand to the edge of the incoming tide. She struggled and shrieked to be released, but Baraball only tightened her thongs. There could be no going back now.

We fed the fire with dried seaweed and peats and roasted the heart and other tasty tender portions of the meat while the carcass with its human content rolled and bounced on the sand, driven back and forth by the waves. The cries of the woman grew hoarse and finally dropped to a moan that mingled with the murmur of the wind.

When we had eaten our fill we began the long Incantation
that was to last till dawn.

> Archangel of Hell hear us,
> Black Donald come to us,
> Night Wanderer fly to us,
> Great Beast of the Sea swim to us,
> Black Worm of the Earth creep to us,
> Master of Witches answer us,
> Grey Grizzled One speak to us . . .

And still the carcass rolled and the moon rose and waned
and the sky grew light in the east. I dozed and the words died
on my lips till I felt Baraball's sharp finger in my back. We fed
the fire from time to time. One snored thickly and would not
be woken, and then as the first gold streak lanced across the
sky, Baraball roused us with a cry.

'It is the mouth of the morning. It is the time.'

We followed her, shivering and yawning to where the carcass lay stranded on the high-tide line. We cut the thongs and
opened the matted pack. The woman was sodden and bloodied,
her eyes wild and her body stiff and still.

'She has spoken with him!'

'Surely she has seen him!'

'What may she not tell us!'

No one dared to say what we all feared, that she might be
dead. There would be no rest for any of our souls if she had
died, but no, she was not dead. She sighed and shuddered and
we pulled her to the fire. Her eyes focused on the crackling
lively flame shooting between the black weed. Suddenly she
began to shriek.

'What do you see?' I cried.

'Tell us, tell us,' the others cried, but all she said was:

'The fire! The fire!'

Baraball took hold of her shoulders and began to shake her.

'We can all see the fire, foolish one. What did you see for
the Lewisman?'

She turned her head away from the crackling flames and looked at us all with bright mad eyes. 'I saw the fire,' she whispered.

The Augur

The boy who was herding that night roused me shortly after dawn. His face was whey-coloured and his tongue in knots. I woke the Lewisman and together we ran down to the shore.

It still sickens me to remember what we saw there. Blood and fire, fire and blood. Blood clotted on the hands and faces of the old women; blood-spattered clothing; hacked and bloody lumps of meat encrusted with sand. Fire diminished in the strong red rays of the greater fire, the sun, which flamed every face and glittered in every eye. I was careful not to meet those malevolent old eyes with my own, for there was evil in the air and I noticed that the herdsboy had turned away.

Then I saw the carcass. The head of the beast was still attached to the skin and I recognized the creature as one of my own cattle.

'This is a matter for the sheriff!' I cried in anger to the Lewisman, but he paid me no heed. He went down to the old women and helped them rise.

'You should be in your beds,' he told them.

'We did it for you, my son, only for you,' one muttered wearily.

'Where is your gratitude?' said another crossly.

'We summoned the Dark One from the Pit,' said the first.

'Aye,' grumbled the other, 'and all to find out your fortune for you.'

The Lewisman stood very still.

'He is angry with us,' said the first speaker. When the Lewisman still did not speak, she added, 'Save your anger. We saw nothing. We should have kept to our beds.'

One who seemed bloodier and madder than the rest suddenly began to shriek.

'Fire!' she cried. 'I saw fire.'

'Pay no heed to her,' said the one they called Baraball. 'Black Donald has addled her mind for her pains.' She sniffed with contempt.

'Come,' said the Lewisman. 'I will take you home.'

I was angered by his behaviour. These women had once tried to kill him. Now they had tried to raise the Evil One on his behalf. Who was he to condone such wickedness? I could not let it pass. Besides, they had stolen my bullock. The herdsman admitted to hearing it bellowing in the early evening, but he had paid no heed at the time for he was lying in a sand-dune with his girl.

'Did you not hear me?' I cried moving in front of the Lewisman and the crones. 'This is a matter for the sheriff. If they are not tried for witchcraft, they will surely be convicted for stealing.'

'No one is thinking of running away,' the Lewisman replied mildly.

That night I called a meeting of the crofters. They crowded into my house but there was no singing, no dancing, though Anna, bless her, brought out ale and bannocks for the sake of hospitality. I told the Lewisman he would be welcome and to my surprise he came, for my tone had not been friendly towards him.

After we had eaten and drunk a sufficiency I began the talking. 'What is to be done with the Women of the Accursed Place?' I asked. 'For too many years now they have stolen our peats, robbed our crops and milked our cows—'

'I am not the man to grudge a creel of peats or a pail of milk,' said Sandy of the Four Fingers hastily.

'Nor I!' cried some others, though I noticed that those who spoke loudest were those who had lost least.

'None of us grudge a little here and a little there, but when it comes to the slaughter of a fat young bullock it is a different story.'

'Aye,' said the Bowlegged One, who could be trusted to agree with me in most things. 'That is a serious matter.'

'There are other things,' said Morag of the Broken Spindle, significantly. 'These should be spoken of at this time. There is one of them who sells the wind. Tell them, Hamish,' she added, nudging her man with her elbow.

'What the woman says is true,' he said, rising to his feet and speaking loudly so that the deafest among us could hear. 'A cousin of mine, the Tall Macrurie, you will have heard me speak of him, I am thinking, for his father's mother was sister to my grandmother.' We listened in silence to the long complicated relationship. 'This cousin is a fisherman like myself. Seemingly he fell out with a neighbour who went to one of the old women of the Accursed Place for a charm. She gave him a cord knotted three times. The first knot was for a favourable wind, the second for a gale and the third for a storm. It was a blessing that my cousin was wearing a powerful charm of protection when the third knot was untied or he would have drowned for certain.'

As soon as this tale was finished others followed and the hours passed quickly as the crofters remembered overlooked cows, sickly bairns and unaccountable deaths. They would have continued throughout the night if I had not interrupted.

'Witchcraft is a matter for the sheriff,' I said firmly.

You will notice perhaps that I did not suggest that the priest be summoned from South Uist. There was no love lost between myself and that man for when he came to Benbecula it was only to condemn my profession. I am not unreasonable in my judgement of others, but I could not take to a priest who has God on his lips but not in his heart.

'Aye,' said the Bowlegged One nodding wisely. 'The sheriff must be summoned. My family lives in terror of those crones.'

'Who is to send for him?' asked one of the women practicably.

'I have thought of that,' I said. 'The Lewisman writes a fair hand. He shall write a letter.'

All turned to look at the stranger in the shadows.

'I will not,' he said firmly.

There was a shocked silence, for we were not used to such

blunt speaking. It was one of the most discourteous remarks I had ever heard.

'If the old ones steal, it is because they would otherwise starve,' he continued harshly. 'If they make charms it is no more than the rest of the womenfolk do. Is it a crime in Benbecula to be old and poor? As for the bullock,' he said, turning to me, 'you will find a cow tethered outside. She is not as fat or as young as your beast but she is the best there is in the Accursed Place. The old women beg that you will accept her in exchange for the slaughtered animal.'

'That is all very well,' grumbled the Boatman, 'but how are we to know that next time the victim may not be one of us? Surely you have not forgotten the hole on the Little Island where you yourself were so nearly destroyed?'

'There is something in every man that needs to be destroyed,' he said strangely. 'The eyes of the aged sometimes see more clearly than the eyes of youth.'

'If only the laird were at home,' Anna sighed. 'He would know what to do.'

'They are saying that the wars are over and that already he is crossing the water,' said one.

'They have been saying that for more years than I care to remember,' said Sandy. 'Is it not time to cast another frith for the laird's homecoming?' he asked, turning to me.

I sighed inwardly. I had cast many such auguries but had interpreted none of them right. By my calculations the laird should have been home for twelve months now.

No one returned to the matter which had brought us together. Reparation for the slaughtered bullock had been made and what the Lewisman had said stung a few consciences, but I was angry, and—I freely admit it—I was wounded in my heart. I had taken this stranger in, treated him like a brother. I expected a loyalty that he had not given to me. Instead I had been made to feel mean-handed and small-minded in my own home among my own people. Deep in my heart I felt shame because he had been the one to show charity to those old crones. Resentment burned in me like a slow candle. Perhaps this was why I allowed my judgement to be clouded by my feelings when tragedy struck the island only two days later.

A child went missing. Such a thing had not happened for many years. Then it had been a simple lad who had fallen to his death in a loch because he had not the wits to keep afloat. This time it was little Sile, a dark-eyed adventurous child of nine years who had disappeared. There was no danger of her drowning were she fool enough to fall into a loch for she could swim like a seal. She should have been born a boy except that she was too pretty.

Her father came to me in a fine state late that night. Sile had not returned at dusk with the other children; no one had seen her since early in the morning and there was no sign of her in the village.

'Rouse the crofters,' I told him. 'Search all night and I will prepare a frith.'

Every man, woman and child who could walk was out that night searching the barns, the byres, the beaches and the moors. Only Sandy and the Bowlegged One were not among the searchers, for they had gone on a fishing trip with supplies to last a week.

I walked the machair and tried to fix my mind on holy things essential to the reading of a true augury, but my mind kept returning to the faces of the old women on the beach, the glittering malevolence in those sunken mad-bright eyes. The wind rose and moaned across the bent grass and seemed to sound like the cry of a child.

At dawn the weary searchers gathered round the croft of the distracted parents. They were all grey and hollow-eyed from exhaustion. We were all perhaps a little mad.

I turned to the rising sun and raised my cupped hands to sound the solemn blast. I looked to the sun-streaked sky and saw—God help me—an image of those hideous crones framed in blood. I looked to the north and they were still there with guilt in their shifty eyes. I turned to the west and still saw them with the sun reflecting from their faces like fire. I turned to the south and saw them as clearly as if they stood in the flesh before me.

Something of the horror I witnessed then must have shone from my face, for Anna cried out in alarm, 'What do you see, my husband?'

'I see the Accursed Place,' I whispered, but all heard me.

The Lewisman pushed forward. There was a terrible expression on his face and afterwards I was sure that he had known then what we had not yet planned to do.

'No!' he cried. 'I myself have searched the Accursed Place. The child is not there. Believe me for the sake of your own souls.'

His words angered us. We ignored him. He was a stranger. His behaviour on the day of the slaughtered bullock had made him an object of suspicion.

'Do you doubt the truth of my frith?' I cried out in anger.

'You see what you want to see,' he answered. 'I have seen what is there.'

'And what does the stranger see?' Morag cried contemptuously.

'Aye, tell us,' they all shouted. 'What does the Lewisman see?'

'The child is safe,' he said, turning to them. 'She is sleeping in a bed of heather covered with a sheepskin. Her thumb is in her mouth.'

The mother of the child began to weep. 'You lie!' she cried. 'She is dead, I feel it here in my heart.'

'She is not lying on any heather bed in Benbecula!' her father cried. 'We have searched every corner.'

'The witches have taken her,' said the mother through her sobs.

The Lewisman disappeared. I thought he had gone to warn the old women, but when we reached the Accursed Place he was not there. What happened next I would like to forget, but this I cannot do, for with the recollection of only the smallest part my mind is forced to relive the whole.

We tore the place apart while the old women screamed abuse for abuse, but we found nothing in those miserable abodes save evidence of their pitiful existence.

I never knew who it was who first cried, 'Burn the witches!' for afterwards it was never mentioned. The thatches were dry and there was a high wind. When the old women saw what we were about to do, they shut themselves inside their huts in the hope perhaps that this would deter us. But it was too late; once alight, the thatches blazed quickly. It would have been impossible to put them out. The Lewisman saw this as soon as he arrived.

'Get them out before you have murder on your souls!' he cried.

Some went to help him, for I swear we did not mean the old ones to die, but we were too late. One was already dead and the others close to suffocation.

That afternoon when the Accursed Place was a smoking waste the laird and his lady rode into the village. He had returned from the wars the previous day and had been celebrating his homecoming in bed with his wife when the Lewisman had roused him.

Would it have made any difference if he had come immediately? It is a question I often ask myself. He could have been with us before the thatches were lit, but in our present mood his word might have carried no weight. The Lewisman was in no doubt, however. He blamed Clanranald.

'Burn the witches?' the laird had scoffed. 'Why, man, we have never brought a witch to trial in Benbecula, let alone burned one, and I'll wager it was no different in Lewis. Go you back to your work. I will ride over sometime later, but it will not be necessary, I assure you.'

When he rode over later, the deed was done. We could not look Clanranald in the face, nor he us.

'Well, well,' he said uneasily, 'what is this that I have been hearing then?'

In the silence that followed there was a shout from the shore. Sandy was hailing us while the Bowlegged One beached the boat. There on the long wide sand a small figure could be seen running towards us. It was Sile.

Seemingly she had hidden under the nets at the bottom of the boat. When she had been discovered a gale prevented the boat from returning at once and they had all spent the night on an island before returning home when the weather had cleared.

The mother of the child ran forward. Hers was the only heart to feel true joy. The laird cleared his throat.

'It seems no great harm has been done. I intended burning those hovels myself many years back. They were a disgrace to the island.'

The Lewisman came forward. He was strange to look at and he held his stone clenched in his fist. His voice was slow and heavy.

'You are wrong, Clanranald. A great harm has been done this day, but the greatest is yet to come. The time is coming when this place will become the roosting ground for monstrous great eagles. They will spread their wings where once your children played and they will carry death where once you carried peats. Smooth-tongued strangers will tend their needs where once you tended cattle and of your line there will be no trace. Your children will be as sand in the wind, scattered and forgotten.'

'As for you,' he cried turning to the laird, 'the day will come when an old wife wearing the footless stocking like the old woman who died here today will drive the Lady of Clanranald from Nunton and the distinguished race of Clanranald will be no more.'[1]

We made what amends we could. Anna took in the old woman they call Marsali and gave her a bed in the inner room. The others found homes in the village, while the one who died was given a memorable burial.

As for the Lewisman, there was no place for him now in Benbecula. Indeed, I know of no place in this world large enough to contain such a one.

Chapter 3

SKYE

The Minister

I have never been so deceived in a man in all the long years of
my ministry both before and since the time of his coming to
Skye. I believe now that he was the devil incarnate.

That is a terrible thing to be saying of a man born in the
image of God, but it is not lightly said. The devil is not always
a roaring lion seeking whom he may devour. He is as likely to
be found in a disciple, as the Blessed Lord knew only too well
when He said to Peter, 'Get thee behind me, Satan'. I have
had time to ponder and to pray and in the light of the events
I do not think that I was mistaken.

It was not an easy matter to minister to a people steeped in
pagan superstition and papist rites. The Reformation had a
quick flowering, but the roots were shallow and had not yet
reached the deeper recesses of the human spirit. Every glen
had its fairy, every township its holy well and unholy women;
every pagan festival was dedicated to a popish deity. I believe
that I was called by the Almighty to stamp out idolatry. I
abominate such practices and not a Sabbath went by in those
days without some misguided soul in sackcloth at the stool of
repentance before my pulpit. It has been my abiding grief and
shame that I was never able to do as much for the Thatcher.
His soul would have been worth a netful of lesser fry to a fisher
of souls such as myself.

I met him on the white coral sands at Dunvegan; a dark
creature he was, sitting on the skeletal strand. He stood at my
passing and—God forgive me—I was taken with him. His man-
ner was deferential, befitting a working man to a minister of

religion, as he waited, bareheaded, for me to speak first.

'It is a fine evening,' I said, brushing away a cloud of midges, for it was one of those calm warm evenings which makes them swarm to human flesh.

'It is indeed,' he said, and I liked the quiet tone of his voice.

'You must be a stranger in these parts,' I said, for I knew every face from Sligachan to Uig.

'I am a Lewisman,' he told me with that hint of pride that is characteristic of the Long Islanders.

'Indeed, and what brings you to Skye?'

'I am looking for employment,' he said simply.

I questioned him about his skills and found out that he was not the simpleton I had expected. He had the English and he could both read and write that language. As I questioned him, a seed of an idea took root in my mind. It had been two years since I had attended a Presbytery meeting on the Mainland, but on that occasion the fathers had been asked to seek out suitable candidates for the ministry. Now I am not usually given to making hasty decisions, but it occurred to me that this young man could well be a likely candidate. He had the appearance, the ability and an air of authority, all necessary qualities for the ministry. He could remain under my guidance for a year or so and then go to Edinburgh to complete his studies. The Macleod would be morally bound to support him on my recommendation, should he prove himself worthy.

All this passed through my mind quickly, prompted, no doubt, by the Lord of Lies, but I was not so foolish as to speak of it. Instead I offered him employment. My house had not been re-thatched for the past two years, for it was a task that I had no time for, either mentally or physically. Besides the thatching, there was enough work on my land to keep him occupied for as long as he cared to stay, by which time I would have assessed his ability for a higher calling.

I began my catechism of him as we walked home together.

'My son,' I began, as we settled into a companionable walk close to the edge of the shore, 'do you love your Maker?'

He was reflective for a moment while our feet whipped the

sweet shore grasses. Then he said, 'Who was my Maker?'

I was taken aback at his answer. For a man who could read and write—or so he had claimed—such a reply was unexpected.

'Why, God was your Maker, my son,' I said patiently.

'Do you say so,' he replied, with an edge to his voice that distressed me.

I should perhaps have reflected longer on the tone of his answer before plunging into argument, but I was filled with evangelistic zeal.

'My son, do you not love God?'

'There is God and there are Gods.'

'Blasphemy!' I cried. 'I have heard that Lewis is an unconverted island, but such ignorance astounds me.'

'The God I know may not be the same God as the one you worship, or the one worshipped by those fishermen yonder,' he replied, pointing to a boat in the bay.

'There is only one God, all-wise, all-seeing and all-terrible,' I told him reprovingly.

'Then your God is not my God.'

'My son,' I said earnestly, for the idea had just struck me, 'are you a Papist?'

'Why?' he said with a hint of humour in his voice that I mistrusted. 'Do the Papists worship a different God?'

'They worship graven images; they bow down to altars and they deify the saints,' I said sternly.

'It seems to me,' he said quietly, 'that God has many faces.'

'The devil has many faces. There is only one God and it is your duty to love him with your heart, your mind and your strength.'

'Love cannot be demanded. It must be earned,' he said, respectfully enough but with a firmness that disconcerted me.

'Do you not think that God has earned your love?'

'How has He done this?' he asked, as if he really wanted an answer.

'He has created you in His own image.'

'I did not ask to be created,' he said, and though he spoke

softly, I detected that same edge of bitterness in his voice.

'Surely the gift of life is all the greater in that it was not asked for,' I told him. 'My son, your knowledge of thatching may be sufficient and your knowledge of English admirable, but your knowledge of Holy Writ is abysmal. It is my duty as a minister of God to enlighten you for the sake of your immortal soul.'

'Can you teach me to love your God when I hate my own?' he said strangely.

I felt the hair rise on the back of my neck at the blasphemous words.

'Never say such a thing to me; never think such a thing in your heart. Only put your soul into my keeping and with God's grace we shall together save it for immortality and the Kingdom of Heaven.'

'The salvation of my soul for the use of my hands,' he said, turning to me with a smile. 'It is a good wage that you pay, minister.'

It was his smile that was my undoing. 'There is good in him,' I told my Maker that night as I strove in prayer. 'Together we shall find it, Thou and I.'

Kate had prepared a mutton broth that caressed every corner of an empty belly. The wine, a gift from Dunvegan, was sweet and strong and the Thatcher ate with a good appetite. How many times have I had good reason to bless my daughter Kate. She is good, obedient and quiet, comely too, in spite of her affliction. The great flame rash that mars her cheek has been there from the time of her birth, and, truthfully, I no longer notice it myself, but it made her shy in the presence of strangers. I suppose she felt that it was in some way repugnant, but I believe they would have noticed it less if she had not drawn attention to it by constantly dropping her head or turning sideways or pulling her shawl across her cheek. Even when we were alone together she would sit with the fiery brand averted from me. Ducking and drooping had become part of her behaviour and it was uglier to my mind than the affliction itself.

If the Thatcher noticed her affliction he gave no sign of it. I have had many strangers at my table; some have gone out of their way to praise a mediocre meal by way of compensation; others have spoken to her slowly and loudly as if she were sick in some way; others have not been able to look away or have done so clumsily. Not so the Thatcher. He behaved towards her with the same courtesy that he would show to any woman and I was encouraged. For one who professed to hate God, he had natural Christian manners.

When the meal was over I took out the Bible and combined my customary hour of study with the task of instructing the Thatcher in the wonderful ways of the Almighty.

The Minister's Daughter

To be a minister's daughter is an affliction in itself. To be a minister's daughter branded by the devil is an unholy contradiction.

Do you see my difficulty? I cannot do the ordinary duties expected of a minister's daughter, teaching Bible stories to the children, comforting the sick and aged, for the crofters have always mistrusted me and would not let their children cross my path. Nor yet can I practise those arts for which I was marked, for I am the daughter of God's representative in the parish and he has made it known that he is determined to stamp out the old rituals.

How did I come to be born this way? It is a question that never ceases to trouble me. Was my mother visited by Satan? Did he come to this very door to beguile her with soft words? Did he overlay her in her bed while the minister was out preaching the Gospel? I could not believe it. My mother was a Macleod of Dunvegan, gently born. She would not have behaved like a crofter's hot young daughter in the summer shielings, or would she? How could I tell? My mother died giving birth to me. Perhaps she died of shame.

For nearly thirty years I puzzled over the secret of my conception. On the night the minister brought the Thatcher to my kitchen, I understood for the first time how a virtuous well-born woman like my mother—like myself—could give herself to a soft-spoken dark-eyed stranger. The moment I saw him, I knew that my mother could have loved such a one. I knew because my mother lived on in me.

There had never been a man for me. The lairds and their sons, though my equal in breeding, would not look at me without a marriage portion and my father, though well-born himself, had given up everything to preach the Word of God. All he had was the house and the land given to him or rather to my mother on her wedding day by the old Chief of Macleod, and the tumbledown church that the heritors whose leanings were still to the old religion would not repair. Even if I had been born with a face like the golden Grainne, I would not have been welcomed as a wife, poor as I was.

As for the crofters, who would choose to wed with one of them? They are animals, less than animals, for I could happily spend my life with my gentle white cow but I could not spend a day, let alone a night, with the likes of Red Roderick or Farquhar of the Hairy Hands. But when the Thatcher sat at my table and ate my meat, I knew that at last I had met a man I could live with.

The reason lay not in his looks, which were not out of the ordinary, nor yet in his behaviour which was unremarkable, but rather because we were two of a kind, devil-spawned and afflicted. Those who are tainted are quick to recognize each other and although his affliction was not as noticeable as mine, I saw it that first night as he sat at meat and listened to the minister. I saw the inward squint of his eye, the rigid limbs, the clenching fists, the sweating brow and I felt the secret thrill of recognition.

The minister was so wrapped up in the prospect of the Thatcher's conversation that he only spoke to me briefly at the end of the meal.

'Did you visit Hector's wife as I asked, my daughter?'

'I did, Father.'

'How did you find her?'

Sick and terrified. When she saw me at the door, the strength went out of her and she sank to the floor. 'Wet your eye,' she had wheezed and crossed herself three times, and then the coughing started so that she could say no more, but she had said enough.

'I gave her the broth as you requested, Father.'

She had cowered away from my offerings. Foolish woman. She believed that it was I who had given her the sickness. She thought she had insulted me by staring at my affliction, and I had repaid her with a dying sickness.

'That was good of you, my Kate, but I fear she is past mortal succour.'

He was right. She would die believing I had killed her. Perhaps I had.

When the Bible had been read, the prayers said and the candles snuffed I showed the Thatcher to the barn where he was to sleep on summer hay.

At the entrance he turned to me and it was so nearly dark that I did not turn away but kept my affliction towards him. His eyes were like black pools.

'Blessings on you, woman of the house,' he said respectfully.

'Blessings on Thee, stranger,' I replied, but whose blessings, I wondered, as I turned back to the house. I had long ago renounced my father's God, and so, I suspected, had he.

The Minister

The Thatcher was a good worker. There was never any doubt on that score. Not only did he cut and lay the thatchings with skill and speed, but he lifted the remaining peats using the pony and his own back. For one who was so small and slight, he had a great strength in him. Besides that, he was a fisherman of skill both in the lochs and on the sea. Kate had more salmon to add to our diet and cod to salt away for the winter. The months passed very quickly.

When it came to Bible study he was less astute. He showed little interest in the God of Abraham, Isaac and Jacob. He had no time for a God who could spoil the Egyptians, ask such a sacrifice of Abraham or turn a woman into a pillar of salt.

'Am I expected to love a God who can destroy and punish and torture?'

I tried to show him that God had to prove and discipline His creatures for their own good and to be an example to future generations.

'Why?' he asked.

'Only listen with open ears and it will all be revealed,' I assured him, but inwardly there was a chill in my heart. My zeal was burning low. He would accept nothing without question and criticism. True faith leaves no room for either.

When we came to the Prophets, I saw that he was interested in a new way, and he questioned me closely.

'Men of God with the Second Sight!' he said with wonder.

He had begun to play with that small stone of his, an irritating habit that had often driven me to the edge of anger. I was never sure why that stone made me so angry and uneasy.

'They were Prophets of God warning against corruption, and foretelling the coming of the Messiah. To say they had the Second Sight is to reduce those holy men to the level of a common crofter who sees a shroud in his whisky-fuddled brain and cries "Funeral",' I said harshly.

'Is the gift of "seeing" right when it predicts the birth of a God and wrong when it predicts the death of a crofter?' he asked.

'You misunderstand deliberately!' I cried. 'The gift of Prophecy in the Old Testament came from God. It was given by God to God-fearing men who knew the importance of prayer and fasting. The art, if it can be so called, of "seeing" is an unholy thing born of Satan to cause conflict, to confuse and to confound. Those to whom it is given are not sons of God.'

'What of Balaam's ass?' he asked softly.

It was a shrewd question implanted by the Evil One himself. I had long pondered on the mystery of Balaam's ass. Balaam was a heathen soothsayer whose methods were not those of the true prophets, and yet God used him. I am one who believes in the fundamental truth of the Holy Book. I believe it to be directly inspired by God and that it is not for man to question His mysterious ways.

'Look at the message in the Oracle of Balaam,' I told him. 'What do you read there?'

He pondered over the verses in the Book of Numbers. When he came to the words, 'There is no spell against Jacob, nor any enchantment for Israel,' I stopped him.

'There is your answer,' I said. 'God chose Israel and Israel will be victorious. That is all you need to know.'

'If God can choose an ass to reveal the truth, may He not also choose a crofter?'

'Such talk reeks of superstition, devilry, witchcraft and all that is impure and discordant in this beautiful island!' I cried, closing the Holy Book, but he was no longer listening. He was clenching and unclenching his fist over the stone and his eyes had become strange and unseeing. I was deeply uneasy. The power that I had recognized in him all those months ago on the coral sand no longer seemed to me to be a power for good.

'Throw away that stone for the sake of your soul, man,' I said sharply. 'You wear it like a talisman.'

In a moment Kate was at my side, her hand on my arm. I had forgotten she was in the room.

'Can you not see?' she said urgently. 'He has an affliction.'

'You may be right,' I muttered.

If so, it was an affliction of the soul. I had never seen a case of possession before, but I recognized it now. I know I should have prayed. I should have fallen on my knees and wrestled with the evil that was in him, but I could not do it. I had a sudden need for air. The peat reek was suffocating, sulphurous. I had to speak to God urgently, but it could not be done here.

'See to him, Kate,' I said harshly, and left the room.

The Minister's Daughter

I watched my father go past the window. When he had gone I turned to the Thatcher. He was staring into the fire, slumped, exhausted, but the strangeness had left him and the stone was hidden once again in the pouch that he carried round his neck. I had seen him in this mood many times, but I had never dared to question him. Now, emboldened by his conversation with my father, I went close to him and stood behind his chair. His head was bent and I stared at the white nape of his neck where the dark hair fell forward.

'You are a seer, are you not?' I said softly.

He sighed but he said nothing.

'Do not be afraid to confess it to me. I care not whether you come from heaven or from hell.'

The living, breathing flesh on his neck drew me like a flower to the sun. I put the tip of my finger on the white skin beneath his hair.

'All my life I have been afraid of men, afraid of their contempt, afraid of the disappointment in their eyes when I turn my face towards them. With you it is different. With you I am not afraid. Why is this, I wonder?'

He stirred and I was afraid he might go from me before I had said what was in my heart.

'No,' I whispered, 'do not turn from me. Do not shut me out.' I eased my whole hand under his clothing so that my fingers spanned the column of his narrow neck. 'We share so much, you and I. Can we not share a little more?'

My hand had found a life of its own. It moved over his shoulders caressingly.

'We are both afflicted, are we not?' My breath was coming queerly and my heart beating fast. I bent down to lay my flaming cheek against his hair. 'As soon as I saw you I recognized you. Are we not both devil-spawned and accursed?'

My fingers closed over the pouch he wore round his neck. He reached up to still my curious hand.

'Is it so plain to see?' he said at last.

'It is there in your eyes as it is on my face,' I said with all the bitterness of a lifetime's disappointment in my voice.

He pulled away from me gently and stood up. He looked at me, his eyes on a level with my own. I wanted to drop my head and turn away my cheek but his eyes held me still.

'Do not look at me,' I whispered. 'I am not a pretty sight.'

'The day is coming,' he began, but I lifted my hand to cover his mouth.

'No,' I cried. 'Do not tell me. I do not want to know. My future is my present and my past. The only change for me will be in the lines of my face and the decay of my body.'

He took away my hand and held it close. 'The day is coming when this room will be full of children, beautiful daughters with smooth cheeks and smooth hair and strong sons with sea-green eyes.'

'My children?' I asked wonderingly. 'And their father, is he there?'

'He is there, a fine man with red hair and a gold beard.'

'And I, where am I?' I whispered.

He hesitated, but for so short a time that I was not aware of it until much, much later.

'You are there,' he said quietly.

I turned away but not to conceal my affliction, only my joy. It was not fitting that a man should witness such a look on a woman's face.

'Say it again,' I whispered. 'Say it all again.'

He repeated word for word what he had seen and I knew that he had not lied.

'So,' I said softly. 'I am to be wed with children of my own.' I did not ask the name of whom I was to marry. I did not

113

need to ask. The description was enough. The Macleod of Dunvegan had as uncle and tutor one Roderick of Talisker. His natural son, Randolphe, born of an English woman long before he married and begat a legitimate family, had flaming red hair and a golden beard.

The Minister

Kate was in good spirits the next morning. She asked me if she might pay a visit to her cousins at Dunvegan and I was glad to give her my permission. She was, after all, a close kinswoman of the Macleods of Dunvegan through her dear mother, and the late laird, Ian Mor, and his lady wife had often told me that she would be more than welcome to make her home at the castle. Lady Macleod had five daughters all younger than Kate and she made no secret of the fact that she would welcome the assistance of an intelligent, gently-born companion.

Kate would not leave me, however, and I was grateful for her care and companionship. My life would have been the poorer without her. Indeed I would have been forced to remarry and after my beautiful Katherine I would have been hard put to find another woman her equal. I was surprised that Kate wanted to go to Dunvegan now and I did not think that she would be gone for long. I wondered briefly if the Thatcher had upset her in any way and hinted as much to her, but she only laughed.

'Perhaps it is time I found myself a husband,' she said with uncharacteristic gaiety.

I was silent. Surely Kate knew by this time that few lairds would welcome her as daughter-in-law. Besides she was past the usual age for marrying and without a dowry.

'Do not look so unhappy, Father. I hope not to be gone for long.'

'Then I will write to your cousin immediately,' I said, 'and perhaps you would find some woman to come in and cook for me when you are away.'

'It is already done,' she said with a little laugh. She was all laughter and chatter that day, but she would give no reason for her strange mood. Indeed, I did not press her.

I sent the Thatcher to Dunvegan with a letter to Lady Macleod. I was glad of the chance to be rid of him for a day. I needed to consider my next move in the doubtful possibility of his conversion. I needed time to think. He was beginning to have an unsettling effect on my personal prayer and Bible study.

My Lady of Macleod sent a warm invitation to Kate.

Dear Minister and Friend,
I was pleased to receive your letter and still more pleased with its request. Kate could not come to us at a better time. Rorie is to celebrate his coming-of-age next month and the Castle will be full of young people and merry-making. Kate will be of great service to me and I shall treasure her as if she were one of my own daughters. . . .

After adding a warm invitation to myself to attend the celebrations she added a short postcript.

If you can spare that personable servant of yours for the week of the festivities I would be much in your debt. Servants of his quality are rare indeed these days. Where did you find him?

So I was to lose my daughter and my Thatcher, but not before I had made a final attempt to convert him to the true religion. The following day was full of rain and mist and wind. I called him in from the barn where he was mending creels. I opened the New Testament.

There is something that I have never rightly understood in myself and that is my preference for the Old Testament revelation of God. I have often wondered why this should be, for I am no Jew. Perhaps it is because the old religion placed too much importance on the trappings of Jesus, the man, His mother, His wounds, His blood. Perhaps I am afraid of His humanity. I do not rightly know, but this I most profoundly believe; the fault is in me, not in the New Testament revelation of God.

The Thatcher surprised me. From the story of the announcement of Christ's birth, his attention was caught. He heard me read and he listened to my explanations without interruption. For fourteen days we read together in harmony and reverence. When it was over he said simply, 'That is the God I could love.'

I was tempted to say that He was the same God indivisible from the Father, but I restrained myself. Let him love the man in God at least. Fear and worship of Jehovah would come.

'Will you kneel at the stool of repentance and be baptized with the water of life?' I asked him solemnly, but the Thatcher was busy with his own thoughts.

'His birth was strange; He saw much and He suffered much. Perhaps it is the same for all men, the journey of the Cross. His life was not so different from my own. It differs only in the way He lived it. He saw as I see, but more clearly than I, for He saw the one thing that I cannot see.'

'What is that you are saying?' I demanded, for his ravings shocked me.

He came over to me, knelt on the floor at my feet and gripped my hands. There was a great shining eagerness in his eyes.

'I would like to tell you how it is with me if you will listen.'

I nodded but with uneasiness. My misgivings increased as I heard about his visions of the future, his dread of them and his fear that they were inspired by the Father of Lies, which of course they were, as I was quick to point out.

'Are you setting yourself up as a Messiah?' I asked, drawing my hands from his in horror. 'Do you dare to compare your sinful birth with His Holy birth, your distorted glimmerings into the future with His supreme knowledge of time?

If so, you have the pride of Lucifer and the conceit of Beelze-bub.'

He stood up. 'Is there no hope for me?'

'Throw away the stone. Close your mind to the visions. Tear this evil from your soul.'

'Words!' he cried, 'all words!'

' "If thine eye offend thee, pluck it out," ' I urged him.

'Ah—if only it were so easy. I do not need eyes to see what I see, or a body to go where I go.'

He turned to leave me, but I called him back. 'God is merci-ful. Only repent and baptism shall bring you back your soul.'

'Will repentance remove my sight? Will repentance give beauty to your daughter's face?'

'Without it, you will die.'

He had moved to the door. Now he turned and looked at me steadily.

'There is a woman in the township here whose cow was suffering from the Evil Eye. She sent for the Wise Woman in the next parish who brought with her several kinds of wood and several kinds of water. She passed the woods through the mixed waters and poured it over the cow. What do you say to that, Minister?'

'I would say that the Wise Woman was practising pagan rites and that you should have brought this matter to my attention at once. It is my duty to stamp out witchcraft and superstition,' I said, impatient of the change of subject.

'Yet the cow lived.'

'The cow would have lived anyhow.'

'And so shall I, Minister,' he said sadly, 'and so shall I.'

I took a step towards him and summoning up the full force of my spiritual strength pointed to him with a long finger.

'Repent and ask for baptism or you shall rot in hell.'

'And what is hell, Minister?'

'Hell is a fiery pit; hell is ceaseless torment; hell is without God.'

'Then it will be the flames for me, Minister, for I have no wish to encounter your God in this world or the next, and the

God I could have served can have no wish to encounter me.'

He left me then and I sank to my knees, knowing that I had failed God, myself and the Thatcher. And yet, I thought, could any human being have succeeded? The devil was an opponent worthy of a Christ. He was no match for a mere minister.

The following day he was due to go to Dunvegan. On his return I would ask him to leave. I did not see him alone again.

Next day Kate was chattering with excitement as he saddled her pony and helped her to mount. His pale face was tinged with yellow and his eyes heavy and shadowed. I was filled with grief for my failure and his stubbornness. While Kate was full of final instructions to the woman who was to take her place in the kitchen, I made myself speak to him.

'Remember, my son, it is never too late for salvation.'

He looked at me and I knew he had not slept that night.

'The day will come when no man will care one way or the other,' he said, but I knew that he was speaking from bitterness and not from knowledge.

The Minister's Daughter

The journey to Dunvegan Castle was less than five miles, but that afternoon it seemed nearer fifty. The old pony moved slower and slower and the Thatcher dragged behind so that I was given the impression that no one wanted to reach Dunvegan at all except myself. Perhaps I was too anxious. I whiled away the time remembering Randolphe the last time I had seen him.

It must have been nearly two years since that day they all rode over to my father's home. Randolphe and his younger half-brother, William of Talisker, were staying at the time with their cousins Rorie and Ian of Dunvegan. Rorie, as heir to the chiefdom, had spent his childhood at Talisker under the tutorage of his uncle, as was the custom, and the four were firm friends, though Randolphe was the older by some ten years.

When the old chief died, Rorie at fourteen inherited Dunvegan and a brash conceited lad he was, though there were some who called him witty. At nineteen he was not much improved and my heart sank low when I saw the four of them ride up to the door with a message for my father.

'Hey, Cousin Kate,' Rorie had cried, 'will you not offer so much as a cup of water to four thirsty travellers?'

Without invitation they crowded into my home, pushing the walls back with their expansive masculinity. I brought them some ale and wished to God my father had been at home.

'Come, Cousin Kate, will you not entertain us with a song or a tune perhaps on the clarsach. You do play the clarsach, do you not?'

Fine they knew I had none of the accomplishments of their sisters.

'At least let us see your pretty face, dear Cousin,' said Rorie teasingly, and tilted up my downcast head with his thumb under my chin. 'Why, how you do blush, Cousin,' he added, staring curiously at my affliction.

And so they continued for fully twenty minutes before they grew tired of the sport. Only Randolphe had been silent. Only Randolphe had turned at the door to thank me for the hospitality. I sometimes dreamed of the tall red handsome strength of him and the kindly look in his green eyes. I had not thought it significant until now.

Dunvegan Castle is as old as time itself and the Macleods descended from the great chiefs of Northland. Every time I see the castle, stark and splendid, with the flat-topped mountains of Healaval Bhcag and Healaval Mhor rising beyond the loch, I am filled with great wonder and pride. I remember the great battles of Ian the Fierce and Black William. I remember the tale of how Alastair of the Hump entertained a lowland laird on the top of Healaval Mhor with food and wine served by a hundred Macleods bearing flaming torches so that from that day forward the mountains became known as Macleod's Tables. I remember the wife and two daughters of a slaughtered

Macleod who were turned into rock stacks and known thereafter as Macleod's Maidens. I remember all these things and
my heart swells with pride in my heritage.

I tried to communicate something of my thoughts to the man
who walked beside me, but he showed no interest. I was a little
disheartened by the heaviness in him, for it contrasted so
strangely with the light he had brought to me.

Rorie's mother, the Lady of Macleod, was in the great hall
when I arrived. She kissed me warmly and soon had me sort-
ing linen and counting plates. Later she took me to the treasure
room and allowed me to polish some of the great vessels which
were to be used at the feast. She herself took care of
Katherine's Cup, a strangely beautiful vessel standing on
four legs, but I was allowed to buff the Drinking Horn
which was reserved for the Chief's sole use. Most of all
I would have liked to have seen the Fairy Flag, but that would
never happen, for if it were taken out of its kist, the fairies
would undoubtedly punish the whole clan. I would have to
content myself with looking at the great iron chest that held
it secure and wonder about what lay within.

There is a wonderful story told concerning the Fairy Flag.
Long ago in the mists of time, an heir was born to the Chief of
Macleod. While the child lay sleeping, his nurse went down to
join in the festivities. When the Chief told her to bring in the
infant so that the clansmen might do him honour, she found the
babe wrapped in the Fairy Flag and when she brought him
into the great hall, voices were heard proclaiming that the
banner was a fairy gift which would save the clan in three
great dangers. It was shown at the Battle of the Spoiled Dyke
where the Macleods were triumphant and it will save them
again if it is not disturbed meanwhile.

'Did you bring that dark-eyed servant of your father's?'
Lady Macleod asked, interrupting my dreams, and when I
told her that he had come, she gave orders that he was to be
well housed and taught to serve wine at the feast.

'Who is he, my dear?' she asked me seriously, and it was
surprising how little I could tell her.

'Is Randolphe to be here?' I asked presently.

'Randolphe!' she cried with a laugh. 'Can you imagine a Feast at Dunvegan without Randolphe? He will be here soon enough.'

The days passed quickly. My little cousins welcomed me warmly. Mary, Marian, Julia, Sibella and Margaret, five sweet flowers to look at but as lively and full of mischief as wild kittens. My cousin Rorie teased me as usual, but this time I answered in kind.

'Cousin Kate's tongue has grown thorns,' he said, not without admiration, or so it seemed.

I saw little enough of him or of the rest of the company, for they went hunting all day and I was busy helping my lady with the preparations.

'And now, Kate,' she said when the work was done, 'we must make you beautiful for the feast.'

Somehow she did not make it seem an impossible task and even I was hopeful as she opened her clothes kist and chose a blue gown for me. I had never seen its like. The full satin skirt was like the sky in spring and the bodice frothed with cobwebby lace that gave my skin a delicate appearance. She gave me gloves of softest kid to cover my working hands and she ordered her own maid to dress my hair.

'No one over the age of twenty should wear it loose,' she said, studying my straight hanging locks. 'You shall have curls to fall across your cheeks, so.'

I looked at my reflection and for the first time in my life I saw more besides my affliction. I saw myself as a bride.

'Why are you doing all this for me?' I asked impulsively.

She hesitated. I wanted her to say that it was for Randolphe's sake, that it was time he was married and that he had shown an interest in me. For a terrible moment I thought she was going to say, 'Because I am sorry for you,' but all she said was, 'It gives me pleasure to see you happy.'

The feast was a splendid affair. The castle was filled with guests and the sombre walls echoed with laughter and hurrying footsteps. When I found myself seated next to Randolphe

I almost felt that the great celebrations were in my honour. I was no longer the minister's unwed daughter, poor and marred. I was a princess enchanted by Randolphe's closeness and the Thatcher's words.

Randolphe was a splendid figure in tartan kilt and hose. If his face had grown a little broader and his doublet tighter in the past year, he was all the better for it. In my opinion he was the finest laird in the great hall. He was courteous to me; Randolphe had always been polite, but he seemed morose. I tried hard to be amusing and companionable. God help me, I even played the cocotte, but he remained cool and distant. He drank a great deal of wine and, under the strain of my unaccustomed role, I drank more than my father would have approved.

My behaviour was beginning to draw glances and laughter from my five young cousins. I heard Mary whisper to her companion:

'Poor Cousin Kate is out to catch a husband.'

'She won't land that particular fish,' said Marian, leaning across the table and not troubling to lower her voice. 'Randolphe is mad for Janet of Sleat.'

I did not believe her.

The Thatcher was serving the wine, a rich red smooth syrup that was all too easy to drink. There were endless toasts, to the young laird, to the clan, to the family, to the piper, to past glories and future successes. The Bard's epic called for another toast, and old Mairie, who had been nurse to the Chief and his father before him, had composed a beautiful wild poem in his honour. The Macrimmon piped a new composition which was cheered wildly. The young unwed girls were becoming coy and the young lairds were taking unusual liberties. Only Randolphe was dull and my shoulders the only ones uncherished by an affectionate arm. Surely now was the time for him to pay court to me. I did not believe he was too drunk to notice me. What had gone wrong?

I drank a glass of wine at a gulp and took matters into my own hands. I was in my cups or I would not have behaved so immodestly, or so I tell myself now. I put my hand on his leg beneath the fold of his kilt and murmured some words of endearment which make me blush to recall. He drew away from me as if my hand had been fire or ice and gave me such a look of loathing that I lost my head.

'The day will come, Randolphe Macleod, when you will be glad to wed with me!' I cried, rising to my feet. 'We will have sons and daughters with red hair and green eyes who will not be ashamed to call me their mother.'

That was what I intended to say but some of the words were mixed up and I don't believe I made much sense, but they all heard me, the Macleods of Dunvegan, and they all laughed.

'Well, you are the close one, Randolphe!' cried his brother, 'and here was I thinking you were hot for Janet Macdonald!'

'I'll be bridesmaid to you, Kate!' cried Marian, with laughter sparkling in her eyes.

'And I'll sponsor the first bairn!' cried Ian.

'If you run short of peats, Cousin, you can always warm yourself at your wife's face,' said Rorie, the witty one.

Randolphe flung back his chair, his face black as night.

'Calm yourself, man,' said his brother. 'Can you not see Kate is in her cups?'

It was the Thatcher who had been my undoing. It was fitting that he should come to my rescue now. He was standing in the centre of the great hall and though his voice was not loud, it had such power in it that the room fell silent at his words.

'Laugh now, Macleod. Laugh long, for the next time the clan meets at Dunvegan the sound of weeping will be heard in the great hall and the laird's seat will be empty.'

I was forgotten. The blackness left Randolphe's face as he sat down in the seat he had just left. My Lady of Macleod gave a short cry of terror. Rorie's face was white. I saw that the stone was in the Thatcher's fist and that the affliction was on him. I wanted to cry, 'He is a liar, the Prince of Liars,' but he held me spellbound as he held the rest of the great company.

'Hear me, Macleods of Dunvegan!' he cried into the listening silence. 'You are a great people now, but it shall not always be so. The day will come when Norman, the third Norman of Dunvegan, the son of the hard-boned Englishwoman, will perish without trace; you shall know the time, for on that day the Maidens of Macleod will fall into the hands of a Campbell. At that time a fox will give birth to four cubs in the north turret of this fine castle. Beware of the day when the Fairy Flag will be shown for the last time; then the glory of the Macleods shall pass, others will possess the broad lands and a small boat be sufficient to carry all the proud lairds of that name.'[2]

When he had finished speaking there was a long silence in the great hall. Even the servants stood still. Rorie was the first to move. He stood and looked at the Thatcher, his wit and his pride forsaken.

'What have I done to you, Stranger, that you should curse my race?'

The Thatcher, so straight and slender and alone among those rich fine folk, had moved to the door. He turned at the Chief's words.

'Look for the coming of another James Breac, for he alone will have the power to redeem the heritage of Macleod.'

In the confusion that followed, I left the table. I went to Lady Macleod's room and took off my finery. A great calm was in me. I knew now that the Thatcher saw clearly and with truth. I was the one to misinterpret his seeing. The golden man and the bright children would yet be mine. What was to be would be, without help or hindrance from me. I found my way to the kitchens and inquired for the Thatcher. After a while he came to me.

'Take me home,' I said wearily.

We did not speak on that night journey back to my father's croft. I did not ask him to explain what he had seen or why he had seen it. His affliction was as cruel to him as mine was to me. I did not need him to tell me this. I knew it in my heart.

It was dawn when he unsaddled the pony and set her to graze in the field among the sheep. I followed him into the barn. In the white new light of morning our eyes met and recognized the reflection of despair. He took me into his arms, and we lay together in the sweet-smelling hay. A wonderful feeling of calm and inevitability comforted every part of my aching body. We fell asleep together in peace.

When I awoke he was making love to me. I put my arms round him and drew him into me. It was the first time I had been with a man and it was to be the last, though I did not know it then. All the pain and the excitement and the shame of the previous night were washed away in that act that was all tenderness. When it was over there were tears on my cheek, but I could not tell if they were mine or his.

He rose and left me to see to the beasts, or so I supposed. Later I found that he had gone. I never saw him again.

The son that was born to me nine months later has red-gold hair. I am already looking forward to seeing his children.

Part Two

THE MAINLAND

Chapter 1

KINTAIL

The Drover

There never was a man like Murdo Morrison, the Bull of Braebost, for fighting, whoring and versifying. He had the strength of an eagle flying on the moon, the sentiment of a courting dove and the conceit of a jackdaw.

He was also the best topsman I had worked for in forty years of droving. No one answered the Bull and remained a whole man. The paths from Kintail to the Muir were littered with the blood of thieving Mackenzies and Macdonnells.

No one, that is, except the Raven.

None of the four men on that September drove from Skye across the Kyle to Kintail and from thence to the tryst at Muir of Ord could understand why Murdo should choose such a one to lead a drove, though none was so foolish as to question the Bull.

'He is not the man to know the difference between a Skye bull and a Hebridean heifer,' grumbled one.

'The first mountain frost will crack more than his skin, I am telling you,' said another.

A drover has to be hardy. Though I have seen more than fifty summers, I can still row a string of cattle across the Kyle. A drover is born of a droving father and grandfather so that knowledge of beasts and mountains is bred in him. A drover is so close to his cattle that he grows to look like them. Murdo was a red bull, hairy from his calves to his wild mane, with fierce pale eyes that turned red in anger. I am a black stot, or I was till my hair turned grey, and although I have not the strength of the younger men, I can still spend a night on the open moor and wake with frost on my beard.

The Raven was a slight man with black hair like silk that lay on a sallow skin. I did not give him two days in the mountains. Man, he did not even have a dog!

There was some talk that he had made an enemy of the Macleods and that Skye had grown too warm for him. As to that, I have no knowledge, for I am no hearth-wife to be always poking into a man's past. Certainly if he had cause to escape the wrath of the Chief he could do no better than cross with the drove into that different world beyond the mountains. If—like so many—he were running from the man inside himself, the narrow teeming streets of Inverness would not hide him.

That first night on the shore of Loch Alsh we were to discover why Murdo had taken him on and if we were surprised we were not the fools to show it.

It had been a hard day, harder than usual, for rain as fine as smoke had swirled about us, chilling us to the core of the belly. As if it were not hard enough to drive our own share of reluctant beasts into the water and rope them jaw to tail in strings of eight, there were the Raven's beasts to see to, for his fingers soon became so numb that he could not easily slip the noose round the lower jaws of the cattle without catching the tongue. As it was, we lost three beasts through drowning and two had their tails torn from their backsides. I set the Raven on to heating pitch, partly to tame his own shivering flesh and partly to seal the wounded cattle.

Mind you, the Raven was not the one to complain. Three trips across the Kyle in a racing tide with a tow of beasts would be enough to finish a stronger man than the likes of him. Maybe the Bull had a better eye for a drover than it would appear.

We had a fire that night made from driftwood and peats sold to us by a crofter who did a good trade with the drovers all summer long. We were able to eat the oatmeal hot, which is not always possible on the high moors where there is no

fuel save the sodden heather. The beasts were grazing con-
tentedly enough considering the upheaval in their lives. A
beast is like a bairn, you understand; he has a yearning for his
old byre and will wander a day's march back unless he is
watched. The rain had stopped and the smoke from the fire
scattered the midges that swarmed in the still warm evening.

Now was the time for tales and songs to cheer the mind
while a horn of whisky comforted the body. I could tell many
a good story about droving in the past and not a night went
past without my repeating the best which grew wilder and
braver on every drove.

Others could sing and one was cousin to the Macdonald
story-teller and knew the Ossian tales by rote. But Murdo was
our bard, a fine enough poet by my standards and a finer one
by his own. He would stand to declaim his verses, sometimes
acting the part and raising his eyes soulfully to the stars;
sometimes tender, sometimes lewd, but never dull. We liked
best his warring verses which told of feuds and raids, but he
had a preference for love poetry and would spend an hour
describing a night's wooing.

> The dart of love as piercing flies
> As the seven grooved spear to fling;
> Brown maiden of the liquid eyes
> Warm as my plaid the love I bring.

All his women were beautiful, gentle and skilled in the art of
love. It was a secret disappointment to me to meet with one of
them and find that she had black teeth and a laugh like a kitti-
wake.

So we sat and ate our oatmeal and the dogs dozed with one
ear alert to the sound of a distressed beast and Murdo rose and
told us he proposed to give us the 'Ballad of Dark Mary', which
the Raven would write down. This then was the reason for his
presence on the drove and I have never heard of a stranger
one.

The poem began with a description of the girl from the top
of her dark head to the tip of her pretty little toe.

Thou art my pretty one, my turtle-dove, thou;
Though dark her hair, her body smells so sweet,
Dark maid, dusky dark, my lovely brown cow.

Thou art my Lady Moon, crown of my night,
Stars are in your eyes, crown of my life,
Fire is in your mouth, hearth of my heart.

'Are you writing it, man? Are you putting it all on the paper?' he would ask every minute or so, and all the time the Raven scratched away with quills made from a quiver of gull feathers.

After a while the Raven put away his pen and folded the paper he had been writing on. It was dusk and already three of the men had wrapped themselves in their plaids and were sleeping exhaustedly. I was to keep first watch so I had been careful to stay awake.

'You have stopped writing, scribe,' said Murdo with surprise.

'I have,' replied the Raven with a yawn.

'I did not tell you to stop,' said the Bull with his hand on his dirk.

'I did not ask you.'

The Bull's hand tightened on his dirk. 'No man answers me and lives.'

'Then kill me. Either way you shall get no more writing out of me this night.'

There was a difficult moment and then Murdo laughed softly.

'Well, Lewisman, what do you think of my versifying?' he asked confidently.

'It is no better and no worse than my droving,' said the Raven, turning his back and drawing his plaid over his head.

Murdo stood over him for a moment. I saw the heat of anger flush his brow. I thought he would plunge his broadsword into the stranger's heart, but instead he turned away and flung himself on to his horse and rode off into the night. As topsman, it was his duty to ride ahead to arrange for grazing or look out for raiders, but tonight he was bound on different business. There was a young widow in a nearby croft who had already given him one son and would not be averse to bearing him another.

When he had gone I said softly, 'It is wise to know the strength of your enemy before you make war.'

He turned his face to me. 'No Braebost Bull insults a Mackenzie Stag.'

I was silent. I had not known he was a Mackenzie and nor had Murdo, I could swear. Not the greatest skill with pen or beast would have induced him to take a Mackenzie on the drove.

There are two clans in the mountains that every drover learns to dread, the cattle-grasping Macdonnells and the bloody-fisted Mackenzies. There is not a tot to choose between them for greed or ruthlessness. Since their clan chiefs— Glengarry and Seaforth—were both locked up in the English fort at Inverness, their clansmen in the mountains were wilder and greedier than ever. And now we had a Mackenzie in our midst. I kept the information to myself, however. A long life has taught me that there are too many trouble-makers in the world.

On the first day or two out, the drove is a cheerful gathering. Pedlars and other travellers stop to pass the time of day and crofters come by to exchange news and gossip. One such old man, Duncan Macrae by name, who had been a fine topsman in his day would have been mortally insulted if I had passed by without a crack. I had driven beasts with him many times in years gone by and we were like brothers. Usually he was out on the road to welcome us, but on this occasion there was no sign of him so when we stopped for the midday grazing, I walked the half-mile up the glen to his croft. I took the Raven with me, for there was nothing Duncan liked better than a young drover to instruct; and there was much the old man could teach him if he had a mind to learn.

Duncan was a lively old man full of talk and information, but on this occasion I found him in his bed.

'So it is yourself,' said his old woman when she had opened the door to us. 'It's glad I am to see you.' She lifted her apron to her eyes. 'Poor Duncan,' she cried, 'I am thinking this is the last crack you'll be having together this side of heaven!'

She stepped aside to let us in and there was my old friend stretched out on his bed. He looked at me with a doleful eye.

'Man, I was just holding out till you came,' he said, putting out his hand to greet me.

'What ails you, friend?' I asked, distressed at the sad change in him.

He shook his head and turned his face to the wall. His woman began a long explanation interrupted at times by sighs of agreement and exclamations of despair from old Duncan. Seemingly he had had words, many words, with a certain woman in Kintail who had cursed him in anger.

'Go to your bed this night, Duncan Macrae,' she had shouted, and a great deal more besides, 'and you will never rise again.'

'Look at him,' the old woman said, shaking her head. 'He has been on his back this past week and every day he grows weaker.'

Duncan had always been a terrible man for charms and superstitions. It did not surprise me to see him brought so low by the ill-wishing of a Woman of Knowledge. In the respectful silence that followed the explanation, the Raven laughed softly.

I turned to look at him with surprise, but his face was shadowed in the dark side of the room.

'Is the end of a man an occasion for humour?' I asked, indignant for my old friend's sake.

'Get up, Duncan Macrae,' the Raven said, still in the same soft voice, 'or your limbs will rot before your heart stops beating.'

The old man raised himself on his elbow and spoke to me with anger livening his eye. 'Is this how the young men of today insult an old grandfather who is on his deathbed?'

'You are not dying, old man, nor near to it.'

134

Duncan was enraged. He threw back the bed-mat and put his wasted legs to the ground.

'Since you are the wise one, since the Book of Knowledge is open to your eyes alone, perhaps you will tell me how I am to die if not in my bed?' he cried, swaying on his feet.

The old woman went to his assistance, but he shook off her arm.

'I am waiting for an answer!' he cried.

I looked at the Raven. There was a stiffness in his body and a strangeness in his voice.

'You will die by the sword, old man.'

There was a cackle of laughter from the old woman and indeed I myself felt inclined to laugh. The spindle-shanked, crooked-backed old bag of bones could scarcely lift a sword, let alone fight. His wife's amusement maddened him. He bent down stiffly and groped under the bed until he found what he had been looking for, a rusty ancient sword.

'By Mourie, you will die by the sword before I do!' he cried, flailing it dangerously.

We left the cottage then in a big hurry, not waiting to say farewell.

'What made you torment the old one?' I asked him as we returned to the drove. 'What has he ever done to you?'

He stopped and looked back. Old Duncan was standing outside his door, shaking his fist and shouting abuse.

'Perhaps I have done something for him,' he said.

It was true enough. My old friend was a great deal better off in his anger than in his bed. I laughed. 'Well, well, maybe you have the right of it.'

Only six months later I heard that Duncan had been set upon by some deserting English soldiers in search of plunder. Not understanding their language or their demands, Duncan had resisted them and been murdered in Glenshiel. Perhaps he would have been better left to die in dignity in his bed.

It takes a strong constitution to stomach the truth and the Raven knew too much. Perhaps this was why none of the men liked him. Did I like him myself? Liking is not a word I am

accustomed to using. A man is useful and he is companionable or he is not. The Raven learned to be useful but he was
never companionable. This was not his fault. Knowledge such
as the Raven possessed sets a man apart from his fellows. I
was dimly aware of his knowledge in the house of Duncan
Macrae; I was to become better acquainted with it on the
third night out in the mountains, but I was never to understand it.

We were on the dawn watch together. It had been a hard
night, for the beasts were not yet far enough from home to
forget the Skye pastures and would keep straying back the
road we had come. But at last they were settled, some sleeping, some munching and some standing motionless except for
a flick of the tail. It had been a dry day, but already great
dark clouds were massing across the Long Mountain of Kintail and fingers of wind ruffled the shaggy hides of the beasts.

'It will rain before dawn,' I said, pulling my plaid closer.

'I am afraid of the mountains,' he said slowly, and I turned
to look at him with curiosity, for it was the first time he had
spoken to me in such a way. That was also the first time I
became aware of his stone. He was leaning forward, his elbows
resting on his knees, tossing a pebble from palm to palm.

'What is there to fear in the mountains except the wolves
and I have only seen two in the whole of my life and they were
but grey shadows.'

I would have added that the Mackenzies who lived in the
glens all about us were much more to be feared than the
mountains, but he was a Mackenzie and might be insulted.

'I am not afraid of wolves, human or bestial,' he said with
that edge of scorn in his voice that I had noticed before. 'But
the mountains, they are another matter. They are part of what
has been and what will be. The mountains see too much.'

I pondered over his words, trying to find sense in them, but
I could not, so I held my peace.

'There is a day coming, old man,' he began in a voice that
was strange and excited, 'when the jaw-bone of the big sheep
will put the plough into the rafters and no man will drive cattle

through Kintail. The sheep will become so numerous that the bleating of one shall be heard by another from Lochalsh to Kintail. You will not see it, but your children's children will see it when they are forced to flee before the march of the great white army, and the mountains will see it as I am seeing it now.'

'How is it that you know such things?' I asked, remembering what he had told the old Macrae, but he did not seem to hear me.

'After that, another day is coming when the sheep will be gone and so well forgotten that a man finding a jaw-bone in a cave will not recognize it or be able to tell what animal it belongs to. Can you believe such a thing?' he added, but not so much as a question to me but rather as a wonder to himself.

'Strange merchants will take away the land of the great clan chiefs and the mountains will become one wide deer forest. The whole country will be utterly desolate and the people forced to seek shelter in faraway islands not yet known.'

'Go on,' I whispered, my spine chilled but my mind enthralled. I did not know what sort of magic there was in this man, but I saw in him a power that few have ever possessed.

He pressed the stone against his forehead and there was a great sadness in his voice as if it hurt to see what he saw and to know what he knew.

'Then will come the time of the horrid Black Rains. They will kill the deer and wither the grasses. Weep for the mountains, old man, and for what they will see in that day; weep for the wilderness of the Gael. After that, long, long after, the people will return and take possession of the land of their ancestors.'[3]

He had begun to shiver. I have seen men in high fevers and men brought ashore half-drowned, but I have never seen a man in such a rigor as this. There was only one cure that I knew of. I took my dirk and opened the hide of the nearest beast so that the blood flowed freely into my drinking horn. I made him drink it to the last drop.

When the fit had passed, I questioned him.

'Who are you?' I whispered.

'A Raven that squawks too much.'

So I called him the Raven.

On the sixth day out we had visitors. We were walking in the shelter of the Little Peak of the Red Bird towards the head of Loch Monar. There was enough grass there for the mid-day grazing and Murdo was about to call a halt before we attempted to cross the treacherous Black Bog that lay ahead of us. Looking up, I saw six Mackenzies mounted and armed with broadswords and poinards. I knew them fine, these mad herdsmen. Their leader was Ruarie of the Red Dirk, one of the bloodiest of his clan. Before Murdo could set the dogs to work to surround the cattle, they charged, shouting and yelling and slashing at the leading beasts with the flat of their swords. The poor creatures took fright and scattered, some up the steep scree-strewn mountains, others towards the bog and some back the way they had come.

The moors and the mountains echoed with the noise as the beasts bellowed, the men shouted and the dogs yapped and snarled in their efforts to drive the creatures up the mountain-side where they would be soon slowed down by the steepness of the ground.

When the deed was done, and a dozen of the beasts had been taken and tethered to the bandits' horses, Ruarie shouted to Murdo.

'Who are you to graze on Mackenzie land?'

'I piss on Mackenzie land!' cried the Bull, enraged. Hitching his plaid, he was as good as his word as he aimed the arc of his water at Ruarie's horse.

'Here are my terms,' said Ruarie with a smile on his black face. 'Two shillings for every beast and you may ride safe from Loch Monar.'

'I spit on your terms.'

This time the spittle fell on Ruarie's leg. Both men watched it dribble to the ground.

'So,' said Ruarie softly. 'It is to be war then.'

Before Murdo could answer, I cried, 'Would you make war on a Mackenzie?'

All eyes turned to me and I knew that I had acted like an old man.

'You must need a tit to suck if you think I would own you as kinsman, old man,' Ruarie cried in scorn.

'Nevertheless, there is a Mackenzie here,' I persisted, and threw my eye on to the Raven. They all turned to look at the stranger and then back at me. I could read the thoughts in them and I read aright. I did not want war. There was altogether too much bloodshed on a drove. I had a longing to die in my bed. Nor did I want to see the Raven killed and if it came to war he and I, the oldest and the weakest, would be the first to bleed.

'Is this true?' Murdo shouted, his anger the greater because he had not known as much as me. He would not have employed a Mackenzie, however skilled with the pen.

'It is true,' said the Raven calmly. 'My mother's father was cousin to the Chief.'

Ruarie began to laugh. He was a great one for laughing when there was least cause to laugh. Still laughing he tossed a rope and the noose fell round the Raven's neck. He was quick enough to slide his fingers under the tightening bridle, but he was hauled off his feet.

'A cousin of Seaforth is a cousin of mine. You shall share Mackenzie hospitality this night, Cousin,' said Ruarie.

The Bull's eyes glowed red. He lunged forward with his sword, but Ruarie's clansmen rode him down, slashing at his sword and shouting abuse. Meanwhile Ruarie rode off with the Raven, who was stumbling and falling over the hoops of heather.

When they had punished Murdo enough they gathered the tethered beasts and rode off, but not before Murdo had brought one of them tumbling from his horse with an arm ripped from the shoulder to elbow.

I would have stopped to staunch the wound, for the blood was spurting forth, but Murdo shouted to me.

'The beasts are more important than any Mackenzie. See to them.'

He was in no mood to argue, so I left the wounded man to stop the blood as best he could.

It took five of us and the dogs till nightfall to round up the scattered beasts. Even then they were restless and hard to settle. Some moaned from wounds inflicted by the sharp prongs of their horns during the stampede.

As for me, I would have been content to let matters rest. We had lost twelve beasts to the raiders and three to the bog. It could have been worse, but Murdo was not the man to part with a single beast without revenge. That night there was no poetry and we ate our oatmeal cold.

When we had eaten, Murdo jerked his head at me. 'You,' he said shortly, 'come with me. The rest of you mind the beasts.'

His plan was simple. I was to go openly to the glen and offer to trade the wounded Mackenzie for the beasts. Meanwhile the Bull would see to his own revenge. It was a cunning plot, for Murdo knew they would not kill me. Old men are of no importance, therefore they are of no value. They would cheat me, torment me, but, if I kept my temper, they would not hurt me. As for the beasts, I do not believe the Bull expected to see them again. By this time they would be well on their way to a fair at Dingwall, or St Duthac's Town, well away from our trysting place. I was to be the decoy, the means whereby the Bull could avenge himself and recover the Raven. The latter had all his verses wrapped in a skin under his plaid.

A good moon shone as I led the wounded man roped to his horse and barely conscious from lack of blood. There was no sign of the Bull, but I did not expect to see him. He would make his own way to the glen. It was an easy matter to follow the trail taken that morning and in a little over an hour we reached the huddle of cottages where Ruarie and his kinsmen lived. A few milch cows were grazing between rigs of unripe corn. Of our own beasts there was not a sign. Certainly they could have been shut in one of the byres, but it was unlikely.

The herdsman, a lad still half a child, saw us coming and ran off to the nearest hut. The door opened as I approached and two women ran out, shrieking and scolding at the sight of the wounded man. Ruarie himself appeared, but came no further than the door.

'What ails the Bull of Braebost that he sends an old man to do his work?' he said, picking his teeth with the point of his dirk.

I jerked my thumb to the fainting man whom the women were untying from the horse. 'There is not a pin to choose between them.'

'Liar,' said Ruarie, as if it were a great joke. 'The Bull was unmarked when last I saw him.'

'I am telling you, the heather on the moor is dyed red with his blood,' I said falsely.

'What is that to me?' he said, lifting his shoulders.

'He asks that you return the twelve beasts you stole.'

'Stole?' Ruarie repeated. 'Do you hear that?' he added in a louder voice and I saw that I was surrounded by his kinsmen who had crept close to me in the dark.

'Did we steal any beasts today?' he asked them innocently. 'Look around you, old man. Do you see any beasts here—or there—or yonder?'

His hand swept the length of the glen. My eyes shifted to the byre.

'The byre? Show him the byre. Show him all the byres. This old man shall learn to respect a Mackenzie's word.'

'Would the Mackenzie you took from our drove tell the same tale, I wonder,' I said boldly.

'You shall ask him.'

And so I was taken into the byre and from thence into the room where the two women were tending the wounded man. In a corner with the noose still round his neck and his hands tied behind his back, the Raven crouched. His eyes were the blacker for the weariness in them. He saw me without interest. He took no part in the banter that followed and it seemed to me that he was the only human being in that reeking crowded room. The rest were animals, as wild and dwarfish and un-kempt as the cattle they raided.

When they had knocked the drink from my hand, pushed a bannock down my throat and amused themselves mightily at my expense, Ruarie came forward with a grin on his face. He placed the point of his dirk against my cheek and nicked it so that the blood flowed.

'Now, old one, tell me if this Mackenzie lies.'

I said nothing, so he nicked the other cheek. His kinsmen roared with pleasure.

'The mouth is the tongue's prison,' cried one of them, so Ruarie seized my face, forcing my mouth to open, and yanked at my tongue. Then the Raven spoke. His words were soft but terrible and such was the power of his presence that all turned quiet to listen to him.

'You are altogether too free with your knife, kinsman. There is altogether too much blood on your hands.'

He paused and then continued before any had time to answer him, and his voice gathered in strength until the sound of it was like the pressure of water under the Kyle.

'The day is coming, Ruarie of the Red Dirk, when the ravens will drink their fill for three days running of the blood of the Mackenzies and glad I am that I will not be here to see that day, for there will be war upon war and Mackenzie men will become so scarce that seven women will strive for the hand of a pox-pitted Mackenzie tailor.'

I swear every skin in that hot room prickled. Ruarie was the first to lift his knife, but the old woman flung herself in his path.

'Touch him not, my son, for he has the Knowledge of Hurting.'

At that moment a scream was heard outside, followed by another and another.

'The Bull!' cried Ruarie, and strode to the door followed by the rest.

The old woman slashed at the Raven's noose.

'Leave this place,' she mumbled through toothless gums,

'but remember that it was the mother of seven Mackenzies who gave you your life.'

The Raven looked mad and strange and his eyes were glassy like a sick beast. I seized his arm and dragged him from that place.

'Make haste, man,' I urged, as I pulled him outside. He stumbled and fell. Seeing his state I was afraid. All round me there was the screaming of women and the raucous shouts of outraged men. I looked down at the Raven. His lips were moving. I put my ear to his mouth and I thought he was crying for his stone.

I remembered the pebble he was always playing with and felt for his pouch. It was there together with his other belongings. I slashed the rope binding his wrists and put it into his hand. At the same time his senses returned and I was filled with fear. The old woman was right. This man had the Knowledge of Hurting just as he had the Knowledge of Seeing and the stone was a thing of power.

'Come, old man,' he said, seeing the fear in my face. 'It is over now.'

It was a long walk. We did not speak for weariness, but when we were nearly back with the herd, the Bull rode up. He was in high spirits, as fresh as if he had woken from a night in a feather bed.

'There was no sign of the beasts,' I told him.

He chuckled. 'I have been paid in full for them,' he said, and drew from his plaid a swatch of long brown hair, a dirk with a jewelled handle and a gold ring with the finger attached.

'I've left at least one Morrison cub in the Mackenzie litter,' he boasted, 'though he will not make mischief for a nine-month yet. Mackenzie women are the best whores in the Highlands,' he added with a sly look at the Raven.

But the Raven did not smile and next day when I woke with the dew on my face, he had flown.

Chapter 2

INVERNESS

Doctor Andrew Beaton MA

Sixteen-sixty-one was a disquieting year to a man of science and order such as myself. After ten years of comparative peace and uncharacteristic prosperity, the citizens of the Royal Burgh of Inverness took ill with the changes brought about by the Restoration.

In saying this, I do not intend disloyalty to my King, but there is no doubt that his return to the throne heralded a new era of trouble mainly brought about by wild and disaffected clansmen whom none could control. Although this is not an admission I would proclaim from the rooftops and few would openly admit, there is no doubt that in spite of the bells, bonfires and bishops that followed on the heels of the Restoration, the burghers of Inverness were sick at heart to see the Commonwealth troopers depart.

Sixteen-sixty-one not only saw the end of order in the streets and straths of the north, it was also the year when the order of my own mind was seriously challenged. In short, it was the year when I first encountered that strange and unpredictable Gael known to me as Kenneth Mackenzie.

I begin with the facts. My name is Andrew Beaton, a descendant of those wild and unconventional Beatons who were well known as physicians in the Highlands some decades past. My methods, fortunately for my patients, are more orthodox. I was educated at the Inverness Academy and at the University of Edinburgh and have been doctor to the good folk of Inverness for the past twenty years. My chief claim to the furtherance of my profession may be said to lie in a short pamphlet entitled *Further Herbal Experimentation* and a *Treatise on the Summer Flux*, both of which have commanded a wide interest. I can also claim some small success in the treatment of plague, that pestiferous 'yellow cloud' that threatened the town every time Montrose or Cromwell stationed themselves up wind.

I have a fine stone house on the banks of the River Ness, a bare half-mile from the Carseland where the English citadel stood. I am unmarried, my profession being both wife and mistress to me, but my household is well governed by a sister of my father, Miss Christine Beaton, who has devoted her life to the furtherance of my career.

My practice ranges over four counties and my acquaintance is widespread. One of my most valued friends was the late Dr Andrew Munro, physician to the English Garrison in Inverness, and it was he who secured my appointment as physician in his place when he was obliged to accompany the Master of Duffus to France. His unhappy death together with that of the young laird was yet another nail in the coffin of 1661. I well remember our last conversation on the eve of his departure to Tours. It concerned the death of the Protector which he had heard from the mouth of his kinswoman, Mistress Jean Munro, who had been in attendance on the Protector at the time. Seemingly, a madness had come upon that wretched man so that he bellowed and blustered like a crazed bull. His chaplains were afraid to go near him for the blasphemies that issued from his mouth. When at last he died, his body was opened and found to contain such corruption and filthy matter that even after the corpse had been embalmed and laid in a lead-lined coffin, the stench seeped through to such an extent that infection was feared and the coffin vaulted immediately.

I suggested to Dr Munro that his sins had corrupted his body, but the good doctor would not hear of it. To me it has always seemed that the line between sin and sickness is very narrow and that a man who has given himself up to the ways of the devil will bear the fruit of corruption.

'Alas for the Protector,' said my good friend, the doctor. 'I fear his name stinks worse than his remains.'

Alas for the doctor, his own end from poison was not so dissimilar from that of the master he served.

During my time as physician to the troopers I became well acquainted with the governor, Colonel Miles Man, and his officers, all men of solid worth and sound mind. Indeed the colonel and I stood together on that unhappy July day when the citadel was finally destroyed by order of His Majesty at the demand of the clan chiefs. My heart was almost as heavy as his as we watched the soldiers themselves demolish the sentry turrets on the rampart walls, crying the while, 'God save the King'.

A great crowd had gathered and I saw the faces of many of the chiefs among them. There was my Lord Seaforth, Laird of Kintail, lately incarcerated in these very walls, and his plain bride heavy with child. Some thought it indelicate of her to appear in public in such a condition, but my Lady Isabella was not one to miss an occasion. It was a sad day indeed for the Clan Mackenzie when the impoverished young laird chose her to be his countess, for she had neither beauty, nor parts, nor portion and Brahan Castle was in dire need of reconstruction after having been occupied for so long by the English soldiery. My aunt would have it that Isabella caught him the day he was released from prison in need of a woman. Some say that a child was conceived before the nuptials, but of that I know nothing.

There must have been upward of a thousand spectators when the soldiers scaled the great gate to ravage the Commonwealth Arms. A thistle of immense proportions had entwined itself in the stone carving, for the fort had been sadly neglected since Cromwell's death some three years previously. The crowd murmured in amazement seeing this as an omen that the Scots Thistle would eclipse the George Cross.

'And do you consider it to be an omen, good Doctor?' the colonel asked me, with a scornful smile on his unhappy face.

I sensed the Englishman's assured superiority over the Highlander and answered him shortly:

'Sir, I keep an open mind on such matters.'

'Surely you as a man of science are not one to subscribe to the supernatural?'

'I have a very strong belief in the supernatural. I have seen too many strange events in my career as a doctor to doubt it. You are a man of God, sir. God is supernatural.'

'And so is the devil, Doctor, and so is the devil.'

He wandered off and as I watched the crowds swarm inside the citadel, destroying, ravaging and plundering, I understood the trend of his thoughts. Destruction for the sake of destruction is always the work of the devil.

As I stood there deep in regret I was joined by the druggist, another Englishman, by the name of Bell.

'Foolish folk,' he said. 'There will be no more labouring at a shilling sterling a day; no more claret at a shilling a pint and no more cheap English viands when the troopers depart.'

'Will you be leaving yourself?' I asked him curiously, for I had heard that many of the English intended to make their homes in the Highlands.

'Indeed no! You will remember I married a Highland lass,' he replied, indicating the fresh-faced buxom woman on his arm.

The air had become acrid and I saw that the Scotch building within the ramparts had begun to blaze.

'What wastage!' said my companion ruefully. 'The wood was bought from Hugh Fraser of Stryes for upwards of seventy-thousand pounds little more than five years back.'

'The citadel was doomed,' said his wife wisely. 'It was built of consecrated stone.'

'My wife is convinced that the citadel is falling because the stones were taken from the big Kirk at Chanonry,' said the druggist with a smile.

'The proof is before your eyes,' said the woman sharply.

At that moment I heard my name called and saw Captain Langridge pushing towards me through the crowd.

'Thank God you are found!' he cried. 'There has been an accident.'

I was not surprised and had come fully prepared for an emergency.

'The fools have set fire to the infirmary. There is no place to take the injured,' he said angrily. 'If only the townsfolk had left the demolition in the hands of the troopers all would have been well. As it is, I fear many lives will be lost before the day is out.'

I had seen the building of the citadel from the day the first trench was dug scarcely eight years before and my heart was heavy as I followed the captain through the growing devastation. Such wastage appalled me. The loss of the citadel's infirmary was particularly vexing. The hospital in Inverness was in a ruinous condition and there had been some talk in the Council of building a new one to accommodate the sick and aged. The infirmary within the citadel would have served the purpose well for it was a well-appointed modern building.

There were about a dozen injured stretched out on blankets on a grassy sward. Mr Mills, the garrison surgeon, was already there, breathing heavily over a man whose legs had been crushed to pulp by falling masonry. His wife was keening over him in the Irish tongue: 'The stones will be avenged. The stones will be avenged.'

I dealt first with a woman and bairn, both of whom had been badly burned. From then on I was too busy to pay attention to what was happening in the fort. A steady stream of injured were brought to me. There were kinsfolk to console and bearers to find who would carry the injured to their homes. It was growing dark when I reached the last of the hurt. At first I thought him drunk, for he lay in a stupor apart in the shadows. I bent to examine him more closely but could find no injury; nor was there a smell of whisky on him. It seemed to me that he was a victim of the falling sickness, and yet I was not entirely satisfied with my diagnosis. His body was stiff and his eyes fixed on a point beyond and through me, but his mouth opened easily enough when I inserted a piece of wood between his teeth to protect his tongue and I noticed that his right hand was working on what later turned out to be a stone. I questioned the man who had indicated him to me, but he could tell me very little.

'He was too close to the flames for safety. When I shouted to him he did not seem to hear me. A burning beam fell close to him and still he did not move. I dragged him to safety and saw that he was in a fit, so I brought him here, Doctor.'

'You did well,' I told him, and he hurried off with an uneasy glance at the stranger, for the falling sickness is greatly feared among some of our less well-educated compatriots. As for myself, it has always interested me greatly being so closely connected with demonic possession.

When I looked back at the stranger I saw that the fit had passed.

'Do you have many of such attacks?' I asked him, and held out my hand to help him rise.

'What is that to you?' he asked, but not rudely. His tone was polite and distant, and he stood up without assistance.

'It may be that I can cure you of them,' I said.

He looked at me and in the glimmering light of the citadel fires I thought I caught a gleam of interest in his eye, but he said nothing.

'Where are your friends?' I asked him, but he shook his head.

I was not surprised. From the state of his plaid and the dirt of his bare legs and the unkempt appearance of his beard and hair, I judged him to be a wanderer. By his Irish, I placed him in one of the Western Isles. It was safe to assume that he, like so many of his compatriots, was alone and probably starving in a strange place.

'Have you eaten today?' I asked him, and when he shook his head I offered him a shilling.

His eyes flashed fire at me as he spurned the coin in my hand.

'Thank you,' he said, 'but I am capable of working for my living.'

Sometimes I can still surprise myself as I did on that day

when I said, 'If you will not accept my charity, perhaps you will accept my hospitality. My house is not far from here. You are welcome to accompany me.'

'Thank you,' he said with simplicity, and followed me at a short distance to my surgery door.

That was my first encounter with Mackenzie. When he had washed himself and eaten, I saw that he was no ordinary peasant. For one thing, he could speak English. He also carried an air of authority which made him immediately an object of interest to me, there being few such men in the world and none that I had ever met from his background. I wanted to know more about him and I was medically intrigued by the queerness of the fit I had witnessed, so I offered him work in my household. Because he was penniless, he seemed glad enough to accept.

Long after I left him in my surgery wrapped in his plaid on a makeshift mattress, I was still poring over my books in search of a remedy for the falling sickness. One I had not tried and which seemed to me to offer the best chance of a cure used the gall of a sucking dog. The choler had to be extracted and given to the sufferer mixed with tiletree flower water during the fit. I decided it might be worth the experimentation.

He was a strange man. From the first he showed little interest in the usual entertainment of the lower orders, dram-drinking, but he was intrigued by the rudiments of pharmacy and diagnosis. Had he been born in different circumstances and given a better education he could have become a good doctor. He was not a man of conversation and made a silent companion when we rode abroad to visit my patients, but as I myself have always been a man content to think my own thoughts, I liked him none the less for that. He soon became skilled at mixing a draught, boiling herbs and distilling essences. He would visit the miserable poor in the hospital and the wretched prisoners in the Tollbooth without complaint, taking with him my physics and advice. After a month or so I began to wonder how I had managed without him.

About his fits he would not speak at all. Indeed after some

weeks all I knew of the man was that he had been born in Lewis and had come east with a party of drovers. When I questioned him on his reasons for journeying so far from his native isle all he would say was:

'I have been told that there is room for every man somewhere on this earth. I am looking for that place.'

I wondered if he had something to hide. If it were connected in some way with the falling sickness, I had only to wait. The symptoms would reveal themselves soon enough. For my own sake, I was eager to be present when the next fit occurred. Epilepsy and the catatonic state have always interested me deeply.

It was, however, to be my aunt and not myself who witnessed his next attack. It happened in this way. It was in August, some six weeks after his arrival, that a great sturgeon fish was taken at the Yarr of Drumchardine. It was reputed to be at least twelve feet in length, and my aunt, in common with the other townsfolk, was in a fever to see the monster. As I was too busy to accompany her, I told Mackenzie to drive her and Miss Fraser, her particular friend, to the north of the Firth. My aunt had taken a liking to the man, and no wonder. Dressed in a new plaid with stockings and bonnet, he had a pleasing aspect. Also he could converse with her in English which she preferred to the Irish tongue, having got it into her head that English was the language of fashion.

Seemingly it was while they were examining the great fish that Mackenzie had another of his fits, though that was not the word my aunt used.

'He looked at the fish and he seemed to go into a dream, Nephew,' she told me. 'His eyes were fixed and staring and there was such horror in his expression that all who saw him were afraid. We gathered quite a crowd about us. Someone cried out that he was bewitched and another asked him what he could see. When he came out of it, he was weeping. I swear to you, Nephew, there were tears on his cheeks.'

'That is not unusual in a case of this sort,' I began, but she had not yet finished her tale.

'He told us then, that he had seen a young man sitting on the shore with two bullets through his breast. He told us to warn the young man, but how are we to do that? We did not see what he saw.'

'What he said he saw,' I murmured ironically.

My aunt was indignant. 'Mackenzie is no wild clansman from the islands and he is no liar.'

I chose to ignore this and returned to my questioning. I was not interested in the nonsense about the young man with bullet holes. This was clearly a dream experienced during the fit, and when I explained this later to my aunt she seemed satisfied. What interested me more were the circumstances surrounding the actual fit, but she could tell me little and Mackenzie was short with me when I questioned him. All he said was:

'Your time would be better employed in looking for the young man of my vision. He is of aristocratic bearing and wears his fair hair straight to his shoulders; there is a tooth missing from the upper jaw.'

'There must be fifty such men who would answer to that description,' I told him shortly. 'Why do you say such a thing?'

'Because he is going to die.'

'We are all going to die. Now do not tell me, Mackenzie, that you are another soothsayer! Inverness abounds in them. Can you not content yourself with being a physician's apprentice? I assure you it is more original.'

He said no more, but barely a month later, everyone knew who the young man with bullet holes in his chest was. Three whales had been stranded on Calder's land. Young Alexander Campbell, a patient of mine and younger brother to the Laird of Calder, went down to the shore to shoot the dying beasts in the maw. His gun misfired three times so he sat down, and setting his gun-butt to the toe of his boot and the barrel mouth to his breast proceeded to draw out the rammer. The gun went off, blasting two bullets through his chest.

On examining the young lad, I noticed that he wore his fair hair to the shoulder and that a tooth was missing in his front jaw. My aunt was quick to remember also and quicker still to tell her friends. Thus Mackenzie's reputation as a seer was established within a couple of months of his arrival in the burgh.

I was in a dilemma. The ordered scientific side of my brain told me that what had happened was coincidence; the Highlander in me was excited. The two halves of my nature warred together and it was about that time that I began to take notes for my *Discourse on the Nature of Second Sight* which I offer with this manuscript for it includes a list of Mackenzie's predictions made during his stay in Inverness and which time alone can disprove.

A DISCOURSE ON THE SECOND SIGHT IN THE HIGHLANDS OF SCOTLAND WITH PARTICULAR REFERENCE TO THE PREDICTIONS OF KENNETH MACKENZIE

By Doctor Andrew Beaton MA, *published 1675*

Second Sight is the ability to see things not apparent to other persons. Three Gaelic or Irish words have been used to describe the faculty. These are *Da Radharc, Da Shealladh,* and *Taibh Searachd*. Of these, *Da Shealladh* or the 'Two Sights' is in most common usage. It is perhaps the most descriptive for it draws the distinction between the world we may all see with our physical eyes and the world of the spirit which is visible to certain people who possess unusual powers and who are known as visionaries, prophets or seers.

There are to my knowledge three categories of Second Sight. In the first, a seer may have a vision of a man dripping water and clad in fish-scales. This will inform him that his friend is shortly to be drowned; or he may see the pallid figure of a man clad in his shroud, another death warning, but in this case the man may expect to die in his bed. Inverness abounds in such prophets all of whom predict disaster. Two butchers of my acquaintance, well known to the local dram-shops, were journeying abroad recently when they found themselves following a spectral army. They could hear the rattle of the accoutrements. This was interpreted as indicating a return of the English army to the north and boded ill for the Highlander. Wells have been known to run red with blood; weird lights and voices have been heard and seen in the aisles of Beauly Priory thus foretelling its destruction. Monstrously sized stones have moved of their own accord. The 'corpse candle' has been seen flickering with a blue light over the home of some unfortunate about to be stricken with mortal sickness.

These seers tend to be melancholics on whom the latest

vision makes such an impression that they can speak or think of little else.

Then there are the seers who interpret natural phenomena and endow them with supernatural meaning. The crowing of a cock at midnight heralded a death in the family. A stranded whale presaged the death of a powerful leader. An unusually good crop foretold the death of a crofter and was known as the 'fey-crop'. A shower on an open grave meant that the soul of the departed was in bliss; a hurricane indicated that Satan had come to claim his own.

In the case of Kenneth Mackenzie, the faculty of 'seeing' falls into a third category. It seems from close observation that some mental or physical abnormality probably seated in the brain can cause the body and the spirit to separate as at death. But whereas at death the soul returns to its Maker thus entering a different world, in the case of Mackenzie, where the body is not dead but merely in a catatonic state, the spirit cannot enter into its promised haven but is in some way free to wander haphazardly into the realms of the future. The soul is still trapped in this world and yet, being freed from the body, has the ability to wander through the realms of time.

Some Arguments Against the Second Sight

It has been said that all seers are touched in the head. This I strongly dispute. Visionaries in any of the three categories before mentioned would be able to control their madness in other ways. Seers are not judged to be mad by their acquaintances. I would state on oath as a doctor that Kenneth Mackenzie was not mad in the accepted sense of that word.

It has also been said that as the learned leaders of our society are not able to account scientifically for the prophecies of seers, they are not therefore to be believed. This too is a poor argument. If everything the wise cannot account for be deemed impossible, then we should not exist at all.

It is said that seers are impostors, and those who are taken in by them are credulous fools. Certainly it is possible that some may be impostors but on the whole they are found to be honest folk who make no profit from their predictions. Besides, the Highlander is no fool. He will not believe in a prediction until it has come true, or at least until the seer has earned himself a reputation for truth.

Some Conversations with a Seer

These conversations were held over an interval of six months during the period of Kenneth Mackenzie's stay in Inverness. For the sake of clarity, I have condensed and collated them into one complete conversation. At first Mackenzie was reluctant to speak of his faculty, but gradually when he had learned to trust my motives, he spoke very freely indeed.

BEATON: Mackenzie, there is much that is wise and intelligent in you, yet your predictions are what many would call superstitious fantasy.

MACKENZIE: Sir, what I see is not fantasy to me but as real as your presence in this room at this moment.

BEATON: If that is truly the case, the fact that there may be a sickness in your head cannot be discounted.

MACKENZIE: Perhaps, but it is a sickness that only death can cure for it is part of my nature.

BEATON: Would you say that your visions are connected with your fits?

MACKENZIE: I would not use those words.

BEATON: How then would you describe your experiences?

MACKENZIE: There is a separation of my mind from my body which leaves my spirit free to move forward in time.

BEATON: This separation you describe is against the rules of nature. I can accept a state of being beyond nature but not contrary to nature.

MACKENZIE: The rules of nature do not always apply to man. You yourself have broken them many times when you have forestalled death on a bed of sickness. The day will come when it will be as simple to see into the future as it is to recall the past. For me that day has already come. The past and the future are not separate states divided from each other by the present. Time is a circle. The end and the beginning are one, just as the womb and the grave are one. Eden will be the setting for Judgement Day.

BEATON: Is this a prediction?

MACKENZIE: It is a truth.

BEATON: Seeing that you object to the word 'fit', let us, for the sake of science, regard this state of 'separation' as at least an abnormality and try to discover its cause. When are the visions most likely to occur?

MACKENZIE: At any time, in any place.

BEATON: What is your physical state before the vision?

MACKENZIE: I believe you would call it choleric. Anger is the knife that cuts my spirit free.

BEATON: Can you describe your feelings more fully?

MACKENZIE: The burn of anger flames up in my head so that there is a great redness before my eyes. When the redness clears my spirit has entered the world beyond the boundary of the present.

BEATON: Is anger the only emotion to cause this strange occurrence?

MACKENZIE: Grief and fear have sometimes taken me out of myself, but anger always.

BEATON: Can you 'see' at will?

MACKENZIE: I do not know for I have never had the will to try.

BEATON: Of what significance is the stone you carry in your pouch?

MACKENZIE: I do not rightly know. Somehow it holds me to my own time. Without it, I could not return.

BEATON: Have you tried?

MACKENZIE: I have tried, and it is an experience I never wish to repeat.

BEATON: Whence came the stone?

MACKENZIE: My mother told me it was a gift from my father.

BEATON: Who was your father?

MACKENZIE: If I knew that I would know the answer to many things that trouble me.

BEATON: Do you believe that the stone contains some magical power?

MACKENZIE: I cannot tell. All I know is that without it, 1 am lost in a world that has no edges, no permanency, where I may slip and slide between the ages and never find firm footing.

BEATON: You speak of this other world. Can you describe it?

MACKENZIE: It is the same world and yet not the same. The sun is brighter, the air is clearer and nothing is hidden.

BEATON: It sounds a pleasant enough place.

MACKENZIE: I hate it. I fear it. My only wish is to escape from it.

BEATON: Why should you fear it?

MACKENZIE: I am afraid my body will die when my spirit is in that place and that my soul will be forced to wander in that world for ever.

BEATON: Do you not believe that your soul is in God's keeping?

MACKENZIE: That is what I fear most.

BEATON: Do you not trust God?

MACKENZIE: Not my God.

BEATON: Tell me this, Mackenzie, have you seen into my future?

MACKENZIE: I have.

BEATON: Then I command you to hold your peace for I have

no desire to know that which should lie only in the providence of God.

MACKENZIE: Now perhaps you can understand something of the curse I carry. It is my fate to look at a beautiful woman and see her shrouded, to see a strong man and know his end.

BEATON: All that you have told me I find interesting but hard to accept. For the sake of science, would you agree to attempt to see into the future without the goad of anger?

MACKENZIE: The idea is abhorrent to me. Why should I do such a thing?

BEATON: If all that you have told me is true then you are gifted in an unusual way. The future alone can prove the truth of your predictions.

MACKENZIE: You speak of a gift. I talk of a curse. It is better to leave the dark side of my life alone.

BEATON: In experimentation we might find a cure.

MACKENZIE: Death is the only cure.

BEATON: I ask only that you attempt under controlled circumstances to see into that other world. I will write down your predictions so that future generations may know whether your sight be true or false.

MACKENZIE: And I say to you that in doing this I may bring about my own destruction. I have never sought to use my sight for my own ends.

BEATON: Nor will you be doing so now. Do you not understand? You will be doing it for the sake of science. You may find it impossible.

MACKENZIE: I fear it will be only too easy.

January—March 1662

As Mackenzie had hinted, he was able to enter the state of trance at will. He sat at a table opposite me, fixed his eyes on a candle flame and his right hand on his stone. In a short time he became rigid and unaware of his surroundings. The results of these experiments are set down as follows:

January 7 1662

Prediction: 'The day is coming when fire and water will run in streams side by side through the streets of Inverness.'[4]

Remarks: This prediction, the result of the first controlled attempt to see into the future, lasted less than a minute. Mackenzie's account of what he had seen was garbled and incomprehensible. I was tempted to dismiss the so-called prophecy as a figment of a disordered brain.

January 10 1662

Prediction: 'The day is coming when long strings of chariots without horse or bridle shall charge from Inverness to the Muir of Ord and there will be soldiers in the chariots.'[5]

Remarks: This trance also lasted less than a minute. The glimpse Mackenzie claimed to have had was so short that he had difficulty in finding the right words to describe what he had seen. The account was once again garbled and difficult to follow. He himself was excited by what he had seen.

January 14 1662

Prediction: 'I see the Fairy Hill under lock and key with spirits of the dead secured within.'[6]

Remarks: An interesting prediction this, for I have long been an advocate for turning Tomnahurich Hill into a burial ground. Mackenzie could have heard me speak on this subject, in which case the prediction should be discounted. It has every chance of coming true in the near future.

January 19 1662

Prediction: 'Strange as it may seem to you, the time will come when full-rigged ships with sails unfurled will be seen sailing east and west by the back of Tomnahurich Hill.'[7]

Remarks: This trance lasted longer than the others at two minutes. It is not a startling prediction. During the time of flood, it would be possible for ships to sail round the mound of Tomnahurich. Mackenzie himself was interested in this prediction and able to describe what he had seen in detail. I have begun to observe that he is more reconciled to the experimentation. So far he has seen nothing to make him uneasy. He admits that what he sees under controlled circumstances is very different from the images provoked by anger.

January 23 1662

Prediction: 'The day is coming when two false teachers shall come from across the seas. At that time there will be nine bridges in Inverness. The streets will be full of ministers without grace and women without shame.'[8]

Remarks: This controlled prediction made on a Sunday afternoon was undoubtedly the result of a fiery sermon preached by the Reverend James Sutherland, Minister of the First Charge, that morning. It should, in my opinion, be discounted as worthless.

January 25 1662

Prediction: 'The day is coming when there will be a ribbon on every hill and a bridge on every stream. I see a mill on every river and a white house on every hill. Dram-shops will be open at the head of every plough-furrow and travelling merchants will be so plentiful that a person can scarcely walk a mile on the road without meeting one. There will be men of law at every street corner.'[9]

Remarks: This prediction lasted three minutes, the longest yet recorded and I was beginning to feel anxiety for the trance was very deep. Mackenzie described fully what he had seen and I am in no doubt as to his sincerity. Time alone can prove his witness.

January 30 1662

Prediction: 'The day is coming when the bridge that spans the River Ness will be swept away while crowded with people.

163

I see a man on a white horse and a woman great with child falling to the water.'[10]

Remarks: This vision caused Mackenzie some distress. It is the most interesting of his predictions for the bridge he described is the bridge that is in use at the time of writing. I have since had the bridge examined carefully by a master carpenter who pronounces it to be sound.

Further Comments, May 1662: After the destruction of the citadel, the townsfolk turned their attention to re-establishing the Great Horse Race. The course round Tomnahurich was cleared, and pillars and posts erected along the way. Smiths and saddlers were kept busy preparing the presentation cups and prize saddles, likewise dressmakers and bakers, for there was to be much feasting and merry-making after the races. The provost and magistrates crowded on to the bridge to greet the clansmen and lairds from abroad. The Silver Cup was hung on hooks from the newly painted port of the bridge with the prize saddles and swords similarly displayed. All was decked in blue ribbon and made a fine show. The Lairds of Murray, Seaforth, Lovat, Grant, Mackintosh, Fowlis, Balnagowan, Macdonnell, Lochiel and a good assembly of the English officers still remaining in Inverness were given a civic welcome by the dignitaries. The riders wore white with distinctive ribbons and a fine showing they made. My aunt and her companion were anxious to go on the bridge, but remembering Mackenzie's words, I dissuaded them and they took up a position close to the start of the race. Mackenzie was uneasy and I scarcely saw the race for keeping my eye upon the bridge. I confess I was almost disappointed when nothing happened and yet I was not surprised. Apart from the prediction, there was no other reason why the bridge should fall and it did not.

March 1663: The bridge was extensively repaired with eighty trees brought over from Norway. There seems little possibility of its immediate collapse.

April 1665: The bridge fell with two hundred men, women and children upon it! There were a number of accidents but no deaths. The cause was a beam inadvertently sawn through by a joiner doing repair work. Though I was in London at the time, it was reported to me that there were several horsemen on the bridge, one of whom was mounted on a grey stallion.

March 18 1662

Prediction: 'Oh, Drummossie Moor, my heart is aching for thee, for the day is coming when thy black wilderness will flow with the best of Highland blood. I pray to God that I may not be spared to witness that day for it will be a fearful time. Heads lie lopped off in the heather; limbs are severed and lost; mercy has altogether deserted mankind while brother savages brother. Red coats are stained black with blood; red blood chokes the flower of the clans. The roar of the great guns has woken the dead in hell while the living weep in the glens. Children rise up against children, old men cut out the hearts of their companions. Oh God, oh Culloden, I am dying with your dead; I am stricken with your injured. Let me die before that day, oh let me die.'[11]

Remarks: This terrible prediction occurred spontaneously on Culloden Moor after Mackenzie had accompanied me on a visit to Mr Forbes at Culloden House. Mr Forbes had said something that angered Mackenzie and he was in a black mood as we rode home in a mist of dark rain. On that bleak afternoon on the moor, Mackenzie looked into hell. He was leading his horse at the time and when the fit came over him, he threw himself down on the black moor. He made me see what he saw, so that the wraithes of mist that rolled down from the hills seemed to turn into the smoke of a thousand guns. I could even hear the shrieks of the tormented. Like Mackenzie, I too prayed that I might not live to witness that day. After such an experience, I did not suggest that we continue with the experiments and nor did he.

Second Sight and Witchcraft

The Second Sight is not normally ascribed to witchcraft. The latter is premeditated evil. Second Sight has a spontaneity that precludes any pact with the devil.

There are some who say that the Second Sight is within the devil's bounty. Our Lord Himself told us to beware of false prophets who are inwardly ravening wolves.

With regard to Kenneth Mackenzie, who knows? He himself believed his visions to be devil-inspired and there were many who were later found to be of a like mind. With regard to what eventually happened to that unfortunate creature, I believe his visions were the product of a deeply disordered mind, but whether that mind was possessed by the devil or disaffected physically, I have not been able to decide. Time alone may settle the matter.

Our experimentation with the future changed Mackenzie in a subtle way that I was not fully aware of until just before he left me. It gave him a pride that he had hitherto lacked. At the same time, I do not think that it improved the character of that strange man, and if that is the case, then I am to blame for it was I who persuaded him to submit to the experiments.

Even without the strange case of the Witches of Strathglass, I do not believe he would have remained in my employment much longer. Whether he acted as devil's agent in that affair or as a man of God, I hardly know. The reader must judge for himself.

Another curse of the Restoration was a return to the old habits of seeking out witches. The civil war had left a back load of petty crimes, but with the return of peace and Episcopacy, there was time to review these offences. I do not say that the Minister of the First Charge in Inverness was entirely responsible for the subsequent outburst of savagery against the older more feeble-minded members of the community, but certainly he and nine members appointed by the council to look into the matter did not refuse to examine parish registers for reports against those suspected of witchcraft.

Now I have always been opposed to this practice, not because I do not believe in witchcraft—I know that it exists just as evil exists—but of this I am sure; not one of the women tortured and burned for the crime was ever guilty. The old, the ugly and the innocent are caught. The truly guilty are too clever, too powerful and often too rich to burn at the stake. Most of the women assembled for examination were victims of fear or revenge and it was a sad day for Inverness when a certain Paterson, known as the 'Pricker', was invited north by the council committee. God knows how many further crimes against humanity would have been carried out without the practical foresight of Mackenzie. Afterwards there were plenty who said that the devil looked after his own and that the women from Ferintosh did not deserve their luck.

The Pricker was an unpleasant man. His skin was grey and smooth and shone with the grease of uneasiness. His hair lay lank to his shoulders and his eyes were like cold grey stones. He wore black silk and fine linen at his neck and a fine cloak that fell to his feet. His voice was thin and high, petulant or compelling as the occasion warranted. Round his neck he wore an ornate silver cross that swung on his breast and drew the eye. As for the tools of his trade, he carried those in a small black cushion attached to his belt, a neat pattern of brass pins differing in thickness and length.

But he was a creature of uncanny power and to members of Kirk and council, a man inspired by God for the work he had undertaken. As for me, I felt only distaste in his company and avoided it when I could. Unfortunately, I had to deal with him more often than most for he would not prick a witch until he was assured by me that the creature was free from infection. He had a morbid fear of the plague.

It was in July 1662, I remember, that I was summoned to Kirkhill to attend a pricking, so I set off on my horse with Mackenzie for the small kirk of Wardlaw. I was somewhat astonished to find that the accused were not feeble-minded hags but fine crofting women, decently clad and well-spoken, all surnamed Maclean. Their accuser was the Chisholm of Comer, a man famed for his meanness, who was Laird of Strathglass where the Macleans had been honest tenants for over two hundred years.

There was, however, no trust or affection between this master and his tenants for he accused the women, fourteen of them and a half-witted boy, of trying to murder him by shooting elf-arrows at images of himself and his brothers made out of butter and of attempting to poison him by witchcraft. The women were deeply insulted by the charge and no wonder. One glance at those quiet well-spoken Highland mothers assured me that had they wanted to poison the Chisholm they would have done so skilfully, without resort to witchcraft. It was clear to the meanest intelligence that the Chisholm wanted the Macleans off his land and that this was his way of getting rid of them. I did not believe that even the Pricker with all his clever methods could find any of these women guilty.

I could not say the same, however, for the women from Ferintosh. Four of them had been brought in by the minister of Urquhart Parish, accused of consorting with the devil. Three were aged hags, mischief-makers, soured by too many impoverished years. The fourth was different. She was beautiful and young. If I had had to choose one of the nineteen unhappy accused to burn at the stake, I would have pointed at her. There was a knowledge in her deep green eyes, an awareness that disconcerted me. As for Mackenzie, he never took his eyes off her. The attraction between them was like a visible cord. Perhaps I am harsh on her because this attraction disturbed me. Mackenzie was no womanizer and he would be soft clay in her moulding hands.

When I had pronounced all to be healthy, they were taken into the kirk for the ordeal. The Pricker, assisted by his two silent black-garbed servants, was offering up prayer. He was a great man for the prayer, that Pricker, which made him popular with the clergy. His smooth words removed any vestige of doubt or guilt that might trouble the minds of the ministers of the kirk. In words that rose and fell like the keening at a wake, he invoked a blessing on the task that lay ahead. His tone calmed the waiting women. Those who knew within themselves that they had nothing to fear from God, felt more easy.

Then at a gesture from the Pricker, the two servants proceeded to poll the women's heads. Their white caps and shawls were removed, not urgently, but with the ease of practice; the hair was cropped close to the skull and thrown in a great tangled heap at the Pricker's feet. He knelt before it and began to mix the grey, black, gold and brown tresses with his long white hands, calling on God to drive the devil from these women so that they might confess with an honest heart. Then he bade the servants bury the hair in the stone dyke that surrounded the kirkyard.

'The devil cannot protect you now,' he said to the women.

'We who are innocent need only God's protection!' cried one of the older women and the others murmured agreement.

'We shall see,' said Paterson, and pointing his long thin finger at her, bade his servants unclothe her and bring her to him. She was stripped of her plaid, her gown and her shift and laid naked on the cold flagstone floor. The Pricker knelt astride her body and proceeded to look for the devil's mark, that bewitched spot which could feel no pain.

I was confident that he would find no such mark on any of them and hoped that he would be content with one or two attempts to find the mark. I have examined witches whose bodies have been bloated and raw from such an examination. I did not usually watch the pricking, for it was a sight that sickened me, but I was interested in these women of Strathglass and intended to help them if I could.

Meanwhile Paterson began to feel the woman's body,

169

starting with her neck and shoulders and then her breasts. He leaned forward so that the cross dangled and swung before the woman's eyes and all the time he whispered to her so softly that I only caught snatches:

'Look at the cross and confess, witch. Look at the cross and confess.'

The woman stared at the cross while the Pricker's hands kneaded and probed in an obscene caress. The woman was quiet, almost asleep, or so it seemed. There was a hush in the kirk as every breath was held.

Suddenly the Pricker plucked a pin from the cushion at his waist and plunged it into the woman's right breast up to the hilt.

I sprang up waiting for the scream of pain, but none came. For a moment the assembly held its breath. Out of the corner of my eye I saw the Chisholm smiling.

Paterson rose and told the woman to stand up.

'See,' he said, 'she does not know where it is. She feels nothing.'

The woman was bewildered. Her hand rose and touched her breast uncertainly. To my astonishment, she could not find the pin.

The Pricker turned to the watchers. 'She is a witch,' he pronounced with triumph. Then he turned and withdrew the pin. A thin line of blood ran down the woman's breast.

So it was with all the fourteen women from Strathglass. The idiot boy could not stop vomiting, so I pronounced him unfit for the ordeal. It was now time for the women of Ferintosh.

First to go was the young woman. Mackenzie moved closer so that he was now standing behind the Pricker. The woman's eyes held on to him as a drowning man to a rope. The Pricker had taken off his cloak and loosened the ruffle at his neck. His grey face was wet from his efforts and his eyes suffused with blood. The woman looked as beautiful shorn as she had done with her gold hair lying on her shoulders. The green of her eyes stained her lids so that she looked like a bruised flower. Her body drew the eyes of all men, and I knew that she gloried in it, but her eyes clung to Mackenzie.

She continued to look at Mackenzie while the Pricker felt her body. She paid no heed to his words or to his cross, but cried out in a voice that was full of disgust, 'This man hath a woman's touch.'

The Pricker jabbed her then with the sneer still on her lips and she screamed so that the hair lifted on the back of my neck. He jabbed her again, this time between the white bones of her clenched hand, and her screams turned to sobs.

'You have proved your point, Paterson!' I cried. 'This lassie is no witch.'

He looked at me, his face filmed with sweat. 'You are mistaken, Sir. She is the thrawnest of the lot.'

He was about to jab a third pin into her nipple when Mackenzie caught his arm and forced it back.

'Did you not hear the Doctor?' he said.

'Unhand me,' the Pricker screamed, and Mackenzie did so, casting the creature from him in a gesture of disgust.

'Dr Beaton,' he cried to me, 'will you not take a look at this man of God?'

Before the servants could stop him he had ripped the creature's silken front apart with his two hands and we all saw a woman's breasts.

In the shouting and confusion that followed, I strode forward and with a swift movement ascertained that the Pricker was undoubtedly a woman. The creature should have been apprehended for fraud but in the general confusion that followed, he—or she—escaped and was heard of no more in these parts. She must have been a rich woman, for I heard later what the Chisholm had paid her for her services.

I offered to treat the Ferintosh woman but she would have none of me.

'I have no need of your assistance, Physician,' she said, and the awareness in her eyes and voice convinced me that if any had escaped justice that day, it was she. I truly believe in the powers of darkness. If she had been protected that day, then

171

the devil's agent was indeed Mackenzie. I last saw her deep in conversation with him, and the expression on his face told me all that I had guessed in the matter.

As for the rest, the Pricker had done for them. They were arrested and taken to the Tollbooth in Inverness where they were cruelly tortured at the instigation of the Chisholm until Sir Allan Maclean of Duart, their clan chieftain, informed by me of the matter, petitioned the Privy Council for their release.

From that day Mackenzie was a changed man. I believe now that the Ferintosh woman had bewitched him if not by sorcery, then by her beauty. He seemed listless and only half aware of me and of my requests. He told me he was not sleeping well. His dreams were haunted by strange disturbing visions. I did not need him to tell me what they were. The face of the woman of Ferintosh was always between us. He was not easy with me until he told me he could stay no longer.

'I am sorry to say good-bye to you, Mackenzie,' I told him with truth. 'Is there nothing I can do to persuade you to stay?'

He shook his head.

'Where will you go?' I asked, though I already knew what he would say.

'To the Black Isle,' he answered. 'There is work there that I know of.'

'In Ferintosh,' I added, and he did not deny it.

I could not have employed him much longer had I been able to persuade him to stay with me, for within six months I was summoned to London to help combat the dreaded plague, my skills in curing the disease having travelled ahead of me with the English troopers. The question I often ask myself is this. Would Mackenzie's fate have been different had I remained in Inverness? I will never know the answer now.

Chapter 3

THE BLACK ISLE

Elsbet of Ferintosh

I returned to my cottage in Ferintosh to wait, for I knew he
would come. He looked like a man in need of a woman, but to
me all men look as if they want a woman. That dreadful day
when the Pricker touched me with a woman's hands and de-
voured me with a woman's eyes, I saw only Coinneach and
I wanted him. As I lay there so close to the torture, I could
think only of him and of the feel of him inside me. When he
ripped the Pricker's shirt and exposed her for what she was,
I knew that Satan had sent Coinneach to save me. He was as
much Satan's son as ever I was his daughter.

When the ordeal was over, it was he who placed my shawl
about my nakedness and wiped the blood from my body. I
would have gone behind a dyke with him then if his master,
the doctor with the sharp eyes, had not summoned him. I had
time only to tell him that there would be work for him in
Ferintosh, and pleasure too for the taking. My man, drunken
Seumas, would be glad enough to be rid of the work of the
croft and I would see to the payment.

I knew he would come. Some nights I sent my spirit-slave,
Farquhar-a-Fearie, winging across the Firth to whisper my
name in his ear. Other nights I smeared my flesh with the flying
ointment and rode on the wind to look on him as he slept.
Once I sent my familiar, the bonnie brown hare, to scratch at
his door and I even threw silver to the woman fairy who lived
deep down in the Findon Gorge—she who knew every man in
Ferintosh—to ask her goodwill.

I took my desire to the meeting of the Great Coven at Culbokie Castle, that strange haunted ruin that men say is older than time itself. Three covens met there that night summoned by Satan himself. The rain was a black flood when the time came, so that none saw us leave the crofts and hovels, the kirk greens and castles, to meet at the appointed place, but it stopped when Satan came so that we knew he had sent it for our protection. Thirty-nine witches and devils there were that night, come from far and near in the Black Isle. Many of the devils had blackened their faces with soot and grease; one was young and fair and he wore a blue bonnet and it was whispered that he was a laird's son from the north. There were fine ladies too in the company whom I could have named, but tonight all were equal under Satan, all his children baptized into his name. He came to us in the likeness of a bull, a black cloak covering his body from his shoulders to his cloven hoof. By day, it was said, he went in the likeness of a man of God in the company of men of God, but by night he revealed himself in his true shape.

As he came, we danced wildly in greeting to the noise of a wailing pipe. Then he desired us to give him the kiss of welcome. Some kissed his ears, others the strange red ring he wore on his white hand. When my time came he desired me to kiss him on the mouth which was hot as glowing peat under the great bull head. This I took as a sign that Satan was favourable to my strong wish. He would be even better pleased when I brought him another soul.

Then followed the great feast which we had all brought ready prepared. Satan blessed our meat but he stayed apart brooding and aloof while we sat down to eat the bread and cheese and meat washed down with raw whisky.

When the feasting was over we started on the work of the night and there was much to do. Satan called down a curse on the evil Pricker and the like including Donald Glas who had betrayed me to the Minister. A storm was conjured to wreck a ship carrying a laird who had evicted a family whose grandmother was in our coven. We fell on our knees and beat the ruined walls with sodden rags repeating after Satan the Incantation again and again,

> 'I beat this rag upon this stone
> To raise the wind in Satan's name,
> It shall not fall till I please again.'

Then there were clay figures and elf-arrows to be blessed, for none was effective without Satan's touch. When it was my turn I took the phial of powder that I had ground from the horn of a stag and told Satan my desire. He beckoned to me to come to him and inquired about the man closely.

'I have heard of this man. Bring him to me. He belongs in this company.'

He took the phial, opened it and spat on it. Then he took me aside and put me on my face and thrust his great cold members into me, saying the while:

'You shall have his body, but I shall take his soul.'

So I knew Coinneach would come to me and that he would come soon. Next day I went to Seumas and found him crouched over the great boiling cauldron in the turf bothy where he made the whisky.

'If anyone comes asking for me I will be on the hill,' I told him.

He peered at me through eyes red and raw from the coarse smoke. His nose dripped and his hands trembled, but he said never a word. He did not like to be interrupted at the sacred rites of distilling. He had his God; so be it. I had mine.

The moor was full of humming bees and the smell of heather but I had little time to enjoy it. I had work to do and I wanted to finish it before Coinneach came to me. There was a great bundle of new wool waiting to be changed into the colour of the sun. There is no one in all Ferintosh who can make a yellow dye like mine and there was always a demand for my wool at the Michaelmas Fair. I needed ragwort for the rich warm yellow of summer, sun-dew for the pale gold of spring and bramble for the orange of autumn. There were other herbs I needed for other purposes, flag and cinquefoil, hemlock and aconite, but their powers are secret and known only to the members of the coven.

When I had finished my tasks and was preparing the evening meal, Coinneach came. The man of the house opened the door to him.

'I was told there would be work here,' he said, and the sound of his voice made my heart leap like a hare.

'And who told you that?' Seumas asked, his voice slurred with the drink he had taken.

'The woman of the house.'

Seumas was silent for a moment. I was holding my breath, for I knew that one word from me and the stranger would be sent about his business.

'You will be the one who exposed the Pricker?'

'The same,' said he.

'And you will be expecting a reward, no doubt?' Seumas laughed drunkenly. 'Man, you have come to the right house for that. Elsbet will see to it personally.'

I flushed with anger. All Ferintosh knew how it was between us but he had no right to scorn me in the eyes of a stranger. He would suffer for that remark.

'I have come seeking employment,' he said quietly, 'but if there is no work, I will trouble you no further. Good evening to you.'

He turned to go, but Seumas caught his arm. We needed help on the croft and labourers were hard to find in Ferintosh, for most men worked at Mr Forbes' distillery. Labourers who would take their wages from the woman of the house were in still shorter supply.

'Wait,' he said, his voice smooth as fish-oil, 'what is your hurry, man? Surely I have the right to ask a few questions before taking a stranger into my house. Will you tell me your name?'

'Mackenzie,' said the other shortly.

'Mackenzie is it?' said Seumas, all affability. 'Well now, why did you not say so? My mother was a Mackenzie, so we

176

are kinsmen, is it not? It just happens that I am looking for a man such as yourself to work the croft. I have other interests, you understand?'

Those 'other interests' he shared with every crofter in Ferintosh, for once the rent of barley was paid to Mr Forbes to furnish his distillery, there was enough left over for every man to brew his own whisky, and drink it too. The men of Ferintosh would be rich indeed if they sold their spirits instead of drinking them. It is a terrible thing to be married to a drinking man. He is no good in bed and he is no good out of it. It is little wonder to me that Satan had so many servants in these parts. He is at least a sober master.

That was the night I sprinkled a little of the love charm in Coinneach's broth. It was also the night I discovered his stone.

As soon as the man of the house had fallen into his usual nightly stupor, I went to the barn where Seumas told the stranger he might sleep. The hens created at my coming, and he turned from examining the hoof of the brown cow which had been overlooked by an old hag who dabbled in hatred, but would have nothing to do with the coven.

'She is bewitched,' I said.

'You are surely not believing such a thing?' he said, smiling faintly, and I knew that I was going to have difficulty in convincing him of the truth in these matters.

'What else is there?'

He lifted the hoof and showed me a swelling, red and full of evil matter.

'A thorn,' he said. 'I can deal with it easily enough.'

'In the morning,' I said softly, for I had begun to tremble at his closeness.

'Now,' he said, and with a secret thrill I knew that I had met my true master. I fetched water and rags as he bid me and an hour later the job was done and the cow on the mend.

'I came here to say thank you for saving my life, not to keep company with a cow,' I said, turning to him.

He turned to me then with his full attention. I swam in those deep black eyes and felt myself to be drowning. He caught me and we moved together, driven by a force both in and out of us. His black beard was soft as silk on my cheek and he smelled of earth and hay and heather.

'Lie with me, my lord,' I murmured again and again until his mouth silenced me.

I have lain with many men, devils, crofters and gentlemen, but none have loved me like this man. His tenderness was like primroses in the glen, his strength like a mighty oak tree and his loving like the words of a bard at a marriage feast.

So this was love. With this I had no need of husband or croft, coven or Satan. There would never be another man for me, and it was the same for him.

'My heart is full of love for you, my queen, my golden fawn, my heart's treasure,' he told me.

He drew me to him again and I was aware of pain in my breast where the pouch that he carried round his neck stuck into me.

'What is this?' I said, drawing it out of the way. He pulled it from me and began to kiss me again, but later when there was no desire left in us, but only tenderness and joy, I took it from his neck and drew out the small smooth stone.

'What is this?' I asked him again.

'The key to my life,' he said slowly, never taking his eyes off it as I held it in my hands.

'Then give it to me,' I whispered, 'and I will wear it next to my own flesh.'

He took it from me gently but firmly. 'You have my heart. Is that not enough?'

'It is enough,' I told him, putting my arms about his body, but it was not enough. The stone contained some secret power and I knew I would not be satisfied until he had given it to me.

We lived for many weeks on the food of love. If the man of the house knew what there was between us, he did not care. The water of life was mistress and wife to him and while he had that to comfort him, he had no other needs.

I was not much troubled by the neighbours at that time.

Since the day I had been taken with the other old women to the pricking, there had been no neighbourliness shown towards me in Ferintosh. Little that I cared! They would come back to me soon enough when they had a grudge to settle. I had my own grievance to settle against Donald Glas who had betrayed me, but that was well in hand. There was a little straw dolly well hidden in the chimney hole; it was already blackened and shrivelled. It was a matter of time and I could wait. I had already heard that Donald was coughing black filth. That fraud of a man! His death could not come too painfully for me. What if I had overlooked his dun bull. It was no more than he deserved, coming at me in the corn rig with his trews unbuttoned like his own bull in rut. I am particular whom I lie with and where I lie, and it is not with the likes of Donald Glas in a barley field at the harvest.

Ah, but I would have taken Coinneach in a cornfield. I would have taken him on a bed of stinging nettles if he had asked me; that is how it was with us in those enchanted weeks. When the work of the day was done, I would follow him out to the fields and we would go together up to the high ridge. When he had eaten my bannocks and drunk some ale, we would lie together behind a broom bush or under the skirts of a silver birch and spend the summer hours in loving.

'Are you happy, my Coinneach?' I asked him once as we lay in a bed of deep dry heather above the shining Firth, with the great mass of Ben Wyvis beyond.

'Is a man ever truly happy?' he asked, looking into my eyes with a tenderness tinged with sorrow.

'What would make you happy? Only tell me and I will do it.'

He smiled. 'I would crown you with riches, my beautiful white swan. I would make you my queen.'

'Tell me the secret of your stone. That is all I want to know,' I whispered, but he did not hear me. A bell had begun to toll in the kirk below. Coinneach rose to his feet.

'Donald Glas has passed to his rest,' he said, crossing himself.

'And none too soon for me,' I murmured.

When Coinneach did not answer I looked up at him. He was staring at the Firth below. His eyes were strange. His body stiff and unaware of mine; his fingers moved on the stone.

'Coinneach, Coinneach, where have you gone?' I cried, but he never heard me.

'The day is coming, however distant, when those sandbanks in the Firth below will become part of the land. Glad I am that I will not see that day, for, of a certainty, troublesome times will be at hand.'[12]

As he spoke, I thrilled at his words. My Coinneach was a true son of Satan, and the stone indeed a key to open the gates of time. When he came back to me, I said to him:

'You have the Gift. Why did you not tell me?'

He sat down tired in his body and his spirit.

'Gift, do you call it?' he said bitterly.

'You spoke of riches and crowns, but you have more.'

'You do not know what you are saying.'

'What nonsense is this?' I cried, impatient with him for the first time in our acquaintance. 'You have a gift that will bring you fame and power and wealth. Only use it right and what honours may not come your way, and mine too, dear heart.'

He withstood my reaching arms. 'I have no joy in this gift, as you call it. To me it has only been a curse.'

Again I was impatient.

'A curse do you say? You have the power to see what many men would give their earthly eyes to see and you are afraid to use it.'

'Yes, I am afraid. I see things only God should see.'

'God,' I whispered, 'or my Master.'

He looked at me strangely, but not with abhorrence, so I took courage and continued:

'Why should you think this gift of yours comes from God? Is he usually so liberal? God's gifts are poverty, cruelty and pain. Satan is a more generous master.'

He looked at me with sudden recognition.

'Yes,' I whispered, 'I am a witch. Am I the worse for it? Would I be here with you now if I were God's woman?'

'You are beautiful and altogether desirable, that is all I know,' he said, coming to me.

'And I am Satan's woman, blood sworn.'

'You are my woman,' he said, his body heavy on mine.

'It is the same thing,' I whispered, and he did not deny it.

He changed after that. He began to talk with pride of his two sights. Instead of trying to hold back the visions, he began, with my encouragement, to seek entry to that other world. With me at his side, and to be there when he returned, he stepped out of the present world with an ease that roused my envy. Often I would ask him for the stone, for I believed that it alone held the secret of entry into the future, but he would not share it. Once I tried to take it from him when he lay sleeping at my side, but he pulled away from me and covered the pouch with his body.

If I could not enter the future with him, I could at least share his revelations, and what a world it was! What changes await the human race. Great events and little details, he saw them all so vividly that he made me see them too, and not only me. His reputation quickly grew so that men would travel long distances to consult with him and to marvel at his revelations. Nor did they come empty-handed; I saw to that.

Not all were pleased, however. The Reverend Andrew Fraser, Minister of the Ferintosh Church and one of my principal accusers at the time of the pricking, was full of wrath. He walked all the way up to the croft to warn us.

'I will not have such devilish practices in my parish,' he stormed at me. 'Elsbet Urquhart, you have already been summoned for raising the devil by the turning of the sieve and the shear and for other outlandish deeds. There are some who would lay the death of Donald Glas at your door. Is there no repentance in your heart? Is there no grace whatsoever?' He turned to Coinneach. 'As for you, Mackenzie, whom they call "seer", you shall not consort with Satan in my parish. I desire that you both come to the stool of repentance on the next Sabbath but one, and confess your guilt before God and the whole congregation.'

Coinneach was angry, so I put my hand on his arm. I did not want him indicted for witchcraft any more than I desired to undergo the ordeal again myself, so I turned politely enough to the minister.

'And what will you do to us if we refuse?'

'God will. not be mocked, woman! Do you think you can escape his wrath for ever? You have been warned.'

He was about to go when I saw Coinneach clutching his stone and I knew that the vision was on him.

'And I am warning you, Minister,' he cried. 'Beware of the magpie who nests in the gable of your kirk. When she has done so for the third year in succession, the roof of your kirk will fall on a great congregation of worshippers.[13] Where will your God be then?'

'Blasphemer!' cried the minister. 'You have not heard the last of this.'

When he had gone, I turned to my lover.

'There is only one who can help us now,' I said.

I found Satan alone in the appointed place by the ruins and I was afraid. Always in the past the coven had been there and though Satan had spoken to me and lain with me, it had always been within sight of the full coven. He stood in the centre of the ruins of Culbokie Castle, a tall black figure cloaked and cowled against a racing moon. I fell on my face, trembling.

'What do you want of me, woman?' he asked in that smooth cold voice that made me tremble. 'Be very sure that your cause is worth while. It is not wise to summon Satan lightly.'

'He is in danger,' I whispered.

With Satan there is no need for explanation. He knew whom I meant.

'I gave him to you! I can also take him away.'

'I will do anything—anything,' I cried.

I dared to look up at the great height of him and for the first time saw his face caught in a beam of moonlight. His pale skin chilled me and his half-closed hooded eyes never moved from mine. Near by, a horse snuffled and shook its bridle.

'I want the stone,' he said at last.

'That will not be easy,' I faltered.

'The stone—or your body in the flames,' he said pointing to me with his long bejewelled finger that flashed a warning fire.

Satan is not one to waste words. I knew that he meant it. Unless I gave him Coinneach's stone, he would lift his protection from me and I would burn at the stake.

'And my reward?' I dared to ask.

'His body.'

With that I had to be content.

I stayed on the ground until I heard him ride away.

It was dawn when I returned to the croft. I went straight to the barn where Coinneach lay in sleep. As I watched, he stirred uneasily and his hand closed over the pouch which contained the stone. It was as if he saw my intention in his dreams. I lay down beside him and fell at last into a dream-haunted sleep.

When I awoke the sun was already warm and he had gone to his work in the fields. I went into the house and saw that Seumas was still asleep. A shaft of light from the door fell on his blotched and ravaged face. I had a longing to be finished with him. When Satan had the stone and Coinneach was mine for ever, there would be no room for Seumas in my life. His drunken existence was meaningless not only to me but also to himself.

When the cow had been milked and the morning work accomplished I went up to the moor. October had flamed the trees and fired the bracken. Clusters of ripe brambles tangled with scarlet hawthorn berries. A great red deer sped past me so close that the wind from his movement lifted my hair. I did not look for Coinneach. There was a ruined stone circle near by where the deadly nightshade grew. I wanted to gather it alone.

The berries were black and beautiful and I filled the little leaf basket I had fashioned from docken with them and tied it safely in a rag which I hid deep in the pocket of my skirt. So absorbed was I in the task that I did not hear the horses until they were almost on top of me. As I stood upright, the first rider reined back with an oath and the others drew up behind him.

'By Holy St Mary, will you make us all murderers, woman?' he cried.

Six men in their prime, dressed and armed for the hunt, looked down on me from their great steaming horses. I knew them all. Who in the Black Isle did not? They were our masters. There was Rory Mackenzie of Redcastle, the oldest and the boldest; Colin Mackenzie of Kilcoy, a sly womanizer; Roderick Mackenzie of Fairburn, the richest laird in Ross; Urquhart of Cromarty, thin-shanked, mean-fisted; Sir George Mackenzie of Avoch, a lawman, by-named the 'Bluidy Mackenzie', and the Caberfeidh himself, Kenneth Mackenzie of Kintail, Earl of Seaforth.

'Have you seen the stag, Mistress?' the Caberfeidh called out to me. 'He was heading this way.'

The deer hounds, great grey wolfish shadows, jostled me, snuffling and nosing at my skirts.

'Call off your dogs, Sir!' I cried.

'They have the nose for a bonnie hind,' said my Lord of Kilcoy slyly and the others laughed.

Rory of Redcastle moved his horse so that he stood behind me and the others closed into a circle around me. Looking at their grinning faces I was afraid, and like the beasts they were, they sensed my fear and drew closer. Though their mouths were still easy, their eyes were hot.

'I know this particular hind,' said Urquhart boldly. He reached down with his riding whip and lifted a strand of my hair.

'There can be few men in the Black Isle who do not know Elsbet of Ferintosh,' said Roderick with a laugh.

'You have lost us our stag, Elsbet,' said the lawman. 'That is a serious charge. What will you give us in return?'

'I have nothing for the likes of you, Bluidy Mackenzie,' I replied hotly.

It was a mistake to show my anger. I would have been wiser to hang my head. The laird enjoyed a quarry that showed spirit.

'That is not what I have heard,' said Rory of Redcastle.

Though he was the oldest of the company, he was the first to dismount from his horse. There was a time when I would have been roused by the excitement I saw in him, but that day was over. My body answered only to Coinneach's touch. Seaforth alone sensed my distaste.

'Come, Cousins, we have wasted enough time. Let us be gone or this will prove a poor day's sport.'

'There is sport to be had here, Cousin,' said Rory, unbuckling his belt.

I turned to escape, but the others moved their horses to bar my way. Redcastle put his hands to my shoulders and swung me round. The heat from him revolted me. I spat in his face.

He flung me angrily to the ground. One of the dogs licked my cheek. Redcastle booted him off and would have fallen on me if Coinneach had not come.

None had heard him approach, but the power in him was so great that the horses shied from him as he thrust himself between them.

'Get up, Elsbet,' he said in a voice that was cold and full of contempt.

I could see that he thought I intended to lie with the lairds of my own free will. I opened my mouth to protest my innocence but I soon saw that it was useless. Coinneach was already far away in the place of visions.

Fairburn was the first to recover from his astonishment.

'Who is this insolent bastard?' he cried, but before any could answer, Coinneach had turned to him. He was white with anger and I saw his hand clenched on the stone.

'Do not be so quick with your tongue, my bonnie Laird,' said he in the power of the stone. 'The day is coming when the Mackenzies of Fairburn will lose their entire possessions and

185

your branch of the great clan will disappear for ever off the face of the earth. The great Castle of Fairburn will stand uninhabited and forgotten and a cow will give birth to a calf in the top chamber of the main tower.'[14]

'What lies are these?' cried Roderick, his face pale with rage as he reached for his sword belt.

Urquhart laughed nervously. 'It seems we have a madman in our midst,' he ventured, his hand to his mouth. Coinneach turned his blank staring eyes towards him.

'Bold words, Laird of Cromarty,' he said, 'but words cannot help you. The day is coming and is close at hand when the grasping Urquharts will not own above twenty acres of land in the Shire of Cromarty.'[15]

'The law has ways of dealing with men afflicted in this way,' said Sir George to Seaforth. 'Let us be gone.'

But Seaforth did not move. He was staring at Coinneach like a man enchanted.

'Hear me first, Lawman!' cried Coinneach, and such was the power in him that Bluidy Mackenzie reined his horse. 'The day is coming when foolish pride without sense will put in the place of the seed of the deer, the seed of the goat and your bonnie lands will fall into the hands of the fishermen of Avoch.'[16]

'I'll listen to no more,' said Colin of Kilcoy. He was shaking.

Coinneach turned to him. 'You cannot escape your destiny, Kilcoy, for the day will come when your fine new castle will stand cold and empty. A loathsome old man shall dwell there, indecent and filthy in his habits, who will not keep his marriage vows nor listen to priest or friend.'[17]

'Be silent, Son of Satan!' Colin cried.

Redcastle was the only one to laugh. 'Let him speak,' he said buckling his belt. 'Words cannot hurt.'

Coinneach looked at him. 'As for you, Redcastle,' he said, 'it is a pity you cannot keep your seed to yourself, for in every generation to spring from your loins there will always be a female fool.'[18]

There was such a silence when he had done that a dog could

be heard barking in Culbokie. Seaforth moved his horse forward.

'And what have you in mind for me, Seer?' he asked softly. His handsome face was pale and his eyes glittered with a strange excitement. But the mood had left Coinneach. He stood with his head bowed, unseeing, unhearing. Seaforth drew his sword. He put the tip of it to Coinneach's chin and forced him to look up.

'There is a place for you at Castle Brahan,' he said, 'if you have a mind to take it.'

Coinneach held his eyes until Seaforth removed his sword, but he said nothing. In a moment they were gone.

That night as we lay together there was a change in him. He was withdrawn and cold and he would not make love with me. I was frightened, for I had never known him in such a mood. I knew that he was thinking of leaving me. He would go to live with the great folk. He would become rich and famous and important and he would forget me and the love we had shared. What if he had offended the lairds? Seaforth had taken a liking to him and Seaforth was the lairds' laird.

What would become of me? With Coinneach no longer in my bed my heart would break; without the stone my life would be in danger. Satan did not make idle threats. Unless I gave him the stone he would show me no mercy. But how was I to get it? Even now as he lay asleep at my side his hand was clasped round the pouch. I fell asleep at last, but I would have been better awake, for my dreams were full of torture and fire.

Next morning as I ladled porridge into his bowl he said what I had been expecting to hear.

'I will be going to Brahan tomorrow.'

'And leaving me?' I saw a great pit opening between us.

'For a few weeks only.' The chasm grew wider.

'And what of the croft and your work here?'

'There is little enough work now that winter is at hand.'

'What of me? What of the love there is between us?'

'I will return,' he said mildly, not meeting my burning eyes.

He rose and put away his plate. I ran to the door and barred his way.

'You will not return. I know it here in my heart. I see it in your eyes. You no longer love me.'

'Let me pass,' he said calmly, but I would not.

'No,' I cried, 'you belong to me! You are mine, mine, I tell you, Satan promised. I will never let you go.' I flung myself against him, beating his chest with my fists.

He caught my wrists. 'I will come back,' he repeated.

'Prove it to me!' I cried drawing back from him and looking him deep in the eyes. 'Give me a token—give me your stone to keep while you are gone. Then I will believe you.'

He dropped my wrists. 'My word is enough,' he said coldly.

Seumas lurched in from the inner room, filthy, stinking and half-crazed.

'What is this—a lover's quarrel?' He leered at us drunkenly.

I poured out my rage on him.

'Hold your tongue, drunken pig. What do you know about it?'

When I turned, Coinneach was gone.

The man of the house laughed and crawled back to his bed.

Tears started to my eyes, tears of desperation and anger. I felt in my pocket for a rag to wipe them from my cheeks and found it stained purple with the juice of the fruit I had gathered in the ruined circle. The berries, wrapped in dock leaves, were a little crushed but otherwise unspoiled. I thought carefully (I am a child of Satan and I do not act without thought); if Coinneach were not to be mine he would belong to no other. Satan had promised me his body in exchange for the stone, but he had not said that the body would be alive. There was only one way to make sure of the stone. Satan guided my deliberations, but I made up my own mind.

I took meal from the kist and bound it with water and the juice of the deadly berries. I kneaded it well, formed it into bannocks and baked them on the great iron girdle over the fire. When they were cooked I spread them freely with butter and cheese and wrapped them in a clean white cloth and took them out on to the hill.

Coinneach was at the peat bank. There were still a few scattered clods to gather. I watched him as he stacked the black peats in a tidy pile for me to creel homewards by and by. My body yearned for him, but there was no pity in my heart.

I gave him the food and without a word, turned to go. I could kill him but I could not watch him die.

'Elsbet,' he called after me.

I stopped and turned my head.

'Will you not eat with me?' he asked.

There was still no pity in me as I smiled at him and went my way.

I went no further than the ruined circle. I sat there for a long time watching the sun set over the western mountains. I noticed that the first fine fingers of snow had touched the heights of Ben Wyvis. The air grew damp and chill and a wind ruffled the darkening firth below. I rose and went back to the peat bank. There was no sign of him.

'Coinneach,' I cried, but only the wind answered me. I saw the cloth that had contained the bannocks glimmering white in the dusk. I opened it carefully and counted. One of the cakes had gone. I looked round again and saw three dead crows.

If I had been human I should have felt relief. As it was I was filled with a burning anger. I scattered the contents of the cloth heedless of the creatures that would suffer from it. Then I went home. Satan may do what he wills with me. I no longer care.

Chapter 4

BRAHAN

Extracts from the Countess of Seaforth's Private Journal

October 18

God, God, God, life is so tedious. There is a great shrieking weariness in my head that makes me lash out at my unruly sons, castigate my servants and chide my Lord.

I look at my reflection in the glass and loathe what I see. God knows I never had beauty with a nose like a gull's beak and great pale eyes fringed with scant lashes, but I had a certain wit and liveliness that compensated. Now I am fast becoming an old hag at thirty with sharpened features and sharpened tongue. God, how I hate myself. I hate my life, my whining brats, my witless husband. Most of all, I hate the poverty that has clung to me like a pall all my life and chains me to this cold and crumbling castle.

I was taught as a child to despise wealth and to admire the finer virtues of courage, loyalty and the like, but I have learned through experience that the finer virtues are easier to practise when larded with wealth.

If I had wealth I would not remain here. I would go to court. King Charles owes me that at least. The Kintail fortune was squandered in his cause and so far he has done nothing to repay it. Sometimes when the pipers are wailing in the great hall, I dream about court. I am surrounded by noblemen whose extravagant wit exactly matches their long purses. Conversation is what I crave; conversation spiced and barbed with wit. Here there is no conversation. The most I can expect from my Lord is a rambling account of the day's hunting, and the rest of the kinsmen are no better. The chase, the dogs and when I am not present the female sex, are all they speak about and of course, the Clan. I was forgetting the most important subject of all, the great Mackenzie Clan. Not that they have much to say about it themselves. It is left to the bards, the story-tellers and the seers, who, God knows, are a wearisome collection of decaying old men, but they listen with a reverence usually accorded to Holy Writ. There is nothing that pleases them more than a story-teller who will recite the bloody details of a bygone feud, or a seer who will predict glory for their sons.

But for tedious talk there is nothing to rival the Church. Bishop Paterson and his chaplain are to be our guests for a few days. Heaven knows how I shall survive it. My Lord escapes to the hunting forest, my children to the nursery, but for me there is no escape. Visiting the tenantry, presiding over my household are the only alternatives and I fancy neither of them. No doubt, the next few days will see an increase in my growing reputation for sarcasm and surliness.

My Lord has returned from the hunt with nothing to show for it but muddied boots and a Feinnian thirst. He prates about some wild Highlander who accosted the kinsmen on the Mill-buie Ridge, another seer by all accounts whom I am expected to feed and house at Brahan, and for what, I wonder: the customary eulogies of the Clan and the flattering predictions of fame and glory. Seaforth is an infant in these matters. His stupidity and conceit madden me. He will believe anything if it is only told to him by a white-headed dotard with a fey look in his half-blind eyes. Well, I have quite made up my mind. There is no room for any more seers, bards or the like within the walls of Brahan. My Lord must make up his mind to it.

October 20

Bishop Paterson is the most married man that I have ever met. No doubt he feels that he is bound to make up for centuries of celebate prelates. His conversation is all on the virtues of his wife, his fine sons and his daughters who are legion. I have constantly complained of the lack of conversation at Brahan; now I complain of its quality. I would rather have silence than the prattle of an uxorious cleric. When he is not recounting the virtues of the fruit of his loins, he is complaining of Masters MacKillichallum and Hogg, two rebel ministers who will not conform to Episcopacy. He is determined that Seaforth shall have them arrested. No doubt my Lord will agree if only to silence the persistent bishop.

The Bishop's Chaplain interests me. He says little but with his master running on like the Conon in spate he has no opportunity to shine conversationally. Nevertheless, in comparison with the Bishop's babbling burn, I feel that there is in him a deep well of intelligence that he could draw from if he wished. His looks are arresting. He is immensely tall, a good hand's span taller than myself who am considered unusually tall for a woman and I find it disconcerting to look up to any man. Unlike his master, the Bishop, who sports a fine plaid, he wears the black gown of the cloister. His only adornment is a curiously wrought gold ring set with rubies which he wears to some effect on his right forefinger. His face is very pale and he wears his black hair closer cropped than is fashionable, but it is his eyes that interest me most. They are large and dark but always half-shuttered by smooth pale lids. He gives the impression of being a holy man absorbed in the inner world of the spirit and yet I am not sure. There is something unwholesome about him that both attracts and repels me.

My Lord informed us at dinner this evening that the new seer had arrived. He bestirred himself sufficiently to relate to the company some of the wild fortunes that this uncouth peasant had predicted for the lairds. The Bishop was silent for as long as it took to eat his venison, but I do not believe he listened to a word my Lord was saying. I did not blame him for it. The ravings of a lunatic seer are as tedious as the ravings of a proud parent, perhaps more so. But the Bishop's Chaplain was interested. I could see as much in the stillness of his body and the turn of his head. I found a certain amusement in speculating on the cause of his absorption. When my Lord had done with his tale I turned to speak to the Chaplain.

'The subject of Second Sight interests you, Master Videl?'

He looked at me keenly through those half-closed lids.

'In so far as it is a manifestation of the devil, yes.'

'Come, Sir,' said Seaforth with a frown, 'I would not go so far as that, eh, Bishop?'

'Second Sight?' said the Bishop, looking up from his plate. 'My dear Lord Seaforth, it is a complaint as common to the Highlander as scurvy is to a sailor.'

My Lord was not pleased. The Bishop's remark was as tactless as it was typical of a brash Lowlander.

'Husband,' I called to him the length of the board. 'You say the Seer has the Gift; the Bishop calls it a complaint and Master Videl here says it is a sin. Summon this Seer to the great hall and let me be arbiter.'

Seaforth looked up surprised and not a little suspicious. It was rare for me to show so much interest in his amusements.

It was the Bishop's turn to be wearied, but he concealed it well enough. Fool though he might be in many ways, he was wise enough to want to keep Seaforth for a friend.

When the Seer was brought before us and my Lord had given him a greeting, I called out to him.

'You see before you three men; one calls you a Seer, one says you are a sinner and the third believes you to be sick. Prophesy, if you can, and let me be the judge.'

He smiled faintly. 'I am not a performing bear to dance to the goad at the Michaelmas Fair.'

My Lord was pleased to see me put down. 'Well answered, man,' he cried.

'It is no answer,' I said coldly, 'and my judgement is this, that you are neither Seer, sinner, or sick, but a charlatan and a cheat.'

The Bishop's Chaplain laid his hand upon my arm and I felt my flesh shrink from his touch. 'I would question this man,' he said looking to me for permission.

'It is said that you carry a charm stone and that you cannot predict without it. Is that true?'

The Seer turned to look at him. 'You wear a ring,' he said. 'Can you preach without it?'

'Of course. The ring is merely a symbol.'

'The stone I carry is neither more nor less.'

'It is a symbol of the devil,' said Master Videl and I noticed particularly that the Seer did not deny it.

'Enough,' said my Lord who had been growing increasingly impatient with the conversation of the clerics. 'I brought this man to Brahan not as devil's agent but to prophesy for my clan. What have you to say to your chieftain, Seer?'

It was then that I saw the Seer's hand clenching and unclenching at his side and I knew that the Bishop's Chaplain was right. The Seer needed that stone.

He looked at my Lord and as he gazed his eyes became strange. It was as if my Lord were made of glass for though the Seer looked at him, he also looked through him. When he spoke his voice was strange and it was apparent to all of us that he was in some sort of trance though whether it was assumed or genuine I had no way of knowing.

'The day will come and will soon be here,' he said, 'when the great stag shall be separated from the deer forests by a wide flow of water and the herd be left to the mercy of the proud hind.'

The Bishop laughed. 'The usual unintelligible riddle. It was the same at Delphi in the days of the Greeks and it will be the same with so-called oracles of the future until Judgement Day.'

This proved to me conclusively that the Bishop is a fool. Even the humblest serving wench in the kitchens of Brahan knew that the great stag is Mackenzie of Kintail and that Isabella is his proud hind.

The Seer shall answer for his insolence. I will see to that.

The Bishop's Chaplain sought me out today when I was struggling with the vintner's account. Seaforth has left such matters in my hands since I uncovered the steward's dishonesty and had him imprisoned. I am gifted, or cursed some would say, with a man's head for such matters and it is as well that I am, for my Lord finds it hard enough to sign his own name.

I confess I was not pleased to see Master Videl and I did not extend him the usual courtesies, nor could I conceal my impatience as I asked him to state his business. There was an inaccuracy in the ledger that I could not trace and my temper was at breaking point.

Master Videl was quick to gauge my mood. He stood at my shoulder and scrutinized the ledger. Normally I would not have tolerated such behaviour in a subordinate, but his close presence had a numbing effect on my senses. I sat silent until his long white forefinger pointed to the error I had missed. As soon as he had pointed it out, the rest was simple. He waited at my shoulder until I had made the necessary alteration. It was a strange sensation having him there. I felt like a child without will or strength and although the fire burned brightly, I found that I was cold.

When I had done, he moved away and the sensation was diminished. I went to the fire.

'You have a head for figures,' I said, holding my hands to the blaze.

'I am glad to be of assistance to you,' he said with a slight bow, 'and I would wish to be of further assistance to you, if you will let me be.'

'Well?' I demanded somewhat less warmly. I do not easily tolerate interference in my affairs, still less unsought advice.

'I do not like to see your hospitality abused. There is one in your household who should not be here. Be wise, Madam, and rid yourself of his influence.'

'Now who could that be?' I asked, my voice knife-edged with sarcasm.

'He who calls himself a seer.'

'The Seer?' I cried with astonishment. 'I assure you, Sir, that he has no influence over me.'

'That I can believe, but there are others in your household who are not so wise-minded.'

The insolence of the man! It was obvious that he referred to Seaforth.

'You exaggerate, I think. He amuses my servants, entertains my guests and belongs to my Clan. There is no more to be said on the matter.'

'He belongs to the devil,' said Master Videl quietly. 'The day will surely come when you will regret having housed him at Brahan.'

'It seems that you too are something of a prophet, Master Videl,' I said with a laugh. 'I shall remember your words and when the day comes I will send him back to his true Master, I assure you.'

'Send him to me,' said the priest, looking at me strangely through his lidded eyes.

'Why?' I demanded impatiently. 'What is your interest in the matter?'

'My concern is his soul,' he said and I could not quarrel with that.

'As you wish, and now, if you will forgive me, I have many household duties.'

He bowed and left the room. It was no doubt my fancy, but it seemed to grow warmer. What a strange creature he is.

November 5

My Lord has received a letter from the King! He is summoned to court immediately and I am to remain here. The unbelievable irony of it! I who so want to go to court must remain, while Seaforth, who grudges a day away from the chase, is to wait on the King within the month. When the letter came and Seaforth told me what it contained, I could scarcely speak for anger, but now that it is settled, I cannot help but see the sense of the arrangement. We cannot both leave Brahan at this time. The estate, which is just beginning to recover under my careful husbandry, would suffer. Besides, we can scarcely afford court dress for my Lord let alone for me, and I will not go in rags. Seaforth has pointed out with unusual wisdom that if the King chooses to recompense him for the loss of fortune during the troubles, that will be the correct time for me to go to court. With this I must be content, though I cannot help thinking that I would be the better ambassador for Clan Mackenzie. There are ways of winning this King's gratitude that are only open to the female sex, or so I have been told.

On the other hand, I will be glad to have my Lord out of the way for a month or two. He is soft-hearted to the point of foolishness and my heart is set on several improvements to the estate which will involve evicting certain unsatisfactory tenants. This can only be accomplished in Seaforth's absence. He has assured me that he will be back before the spring which will give me time to do what is necessary in these matters.

There is much chatter in the castle about the Seer's prediction concerning the absence of the great stag and Seaforth is as proud of it as if he had made it himself. He is altogether too thick with the Seer and I do not like it. The kinsmen are surly on the subject and I do not blame them, considering the Seer's insolent behaviour to them. I had hoped to be rid of him as soon as Seaforth left for court, but my Lord has made me swear to shelter him until his return. I have said that I will do so provided he keeps to the bothies at the back of the stables. I have made it plain that I will not have him in the Castle. With that both my Lord and his Seer will have to be content.

A letter today from my Lord, the first since Christmas. I fully expected it to contain word of his imminent return, but far from it. The King has ordered him to France. It seems that His Majesty has taken a liking to my Lord and has entrusted him with a personal matter. I should no doubt feel proud of Seaforth's success, but I do not. I seethe inwardly with jealousy. I should be the one to go to Paris. I am the one with the cultured mind and the French language. Such an honour is wasted on Seaforth. He has neither the grace to appreciate it nor the wit to enjoy it, whereas I . . . but I will write no more on the matter. It pains me too much.

I have sent word to Master Videl to visit me. I find his company increasingly stimulating. Without his visits I should have gone mad from the tedium of the longest winter I have ever endured.

The Seer's name has been much to the fore today. They are all saying that the 'great stag' has indeed been separated from his herd by a wide flow of water, and even I must concede that he made a clever guess.

I confess I broke my own rule of silence on the subject of the Seer this evening when I questioned Agnes about him while she was dressing me for the evening meal. It seems that he has been making a name for himself in the district with his prophecies. At my hint of interest, the flood gates broke and Agnes burst into a flow of weird and extraordinary predictions concerning overflowing lochs, drowned villages and a great deal of incomprehensible rubbish to do with the reeking wells at Strathpeffer.[19] I do believe the Seer says such things to confuse the minds of simple folk and set himself up as a sage. If it were not for my promise to Seaforth, I would have dismissed him from Brahan months ago.

Master Videl has been with me for the past two days. I find I have become dependent on him for many things. He has a clear mind and his advice on matters of business has been profitable on every occasion. I still cannot admit to liking the man. There are times when I almost fear him and yet I am drawn to him in a way that I cannot explain. There is a streak of cruelty in him that matches my own. We are two of a kind, he and I, and yet having said that, I still do not know what he is thinking, what he admires, if anything, in me. Certainly it is not my body. He is no more drawn to me in that way than I am to him. The bond that unites us is different. I believe that he reads my mind and knows what I am thinking before I know it myself. This I find disconcerting, but at the same time I am flattered. I am one of those few women who prefer to be admired for their mind.

He visits the Seer when he is staying at Brahan. Only today I saw him leave the bothy behind the stables. Wrapped in his long cloak, his head sunk on his breast, he strode across the courtyard as if all the devils in hell were at his heels. There are times when I wonder if the Seer is not his main reason for visiting Brahan. His conversation often includes the Seer. Only this evening he opened the subject again.

'How much do you see of that man?'

'Nothing, if I can help it.'

He looked at me under those hooded lids and told me that I was wise and yet I wonder if he is sincere. Sometimes I gain the impression that he is disappointed that I have not more to say on the matter.

Still no word from my Lord. Rumours buzz round the castle like summer flies. He is sick; the French King has cast him into prison; his ship is lost at sea. The kinsmen frequently ride over for news and I am weary of telling them that there is none. I am weary of worrying over my Lord's safety, running the estate, my children, the clan affairs. It is altogether becoming too much of a burden. I need to know what it is that prevents Seaforth from returning to his home. Tonight Agnes whispered to me as she stroked my hair with the brush:

'There is one who could help you, my Lady.'

I did not need to ask whom she meant. I knew because she had only repeated what had been in the back of my own mind for weeks now.

'Bring him to me,' I told her looking at my face in the glass. Was this the proud Isabella of Seaforth, this pale-eyed scarecrow of a creature who was reduced to asking help from a superstitious Highland peasant?

'Now?' Agnes asked, surprised, for it was past midnight.

'Now,' I told her. By daylight I would have changed my mind.

She brought him to my room and left us together. I could not think of a word to say to him and he did not help me. I was aware of the same antagonism that had been in me the first time I saw him. We would always be at enmity, he and I. He regarded me with dark consideration. When my words came they sounded strange to my ears. I had never in my life pleaded with anyone.

'Where is he?'

His expression did not change. 'Your Lord is well and happy,' he said.

His complacency angered me. His hands lay slack at his sides and I could see that he did not hold his stone.

'Answer me properly,' I commanded him. 'Prophesy for me. Where is my Lord? What is he doing? Is he preparing to come home?'

Still his expression did not change.

'Your Lord is in good health and a contented mood,' he repeated.

'How do you know?' I cried, infuriated by his calmness.

200

'How can you stand before me and lie. What is it that you know?'

His eyes darkened but he answered me nothing.

And then I did something which I can hardly bring myself to write, something I have never done in my whole life not even as a child. I burst into tears. God, the shame of it. Tears flew from my eyes like rain and sobs clogged my throat. I wanted to scream at him to get out of my sight, but I could not speak. By the time I had recovered, he had gone.

June 30

He knows. Of course he knows. Why then will he not tell me? Why will he not take out his stone and tell me what he sees? What is it that he does not want me to know? Is my Lord sick of the plague or the pox perhaps and he fears to tell me? I would rather hear an uncomfortable truth than put up with this uncertainty.

My pride has all gone. I am fast becoming a broken wreck of a creature. I will write here what no one knows, not even Agnes who must know me as well as I know myself. Perhaps in the writing of it, I may be able to forget the humiliation.

I went to his bothy tonight. Aye, the proud hind of Brahan crawled on her belly to the runt of the herd. He was there alone and he stood waiting for me to speak.

'Why will you not tell me what I seek to know?' I cried. 'Have I not fed and housed you these past months? And for what? You prophesy for my servants, my kinsmen and my Lord, why will you not prophesy for me? What have I ever done to you?'

'Your Lord is in good health and he is in fine company,' he said, as he had said before, but this time I fancied there was pity in his tone.

'Fool!' I cried, and raising the short whip I always carried for fear of the dogs, I brought it stinging across his cheek.

'Fool to think that I am to be cheated by soft words.'

He caught the whip before I could strike again and drew me close to him.

'What do you want me to tell you,' he said locking me to his eye, 'that he is dead?'

'I want the truth.'

He took his hand off my whip and opened the door.

'There is nothing more I can tell you,' he said, but his eyes slid away uneasily and I knew he was lying, yet I could do no more.

July 4

I have told Master Videl everything concerning my dealings with the Seer. I expected him to be at least contemptuous, at worst incensed, but he said little and there was a thoughtfulness in his tone and a gleam of excitement in his eye.

'Have you never thought, Countess, who might be responsible for Seaforth's long delay?'

'Speak more plainly.'

'They say many things about the Seer that come to my ears alone. Some believe that he practises witchcraft.'

'Witchcraft?' I scorned. 'What nonsense is this?'

'That is the first careless remark I have ever heard you make, Countess,' he said softly.

'Explain yourself.'

'Faith in God can remove mountains, it is said. Faith in the devil is also not without power.'

The strange coldness that I have felt so often in his presence made me shiver.

'I do not understand. Seaforth was good to him—too good in my opinion. Why should he use the Black Arts to keep him from his home?'

'Seaforth is not unhappy now—by the Seer's account—but,' he paused, 'you are.'

All became clear to me. 'What am I to do?' I whispered.

'Forget the Seer, for a time at least. Forget your anxieties. Invite your kinsmen and friends to a great feast.'

'Without my Lord?'

'Show this impudent Seer that you care nothing for his dark ways. Show him that you are not concerned for your Lord. Invite him to your feast and make a mockery of his predictions.'

'How am I to do that?'

'There are many ways,' he told me.

'I'll do it!' I cried.

July 16

The Bishop's Chaplain has indeed been a wise counsellor to me. Thanks to him, I am my old self again. Indeed I have been so busy preparing for the feast which is to fall on my birthday than I no longer brood over my Lord's absence. If the clansmen think it strange for me to celebrate in such a way, they have not shown it. All the lairds and their ladies from Caithness to the Great Glen are coming. The Bishop is bringing his entire family, though where they are all to be housed, I do not know. I pray for favourable weather so that the lairds may have good hunting and the ladies take pleasure in the gardens.

I am determined that the Seer shall be humiliated and I believe I know how it is to be done. I shall ask him in the presence of the whole company to predict the whereabouts of my Lord and when he tells me in that sneering voice of his that he is well and happy, I shall inform my guests that I have just had word from my Lord that he is laid low of a fever, chained to his bed, disenchanted with the court of King Louis and longing to return to the Highlands. I can hear the ringing laughter of the whole clan. No doubt my Lords of Redcastle, Kilcoy, Fairburn, Urquhart and Avoch will laugh the loudest.

The feast is over. Master Videl has just left me. I will do as he advises. I have no alternative. I scarcely need to write to-night's happenings in this journal for they are burned into my brain. Nevertheless I will record them. I lay the blame of to-night's humiliation at my Lord's door. If he had been here, none of it would have happened.

The devil is not to be mocked. I learned that tonight. I learned many things tonight, and yet all started so auspiciously.

The weather was fine, the hunting good, the feasting excellent, the company cheerful and loud in their congratulations. I received many fine gifts. The Bard, contrary to my expectations for I have not always been complimentary to him, composed a beautiful verse in my honour and my piper played a new reel which he entitled 'Lady Isabella's Feast'. I was toasted and fêted like a queen. All went well until I summoned the Seer. I could see that many of my guests were uneasy at his coming. Fairburn who was seated on my right hand frowned his disapproval.

'Leave well alone, Bella. He will only sour the wine,' he murmured and perhaps I would have listened to him if I had not felt the eyes of the Bishop's Chaplain upon me across the length of the great hall.

'I have a score to settle and so have you,' I told Fairburn.

He did not deny it, so the Seer was summoned to the great hall.

'Welcome, Seer,' I called out to him. 'It is my birthday feast and it is customary to honour a lady upon that day. My kinsmen, my bard and my musicians have all done me much honour. What have you to say to your chieftain's lady on this auspicious day?'

'What would you have me say?' he said in that quiet voice that has the power to madden me.

'I would have you tell the company why my Lord is not at my side this day.'

'I do not know,' he said, his eyes to the ground.

'He does not know,' I cried mockingly to the company. 'The great Seer of Brahan does not know the answer to such a little question. Come, man, take out your stone and try again. Perform for the clan. I demand it.'

I had angered him. I saw his hand clench suddenly and I knew that he held the stone. His eyes changed and there was a great silence in the assembly. Presently he spoke:

'Since you must know what can only distress you, so be it. Your Lord has little thought for you on this your feast day, nor does he remember the deer forests and glens of Ross. I see him in a gilded room, dressed in silks and cloth of gold. He is on his knees to a fair lady and his arm is round her waist and his lips pressed to her hand.'

I could not believe that I had heard aright. My hand clenched on the false letter telling of Seaforth's sickness, his longing for home and me. No good to read it now. None of the company would believe it for the Seer's words had the ring of authority. Not one eye met mine as I rose shaking to my feet.

'You have spoken a great evil of my Lord in the house of his ancestors. You have insulted a lady at her own board. You have defamed a mighty chief in the presence of his clan. Never fear, you shall receive your reward.'

I looked to my guard and without a word of instruction they seized him and took him to the dungeons. I left my guests. I could not face the pity in their eyes.

Master Videl offered neither pity nor comfort. He brought me a bundle wrapped in a cloth and opened the contents. It contained a doll made of clay, crudely fashioned with a great beak of a nose. It was dressed in a scrap of silk that I recognized as coming from an old gown of my own. It was pierced with a honey-coloured elf-arrow of great beauty and great evil.

'What is it?' I whispered, horrified.

205

'The evidence you will need.'

'Evidence?' I still did not fully understand.

'I found this monstrous thing hidden in the Seer's bothy. It is the work of one—Elsbet of Ferintosh—a notorious witch lately mistress to the Seer.'

I looked at him curiously and saw the answer to my unasked question in the exultant glitter in his eye.

'It is proof that he is a tool of Satan, a sorcerer and a witch. It is your duty to bring him to justice.'

Even then at that dark moment I knew the Seer had had no part in this sick bewitchment, but I did not care.

'It will be my pleasure,' I told the priest.

Chapter 5

THE CHANONRY OF ROSS

The Seer

That filthy body is propped against the sweating stone of the
dungeon in the half-ruined castle in the Chanonry of Ross. The
clothes are stinking rags. Those tangled strings at the
extremities were once fingers with nails. The head is bowed
and the mouth falls open in a moan. The Stone lies unheeded
in the pouch around the neck.

That body is my body. That tortured remnant of humanity
houses my spirit. I am two creatures. The body that bleeds
and lies chained to the ground, the spirit that hovers a hand's
span above, both are mine, both are me. My spirit rises higher
through the dripping dungeon roof for walls are no barriers to
the soul. I tremble in the blue air between the doves that flit
across the Kirk Green. I can see my broken body dimly like
a shadow hunched over the Stone. The Stone I always see.
It is the anchor of my soul.

Below my hovering spirit the Kirk Green swarms with folk
in festal mood. They run this way and that like flies on a dung
heap. I know each one, their names, their temperament. Am
I then God? Who am I? Enough, my soul. Such thoughts
destroy.

The body below lifts his mangled hand and presses it to the
pouch. My spirit shrinks down, down, down from the
tumbling sky to the dark imprisonment of flesh. Spirit and
body, body and soul, we are indivisible again.

The key scrapes in the lock. The great rust-bound mildewed
door creaks open and my jailer admits Master Videl. Strange,
I cannot predict for him. When I force my spirit into that

place where I have seen so much sorrow, so much evil, so much change for so many people, for him there is nothing, dark nothing, an abyss. I stand at its edge and tremble. I am afraid of the Black Priest, not of what he has done to my body, but of what he would do to my soul.

He tells me that the court is ready. He bends his great height and whispers for my hearing alone.

'You can still save yourself. Only give me the Stone.'

His breath is foul, more foul than the sodden straw in my cell.

'From your hands to mine, your power to me,' he urges.

But I am not yet ready to abandon my soul.

'Fool,' he whispers, 'do you not know that I have the power to save you from the ordeal?'

The fire or the abyss. The choice is mine. I welcome the fire.

Outside, the white sunlight bursts on my eyes. The swarming flies have turned into wolves. They would tear me apart. A woman with black teeth opens her mouth and venom pours out; a small mean man as filthy as myself spits in my face. I am touched by a dozen hostile hands. Pain shoots up from the torn tips of my fingers and explodes in my head. The Black Priest walks before me, cutting a path through the forest of wagging heads. The jailer prods me with the tip of his sword. A seed of anger swells in my gut but I will not nourish it. Anger is my undoing. Look up at the great cathedral, oh my soul. Take its peace into your disquiet.

Beautiful Chanonry Kirk. Rose-red splendour of stones. Your days also are numbered. Only the dead who sleep beneath your nave are at peace. They will not hear the tumble of your walls. Their ghosts will chant in the empty aisles. Ghost singers within ghost walls.

A dove flies up to the high spire, above the mob, the dram booths and the sugar-cake stalls. My spirit yearns upwards to that dove but it is chained by fear. I dare not abandon my body to the crowd.

The Chapter House is dark and full of the great folk. I am

hustled between the silks of fine women and the rich plaids of the lairds. The old she-cat who is mother to Seaforth grips my arm and commands me to repent.

What is repentance? A word, an act of will too weak to remove the mountain of my guilt. The day I first lifted the Stone and willed my spirit to leave my body was the day of my downfall. On that day my curse became my shame. Now I no longer know if my predictions will happen because I wish it, or because they are already grooved into the circle of time. Did Seaforth give his heart to the French woman because I willed it, or did I 'see' only what my Chieftain himself had willed? I do not know. Yet, curse or vision of truth, the outcome is the same. Not even time itself can tell me whether my predictions are born out of truth or out of anger.

The Sherrif, Sir John Urquhart of Cromarty, has come in. His small close eyes flicker uneasily on and off me. The lairds settle into their places and the jury, all clansmen of the Mackenzie, are sworn. None look at me with their eyes, but in their thoughts they stare. There is a stir at the back of the Chapter House and the Tall Woman enters. She is welcomed by Sir John and given a chair at his side. She is not afraid to look at me. Her eyes never falter as the Charge is read:

'Kenneth Mackenzie, you are indicted and accused by Isabella of Tarbat, Kintail and Seaforth that you did practise to deceive and injure by means of the most foul witchcraft, prophecy, enchantment and diabolic incantation, the person of the said Isabella and did thereby attempt to estrange and separate the said Lady from her most noble Lord and Chieftain, Kenneth, fourth Lord Mackenzie of Kintail and third Earl of Seaforth, by fashioning a clay image of the said Lady thus attempting to cause Lord Seaforth to remain in foreign parts away from his family and his clan; and did also consort with other witches to bring about the downfall of the said Lord and Lady by vile prophecies and incantations.

'How say you, Prisoner, guilty or not guilty?'

I am expected to answer this charge when I do not know the truth of it myself. If my prediction was a curse born out of anger, then I am indeed guilty of much of that of which I have been accused. The court must decide.

'Not guilty.'

The Black Priest is my accuser. The Tall Woman watches him from pale cold eyes. From time to time she beckons to him to instruct or question him, but he has no need of her assistance. He lifts the clay doll for all the court to see. It reeks of Elsbet and her profession. Ah, Elsbet, your arms to me now, your lips to mine. Your breath was honeysuckle and sulphur; your golden skin covered a tarry soul.

The Black Priest has woven a spell round the court. He has plenty to say and his words drop into cold hearts.

'Members of the Jury, you will have heard it read from the pulpit many times that the gift of prophecy comes from God. It is true that the Scriptures are full of incidents of prophecy divinely inspired. Jesus of Nazareth Himself was a prophet. But just as there are false gods, false teachers and false friends, so also there are false prophets. Hear the words of the Holy Writ:

' "Many false prophets shall arise and shall deceive many," and again, "false prophets shall rise and shall shew signs and wonders to seduce if it were possible even the elect".

' "Beloved," said St John, "believe not every spirit, but try the spirits whether they are of God because many false prophets have gone out into the world." '

The words blur in my mind. I have a longing for Lewis, for the black moors and the white sands, for the wet green grass of the summer shielings. Was there room for me in Lewis and I never knew it? Certainly there has been no other place. The Black Priest's voice grows louder.

'There are some who would say that this so-called "seer" in the dock is a true prophet. You quail and tremble at his words. Misguided fools that you are! Have you not yet learned to tell truth from falsehood, good from evil? The great prophets of the past did not need a charm stone to see into the future. They needed nothing but their faith in God. It is the Stone that betrays the false prophet and makes him a witch. It is the Stone that proclaims louder even than that image of clay, that Kenneth Mackenzie is guilty of terrible crimes not only against a gracious lady who has shown him hospitality, but against every laird in this land. It is the Stone that he wears next to his heart that betrays the sorcerer.'

The Black Priest has the gift of oratory. The lairds are very still as once again he lifts the Holy Book.

' "There shall not be found among you anyone that usest divination or an observer of times, or an enchanter, or a witch, or a charmer, or a consulter with familiar spirits, or a wizard, or a necromancer, for all that do these things are an abomination unto the Lord." '

He shuts the book and the mother of Seaforth cries into the silence:

' "Thou shalt not suffer a witch to live." '

In the uproar that follows, the Black Priest comes close to me.

'Give me the Stone,' he says, 'give it to me and all may yet be well. Put it into my hand.'

The jailer hears him. He rips the pouch from my neck and shakes it out. The Stone falls to the ground. It rolls to the feet of the jury who shrink from it as from a serpent. No one dares to touch it.

'Pick it up,' the Sheriff orders, and the jailer thrusts me forward so roughly that I fall to my knees with my palm across the Stone.

I cannot pick it up. I cannot lift my hand, for the Black Priest's foot presses down, imprisoning the Stone beneath my palm. Flames of pain consume me. The jailer bends, but the Black Priest dismisses him. He stoops himself to take the Stone.

'Your hand to my hand; your power to me,' he whispers so that only I may hear him.

I know now what I have always suspected. Master Videl is vassal to the Lord of Lies. He lifts the Stone with triumph from under my hand and the Tall Woman cries:

'Let him die the death!'

The seed of anger has swollen. It bursts in my head. My spirit rips through the curtain of flame and soars about the court. I see below me the squawking crows crowd closer round their prey. I am caught up in the great whirling circle of time. I see what I want to see, I hear what I want to hear and the words stream back through the centuries and issue forth from that bruised and tortured body I have left behind.

'Woman, heed me well for I see far into the future where lies the doom of the House of Seaforth. Mackenzie to Mackenzie, Kintail to Kintail, Seaforth to Seaforth, all will end in extinction and sorrow. I see a chief, the last of his house, and he is both deaf and dumb. He will be father to four fine sons, but he will follow them all to the grave. He will live in sorrow and die in mourning, knowing that the honours of his line are extinguished forever and that no future chief of Mackenzie shall ever again rule in Kintail. Lamenting the last of his sons, he shall sink in sorrow to the tomb and the last of his possessions shall be inherited by a widow from the east who will kill her own sister.

'As a sign that these things are coming to pass there will be four great lairds in the days of the last Seaforth. Gairloch shall be hare-lipped; Chisholm shall be buck-toothed; Grant shall be a stammerer and Raasay an idiot. These four chiefs shall be allies and neighbours of the last Seaforth and when he looks round him and sees them he will know that his sons are doomed to die and that his broad lands shall pass to strangers and his race come to an end.'[20]

The body moves its hand to touch the Stone, but it is not there. The moment I have dreaded is at hand. My spirit cannot return to that poor empty shell. I am outlawed, exiled, borne away on the wind of time, tossed like a grain of sand in a storm . . .

Such sights, such visions! There are no words left. Exploding fires consume the earth, the world is a desert. The air is thick with the black rain that brings destruction. I am lost in eternity. Let me return, only let me return . . .

The body stands rigid in the dock. Spittle seeps from a corner of the mouth. The eyes are empty: the mouth has no speech.

'He is possessed,' cries the mother of Seaforth and crosses herself.

'What need we of further witnesses?' cries the Tall Woman into the silence. 'Enough is enough.'

Fairburn cries, 'How much more must we hear? Will you wait until the whole of Ross is a wilderness peopled with peasants before you silence this sorcerer?'

The jury whisper together.

'We find him guilty as charged.'

The court is engulfed in noise and Sir John beats the table with his fist.

'Hear the judgement of this court. Kenneth Mackenzie, you will be taken away to the Ness of Chanonry between three and four in the afternoon and there you are to be strangled to death by the hand of the hangman and thereafter your body is to be burned in a barrel of tar and the ashes scattered on the wind: all your movable goods and gear are to be brought to His Majesty's use.'

The body hears nothing, sees nothing: the flesh feels nothing. Mindless, he is kept alive only by the beat of his heart. He is dragged through the court on senseless feet. None look him in the eye or dare to touch his limbs for fear of enchantment. Outside the surging crowds shout abuse, ribaldry and scorn. A drunken crofter raises his horn cup and cries:

'Good health to you, Seer, in hell!'

A child is screaming because the crowd has separated her from her mother.

Still the body feels nothing, hears nothing, sees nothing.

The body is thrown on to the cart that has lately returned from carrying the peats down to the Ness for the burning. The jailer rides with his prisoner. The Sheriff and the lairds withdraw to drink a dram or two. Time enough for them to leave for the Ness. The burning will wait. The Tall Woman stands apart and alone. She has at last had word that Seaforth is on his way home. She is in a fever of impatience for the burning to be over before he arrives. The dead tell no tales.

The Black Priest is hurrying across from the back of the Kirk Green towards the Bishop's palace. The house is silent for the Bishop's family are all on the green. The Bishop himself is away in Edinburgh on ecclesiastical affairs. He finds it convenient to be out of the diocese at such a time.

The Black Priest climbs the three flights of stone steps to his room in the west turret. It is quiet here. Only the noise of the incoming tide below his window intrudes. His long thin fingers caress the Stone. The ring sprinkles red light.

Meanwhile the cart lurches over the rough ground down the Greengates to the great flat tongue of the Ness where already the pitch in the spiked barrel is beginning to smoke. Sun sparkles on the sea and lightens the faces of the crowd. It is a perfect harvest day, but the cornfields are empty. The whole world has come to the burning.

The body is dragged from the cart and propped between two clansmen armed with broadswords. The crowd sways as the wind swirls smoke in their faces. The provost and the bailies stand in dignified rank as befitting their position and the occasion. There is a scatter of children as the lairds' horses thunder down the Greengates. The parish minister, the Reverend George Munro, stands alone, his brows drawn in disapproval. He is composing his Sunday sermon and the text will be, 'He that is without sin amongst you, let him cast the first stone.'

A dram shop has been hastily set up out of reach of the smoke and a fiddler is playing a reel. The executioner, a Cromarty man, slips a noose round the prisoner's neck. When the time comes he has a mind to be merciful. Last to arrive is the Tall Woman. The crowd parts to let her through and a boy runs to hold her horse.

The Clerk to the Court moves up beside Sir John Urquhart

and clears his throat. He begins to read the sentence for the last time. The Reverend George Munro looks about him for Master Videl. His frown grows fiercer when he realizes his colleague is not present. Master Munro is angry. It is not the first time the Bishop's Chaplain has been found failing in his duty to a soul in need.

The minister goes up to the prisoner and looks him in the eye.

'Repent, for the kingdom of heaven is at hand,' he says, but there is no flicker of response in those soulless eyes, no sign of recognition. The minister's anger increases.

'So now they convict idiots and the feeble-minded,' he says to the hangman. 'God save us.'

He reaches into his pocket and takes out a small silver cross. It was his mother's and her mother's from the time of the old religion. He has nothing else to offer this poor half-wit, no other key to paradise. He puts it in the mangled hand and closes the fist over it.

'God go with you, my son.'

The hand is blind. It cannot tell silver from stone. It recognizes only the hardness in its fist and the old familiar anchor draws the soul back into the safe prison of flesh.

At last I can return to my body which leaps into the present reality of pain. My senses awake to the smell of pitch and peat, the sound of the clerk's voice and the feel of the rope on my neck. I look up. Above me a raven and a dove fly in widening circles. I watch them, my hand on the hard silver and I am not afraid.

Urquhart raises his arm and the Tall Woman gives a cry of triumph.

'So,' she cries, 'the time has come at last for you to join your fellow devils in hell!'

I see the hate in her and I am afraid, but not for myself.

'I am finished with hell,' I say strongly, without effort or aid, 'and I will leave a sign that you may all know that I speak the truth. Look up at yonder birds.'

All eyes lift to the raven and the dove still encircling my pyre. There is no laughter now.

'When I am dead and my body consumed, they will return. If the dove alight on the ashes and is consumed then you have spoken truly, but if it be the raven, then look to your own soul, woman.'

She flames with anger.

'Hear him,' she shouts to the crowd. 'So now he has influence over eternity. Cast him into the pitch—alive!'

The hangman hesitates. It is the clansmen who lift the rope off my neck and throw me into the fire.

A moment of shrieking agony and it is over. The body chars, stinks and shrivels. Poor creature of flesh; poor mortality. It is time for my spirit to go to the place beyond, and yet I cannot rise above the blue air. My soul is still in chains. The Black Priest would chain me to hell. I see him below me in a round room. The Stone is in his hand. He presses it to his eye and his body sweats with strain. He stands in a circle within a star and holds the Stone towards a single black candle. He prostrates himself again and again. Then he stands up and looks at the Stone intently. He looks for a long time.

The fire dies, the folk go home in slow weary procession. Some snore drunkenly on the grass. Only the Tall Woman remains. She is watching a raven pecking at the scattered crumbs of meat and bannock. It moves closer to the hot ashes. The Tall Woman frightens it away, but it returns. There is no sign of the dove.

The Black Priest is still looking at the Stone. Suddenly he loses patience. He flings wide the shutter of his window. He takes back his arm and throws the Stone as far as his strength will take it. It falls on the shingle at the edge of the sea. A long arm of water closes over it and draws it back and back into the water from whence it came, and I am free, free of the flesh, the devil and the world . . .

There has always been a place for me here.

APPENDIX

The Predictions

1. (Page 102.) The Macdonalds of Clanranald were the great family of Benbecula for many centuries. Their downfall started with the death of the chief at the Battle of Sheriffmuir and was completed in 1745 when Prince Charles Edward Stuart escaped to Nunton after Culloden. It was here that Flora Macdonald and Lady Clanranald dressed the Prince up as 'Betty Burke', an Irish maid, so that he could escape to Skye. Shortly afterwards General Campbell arrested the Clanranalds thus ending a long and glorious chiefdom. Eventually the direct line was to die out altogether. The prediction concerning the old woman with the footless stocking (a primitive form of footwear) came true when a certain old Mrs Macdonald known as the 'Cailleach nam Mogan', because she was the last to wear this form of footwear in the island, took over Nunton which her descendents occupied long after the Clanranalds had fallen on hard times.

2. (Page 124.) Part of this prediction was to come true in extraordinary detail. In the summer of 1799, the Reverend Norman Macleod visited Dunvegan Castle and recorded that an English smith told him that he intended to open the iron chest which contained the Fairy Flag, the next day. The minister asked to be present and permission was given him by the factor provided he said nothing to the chief. Next day, therefore, the smith forced open the chest; with unnecessary violence as it happened, for a key was found under part of the covering. Within the inner case, the flag was found enclosed in a sweet-smelling wooden box. The flag consisted of a square piece of rich silk embroidered in gold thread with crosses and 'several elf-spots' stitched with great care on different parts of it.

At the same time news reached the castle that 'Norman, the third Norman' and heir of Macleod, who was a lieutenant on HMS *Queen Charlotte,* had been lost at sea. Within a week, Macleod's Maidens had been sold to Angus Campbell of Ensay and a fox which belonged to a certain Lieutenant Maclean who was staying as a guest at Dunvegan had a litter of cubs in one of the towers.

The rest of the prophecy has not yet come true and fortunately the Clan has had no need of the services of 'John Breac'.

3. (Page 137.) This is one of Coinneach Odhar's most fascinating predictions for in it he foresees the history of the Highlands from the time of the evictions through the present day and into the future that lies ahead of us. Shortly after Culloden, the landowners and clan chiefs began to replace the crofters and their old form of agriculture with sheep and shepherds from the south. This caused unbelievable hardship to the evicted tenants many of whom were forced to emigrate to Newfoundland and New Zealand—islands unknown to Coinneach Odhar.

During the nineteenth century many of the old clan chiefs were forced to sell their estates to the new rich industrialists or to low-land sheep-farmers who took up leases of glens evacuated during the clearances. Thus vast tracts of the Highlands became the property of absentee landlords who stocked the mountains with deer and grouse in order to indulge themselves in an orgy of slaughter for a few months in the year.

Thus the desolation and depopulation which started after Culloden has continued right up to the present day when real efforts are being made by such organizations as the Highlands and Islands Development Board to bring prosperity and employment to the north.

Highlanders today often speculate on the significance of the 'horrid Black Rains' and wonder if they could be connected in some way to the Oil Industry which is finding a footing in the Highlands, or perhaps there is a more sinister explanation such as nuclear fall-out. A disturbing thought!

4. (Page 161.) This prediction is believed to have come true with the arrival of piped gas and water to the streets of Inverness.

5. (Page 161.) Obviously a train with railway carriages.

6. (Page 162.) The first burial at Tomnahurich, or the Fairy Hill, took place in 1846. The cemetery is surrounded by a fence with a gate which is locked at night.

7. (Page 162.) This prediction foresees the Caledonian Canal built by Telford in 1822. Although never a great commercial success, the canal meant that ships were no longer so vulnerable to the storms of the Pentland Firth.

8. (Page 163.) There is some doubt as to the fulfilment of this prophecy though there are some who claim that the 'two false teachers' were the evangelists Moody and Sankey who made an attempt to revolutionize the religion of the Highlanders. Certainly there may be some ministers who might admit to being 'without grace' and plenty who would do it for them! Perhaps Coinneach foresaw the mini-skirt when he talked of 'women without shame'.

9. (Page 163.) The fulfilment of this prophecy speaks for itself. The 'ribbon on every hill' refers to the tarmacadamed roads and the travelling merchants must be the modern travelling vans by which so many Highlanders do their shopping today. In Coinneach's day, rivers for the most part had to be forded and a dangerous journey it often was; 'a bridge over every stream' was to him a luxury indeed. It is certainly true to say that in Inverness and particularly in Dingwall there are policemen at every corner!

10. (Page 164.) Some believe that this prophecy foretold the great flood of 1849 when the Inverness bridge was swept away. There were only two people crossing at the time, a man called Matthew Campbell and a woman who just managed to reach the west shore before the last arch collapsed. The prediction could equally well have referred to the fall of the old wooden bridge in 1665.

11. (Page 165.) This prophecy was made on the battlefield of Culloden nearly a hundred years before the last battle on British soil took place in 1745.

12. (Page 180.) With the proposal to build a bridge over the Inverness Firth, a causeway across the Cromarty Firth roughly at the spot foreseen by Coinneach and a bridge across the Dornoch Firth, this prediction is in imminent danger of coming true.

13. (Page 182.) When the famous Reverend Doctor John Macdonald known as the 'Apostle of the North' for his evangelistic zeal and remarkable preaching powers was minister of Urquhart Parish which included the district of Ferintosh, a remarkable event took place which could be said to fulfil this odd little prediction.

Magpies had been nesting in the church gable as foretold and this combined with the fact that there was an ominous crack in the church walls caused a great deal of uneasiness among the congregation. One Sunday when the church was so full that it was necessary to connect the seats with planks so that everyone could sit down, one of these temporary benches collapsed with such a noise that the congregation was terrified. Remembering Coinneach's prophecy, there was a stampede for the door and many were crushed and seriously injured.

14. (Page 186.) At the time this prediction was made, it seemed a ridiculous prophecy. Roderick Mackenzie, fifth Laird of Fairburn, was one of the richest and best respected chiefs in Ross-shire. He entertained lavishly in his castle of Fairburn and was waited upon by liveried servants. The line was, however, to die out with Major-General Sir Alexander Mackenzie of Fairburn who died unmarried in 1850.

The castle had been left to rot for some time previous to this and by 1851 it was being used as a barn by a local farmer who used the tower to store hay. One of his cows who was in calf at the time followed a trail of straw up the winding staircase to the turret room and being unable to get down again was forced to remain there until the calf was born. This prophecy was so well known that a special train was laid on from Inverness to Muir of Ord to enable curious sightseers to see the fulfilment of the old prediction for themselves.

15. (Page 186.) To the Urquharts who—due to the eccentric and delightful Royalist, Sir Thomas Urquhart, could trace their ancestry back to Adam and Eve—this was a bold piece of insolence. At that time the family possessed not only vast tracts of land but had been hereditary sheriffs of Cromarty since the time of Robert the Bruce. True to Coinneach's vision, by the second half of the eighteenth century practically all their possessions had gone. Their great castle at Cromarty last inhabited by an old woman and a

young girl, was razed to the ground and a new mansion house built close to it by the new laird of Cromarty, a certain George Ross who had made a fortune as an army agent and bought the estate.

The present laird of Urquhart is an American and all he owns in the Black Isle is the ruin of Castlecraig, another ancient Urquhart stronghold, perched on the south shore of the Cromarty Firth.

16. (Page 186.) Sir George Mackenzie of Avoch, or Rosehaugh, as he was to call it because of the profusion of wild roses that grew there, was one of the most distinguished men of his day. He was Lord Advocate for Scotland during the reign of Charles II and his 'Institutes' are still considered to be important by the legal world. He earned his byname, 'Bluidy Mackenzie', because of his harshness to the Covenanters. On the other hand he was particularly gentle to the poor and weak and renowned for his leniency towards witches. The 'seed of the deer' refers to the armorial bearings of the Mackenzies while that of the goat refers to the Fletchers who bought the estate of Rosehaugh about a hundred years ago. James Fletcher was himself the son of an Avoch fisherman who had made a fortune in the business world, thus enabling him to buy the estate from the impoverished Mackenzies. The Fletcher line was to come to an end with the death of the grandson's widow some twenty years ago. The estate was then bought by an insurance company, but the fishermen of Avoch now own their village and the cottages that were at one time part of the Rosehaugh estate.

Sir George Mackenzie was succeeded at Rosehaugh by his third son, George, who married and had a daughter who died without issue.

17. (Page 186.) The Mackenzies possessed Kilcoy Castle for nearly three hundred years and the last to live there—Charles Mackenzie —died in 1813. Thereafter the castle remained in a ruinous condition for nearly a hundred years. In this instance however, Coinneach did not see far enough, for the castle was thereafter twice restored and is now a very fine private property. Who the filthy old man who did not keep his marriage vows was, history does not relate.

18. (Page 186.) Redcastle was originally built in 1179 by William the Lion and did not fall into Mackenzie hands until 1608, when

the famous 'Rory Mor', Tutor of Kintail, received a charter under the Great Seal for the land of Redcastle. It was to remain a Mackenzie stronghold until 1790 when the impoverished Roderick Mackenzie was forced to sell it to James Grant of Coriemoney. Roderick was the last direct male representative of the House of Redcastle, for he died unmarried and the family was thereafter represented by the Mackenzies of Kincraig. Highland legend relates that there was much truth in the prediction concerning the unfortunate women of Redcastle.

19. (Page 198.) Coinneach Odhar had much to say about Strathpeffer and the surrounding district. The best known of his predictions concerns the mineral spring there.

'Uninviting and disagreeable as it is now is with its thick crusted surface and unpleasant smell, the day will come when it shall be under lock and key and crowds of health and pleasure seekers shall be seen thronging its portals in their eagerness to drink the waters.'

This prediction became true in the nineteenth century when Strathpeffer became a holiday and health resort.

20. (Page 212.) This is the most famous of all Coinneach's predictions and the one that has caused the most wonder and speculation among Highlanders from the time of its utterance up till the present day. There is no possible chance that the prophecy was made after the event, for at least three writers of unimpeachable reputation knew about it when the last Earl had two sons alive and in good health. These were Sir Humphrey Davy, Sir Walter Scott and Mr Morritt of Rokeby.

The tenantry were, of course, deeply impressed by the prophecy and when the last chief was impelled by his own munificent extravagance and generosity to sell part of Kintail, they offered to buy the land for him so that it might not pass from the Mackenzies. At this time one son was still living and there was no immediate prospect of the succession dying. Before this could happen, however, the last son, a man of great promise who represented Ross in Parliament died suddenly and the prophecy was fulfilled.

The last laird, Francis Humberston Mackenzie, was a man of great character and distinction. Although not born deformed, he became stone deaf after an attack of scarlet fever as a boy which in the end resulted in a complete inability or reluctance to speak. In spite of the fact that most of his communication had to be done in writing, he raised a regiment, was created Baron Seaforth of Kintail, was Governor of Barbados and in 1808 was made a Lieutenant General. He had four sons, the eldest of whom died in infancy, the second died young, the third died in 1814 and the youngest in 1813. His six daughters included Mary who was widow of Admiral Hood. She later married a man called Stewart and inherited Brahan. It could be said that she was responsible for the death of her sister Caroline, for she was driving the pony trap when the horse bolted and Caroline was killed. In 1815, Lord Seaforth himself died, the last of his line. One by one the remaining estates were sold, first the Island of Lewis, then Kintail, the church lands of Chanonry, the Baronry of Pluscardine, even Brahan Castle itself of which nothing now remains except a plain of grass watched over by a magnificence of trees.

Strangest of all, the four lairds of Chisholm, Grant, Raasay and Gairloch were all deformed in the way foreseen by Coinneach all those years before.

Perhaps Sir Walter Scott's 'Lament for the Last of the Seaforths' best sums up this tragic Highland chief.

> In vain the bright course of thy talents to wrong,
> Fate deadened thine ear and imprisoned thy tongue,
> For brighter o'er all her obstructions arose
> The glow of thy genius they could not oppose
> And who in the land of Saxon or Gael
> Could match with Mackenzie, High Chief of Kintail.
>
> Thy sons rose around thee in light and in love
> All a father could hope, all a friend could approve;
> What 'vails it the tale of thy sorrows to tell?
> In the spring time of youth and of promise they fell!
> Of the line of MacKenneth remains not a male,
> To bear the proud name of the Chief of Kintail.